The broad smile on
same day as his par   ie
went through life witl
everything around hii
moved in with their paternal grandfather, who was equally heartbroken, having lost his wife and his only child, long before their time. The drunken driver who caused the crash witnessed only an alcohol-induced stupor for the last few seconds of his life, unlike the driver and passengers in the car who he hurtled towards, where everything was clear and in slow motion, without the time to avoid the vehicle on the wrong side of the road, but with just enough time for Tom's grandmother to say "Thomas", before the fatal collision.

In the 1960s, when Tom's grandparents' bank balance had increased in line with the success of Grangers, the company they were heavily involved with, they could afford to move to a bigger and better house, Tom's grandmother had chosen an old mansion with a view to restore it to its former glory, and to fill it with children. After the first child was born, a much loved son, nothing else happened, so she filled her spare time away from helping to run her father's rapidly expanding company to working with the gardener to make the grounds as spectacular as any she'd visited, and giving the local builder specific instructions for repairing the stone walls and organising the restoration of the ancient large wooden doors and window frames, ensuring that the old-fashioned locks allowed entry with only a small amount of effort. Tom's grandfather was more practical and arranged for a modern central heating and hot water system to be fitted throughout the house and ensured that the outer doors could be bolted securely plus installing a new burglar alarm system which covered the entire house, including the six bedrooms.

The long summer holidays from school came and went, without Tom moving outside the grounds of his grandfather's large house in Oxford. Tom's grandfather had been the chairman of Grangers for some time, and both Tom's father and grandmother were on the board, but Tom's father thought that he would learn more if he spent the Summer holidays away from the spotlight at his friend's company. However, Tom made no effort to spend a single day working during the summer holidays, and lost himself in his favourite engineering books, making no attempt to join in any conversation with the many regular visitors to his grandfather's house.

Tom was equally as quiet when he returned for his final year in school, and his grandfather started to become worried that Tom's academic success in his previous years would not conclude with good enough grades at A level to get into a top university. Tom had always been large for his age, both in height and build, and had put this to good use on the rugby pitch, which was beneficial because his school's main sport was rugby, instead of the more common, in both meanings, football. He had been in the school senior team, since the fifth year, and held the number 8 position on merit. The new school year coincided with the start of the school rugby season, and he continued where he left off, as team captain. The headmaster, who was a huge supporter of the school rugby team, became concerned that Tom's focus on the game was missing, and instead of running the game, and seeing moves long before they became apparent to the other players on the pitch, he was merely going through the motions. At half time of the opening game of the season, the school team were losing by ten points against a team they would usually beat quite easily, resulting in a change to the Headmaster's usual half time team talk.

"We really should be beating this rabble, what's going wrong?"

The unusual silence was answered by the hooker, who had taken more punishment than the others. "Well sir, we lost some good players at the end of last term when they left to go to university, but the opposition seem to have the same team as last year, and they're bigger and better."

The Headmaster instantly dismissed this comment and looked for a more positive response. "Harbod, is there anything that you can do to turn things around?"

Tom looked at the rest of the team and responded with a lack of passion. "The full back is smaller than the rest of the back line, if I tried a high kick towards him, I'm sure that we could rush him before he catches the ball and go for the line."

The Headmaster was unimpressed. "That will be successful once, but they'll move enough people to cover for him."

Tom nodded. "Yes sir, they will, but it will be successful twice, they'll move someone over, so I'll put more speed on the ball for second time, and we'll need to move faster. After that, they'll move another person over, and we'll exploit the gap further along the line, and try something different."

The first scrum of the second half went as planned, and Tom took the ball out of the back of the scrum and launched a high kick towards the opponents' back line, the right wing ran through the opposing full back, collecting the ball on the way, and they had reduced the deficit to five points. Tom nodded at the try scorer as the ball flew between the posts for another two points. The Headmaster had difficulty breathing as his team held out despite the expected onslaught. Tom spoke to the kicker when they had a penalty kick ten minutes later, the ball reached the touchline further up the field and the resulting line out from the left also went the way Tom had said, and despite there being another player next to the full back they ran through for another try. Whilst they were waiting for the conversion kick, Tom spoke quietly to the winger. An un-converted try and a penalty gave the lead back to the opponents, and constant pressure remained on Tom's team. Tom had his chance just before the end, when his team was awarded a penalty deep in their half, which was kicked into touch on the left, for a line out just inside the opponents' half. The defensive line moved to provide more cover to the full back. Tom shouted "seven" their code for a long ball, and the hooker threw the ball to the end of the line. The catcher was lifted high enough to take hold of the ball easily. Whilst the ball was in the air, Tom had sprinted to the right of the end of the line out to catch the ball as it was passed out to him. The opposing team expected this, and two defenders rushed at Tom to bring him down before he could kick the ball, whilst two other defenders moved closer to the opposing full back to protect him. Tom changed direction and lofted the ball towards the left wing a split second before he crashed to the floor underneath the two opposing players. The winger ran at full pelt towards the ball, well away from the action, and the opponents stared in disbelief as he caught the ball and had time to cut in to place the ball close enough to the posts to make the conversion easy. Tom was hauled to his feet by his jubilant teammates and looked to be in far better shape than the two players who had tried to cause him severe GBH. The ball went between the posts well after the eightieth minute, and the game was won. Tom shook hands with his teammates, and the opposition, but his face did not match the look of joy on the Headmaster. The Headmaster knew Tom's grandfather well enough to make a private visit and lost no time in raising his concerns about Tom's lack of passion on the rugby pitch.

"I had expected Tom to be back to his normal self by now, but he's quiet and no longer has the spark that made him so special."

Thomas knew the Headmaster was correct but felt that he had to stand up for Tom. "He's still grieving and needs more time."

"I'm sorry but I can't agree with you Thomas. The accident was nearly six months ago, I've seen plenty of children who have lost one or both of their parents, and they have all shown some sign of recovery after this time. We need to do something, or he could stay like this until he needs treatment for depression."

Thomas knew that Tom was much quieter than before his parents died, but Tom was still doing everything expected of him at school. "Is his schoolwork suffering? Do you think that there will be a problem for him not getting good enough grades for University?"

"His schoolwork is fine; no, it's better than fine. He seems to put all of his focus into his studies. I'm concerned that we need to do something to get his personality back to how he was before the accident. He just went through the motions on the rugby pitch last

Saturday until I pointed out to him that he should be making things happen."

Thomas didn't see this as a great problem. "So what do you recommend?"

"I have a friend, an ex-pupil actually, who runs the local boxing gym; he's been highly successful in turning young lives around. They like the challenge and are happy to raise their concentration level and they change to meet the discipline required.

Tom wasn't sure why his routine was being changed, especially when he was busy studying for his A levels at home each evening but did as his grandfather asked him to without argument. He parked his car outside the boxing gym the following Tuesday and walked into the smell of sweat to meet the owner. Two people wearing huge gloves and head guards were circling around the inside of the boxing ring, hitting each other with far less force than Tom usually encountered on the rugby pitch. The dimly lit room only allowed him to see the others who were busy being shouted at on the multi gym. As he moved further into the gym he could see one person punching his trainer's hands, and another was grunting in time with his punches against a large leather bag, hanging from the ceiling. When the pair in the ring stopped their dance, their trainer came down to meet Tom.

"Tom?"

"Yes, sir."

"My names Rob, there's no formality here. Swifty said that you would be here tonight and asked me to have a look at you."

Tom had never understood why the Headmaster was called 'Swifty', it had nothing to do with his name or demeanour, but he had seen old pictures in the Head's office dedicated to the name, and had never really thought about it.

"Have you boxed before?"
"Not properly, I've had to protect myself on the rugby pitch a few times, but that usually turns into a free for all, not one on one, and I'm usually the one dragging people away from each other."
Rob smiled at the comment. "I usually get the ones who start the fights or join in for no reason so this should be interesting. Wait there a sec."
Rob walked back to the ring and came back with a large pair of boxing gloves. "Try these on, we'll see how you manage against a bag that won't hit you back." Rob tied the laces tightly, and stood behind the bag, holding it in place. Rob noticed the vacant look on Tom's face, which remained the same whilst Tom punched the bag a couple of times. It was Rob's face which changed; "Whoa; who taught you how to punch that hard?"
"My father. He used to box when he was younger, we had a gym at home with a bag like this one."
"Amateur boxing's a young man's sport. How long did he keep going?"
"He didn't really box competitively, but he told me that it was the best way he knew to keep fit and strong. He never liked to train on his own, and when I became old enough, he preferred my company to a personal trainer. He said that a few minutes hitting the bag relieved him of a day's worth of stress and frustration from work."
"Let's see if you can step up the pace and keep going for a minute."
Tom moved slightly faster, increasing the power until Rob told him to stop. Rob was surprised that Tom was hardly breathing any heavier than when he started.
"Let's try again, this time as fast as you can for a minute."
The bag was in danger of extreme damage, and Tom took a deep breath when the minute was up. The expression on his face remained the same, and he looked like he could keep this up for much longer.

"You're a lot fitter than most people I know. What training do you do?"
"Not much at the moment. I play rugby twice a week, and we have some PE training at school, but I no longer have a multi-gym at home."
Rob knew about Tom from the local paper, and the update from the Headmaster. "Well, you can set your own regime on our multi-gym or join the circuit that we run at seven and eight o'clock every night."
This was more than Tom had spoken to anyone since his grief counselling three months ago. He held his gloves out for Rob to undo the laces and walked over to look at the now unoccupied multi-gym. Tom nodded to Rob, murmured "See you next week" and left.

Tom quickly fell in with the usual regime in the boxing club; arrive at the gym at a quarter to seven, change into training clothes, take part in the warm up and join in with the seven o'clock multi gym circuits followed by the punch bag. Rob walked over to Tom and watched him attacking the bag at full pelt.
"How much time have you spent in the ring?"
"I haven't really. I sparred with my father and his personal trainer a little bit, but that's all."
"Could you spar for a couple of rounds with Danny, both of his usual sparring partners are away tonight, and he needs to keep sharp for a competition next week?"
"What do you want me to do?"
"He's a bit smaller than you, but has very fast hands, so could you hit him every now and again, to make him concentrate on his defence more."
"Ok."
Tom stepped into the ring, and most of those in the gym stopped what they were doing and moved closer to the ring to see the new boy against the star light middleweight. The onslaught started straight away, but despite being hit in the face on a regular basis, Tom

ignored the punches. After thirty seconds of non-stop punching, Danny dropped his guard, and his next recollection was being picked up from the floor by Rob.
"What happened?"
"You didn't concentrate. If you do that next week, the same thing will happen."
"I doubt if I'll get hit as hard as that. Are we going again?"
Rob shook his head. "No, I think that you've learnt your lesson. Do you feel ok?"
"I'm fine, I must have slipped."
Some of the crowd laughed, but Tom stood next to the ropes looking at Danny with a slight look of interest, but with no great concern of what he'd done. Rob took a mental note of Tom's reaction for his update to Swifty and checked Danny's eyes again.
"That's all for you tonight Danny, we need you in one piece for next week. Go and have a shower and get changed, I'll see you on Thursday. Tom, can I have a quick word in the office?"
"Did I do something wrong?"
"No, I just want to check you out. Danny caught you with some good punches."
Tom's face had started to show some marks from the punches, but they seemed to have no effect. "Did any of the punches hurt you?"
Tom shook his head. "They didn't really hurt me. They were good solid punches and I could feel him hitting me quite often, like you said he would, I just waited until I could get a clean shot at him. Even then, I didn't really hit him that hard."
"Are you interested in taking up boxing seriously? You could get to quite a high level, even though you're starting very late."
"No thanks, I'm going to University next Summer, so I need to concentrate on my studies now, and then I'll be away."

"Ok, will you be back next Tuesday?"
"Definitely. I can manage one night a week away from my studying, but anything more could be difficult."
"Thanks for the spar tonight, even if it didn't last very long. Are you ok to go again if we need you to?"
"Yes, no problem. See you next week."

During the following two weeks, Rob took Tom to one side and gave him guidance on defence. Tom quickly understood how to deflect punches with his arms, but his footwork was too slow to move his body out of danger. Rob continued to work with Tom on defence, especially his footwork over the next few months. Four weeks after sparring with Danny, Rob gave Tom a larger opponent after the usual circuit on the multi-gym.
"Tom, could you help me in the ring please? We want to see what Dave.is like with someone who can take a punch, his usual sparring partners never seem to last a round, and he's a bit too fast for me. Could you try to stop Dave from hitting you as often as Danny did last time?"
Tom had seen Dave in the ring and was surprised how a white man with such large muscles could move as quickly as he did; Tom wasn't a racist but couldn't help but notice that his black team-mates who were the two props in the school rugby team were faster and more agile than the white players who were smaller and less muscular than they were. Not only was Dave about two inches taller than Tom, he was well over a stone heavier, none of which seemed to be fat. The first two minutes against Dave were completely different to the previous sparring session, the punches were twice as heavy, but nowhere near as fast and often. Tom managed to block or dodge most of the punches, which came from a variety of directions, and absorbed the ones that made it past his defence. Tom only managed to hit Dave properly twice but noticed him wince when

the punches landed. During the break, Tom swilled his mouth out with the water from the communal bottle, and Rob noted that Tom looked at the amount of blood that hit the bottom of the bucket with a certain amount of curiosity. Rob was impressed with the way that Tom was sticking to his task.

"In the next two minutes, try to hit Dave a bit more. A few punches to the ribs and belly would be good, no need to go head-hunting all of the time as most boxers do; if you hurt an opponent's body enough they will eventually drop their guard, and it will be easier to punch his head."

The defence of the lower areas was much easier to breach than Dave's head, and Tom was punched far fewer times during the next two minutes, as Dave had to concentrate on an attack which was much stronger than he usually faced. At the end of the third round, both boxers were breathing heavily, and had taken more punishment than Rob had wanted, but it was exactly what Dave needed. All of the other boxers had watched the third round in complete silence and applauded loudly when the bell sounded. Dave touched gloves with Tom and nodded with respect.

"Can Tom and I have another go next week?" Rob was happy for this to happen on a regular basis but didn't want Dave to get injured before any of the regular competitions, especially as Dave was Rob's best ever chance of winning something important. He also hoped that improving Tom's footwork and co-ordination would result in a corresponding improvement in Dave's boxing skills.

As is usual with teenagers, time goes incredibly slowly whilst they are waiting to reach a certain date, such as their birthday, examinations, or better still, the end of the school year.

The regular boxing training on Tuesdays, and Rugby on Wednesday afternoons and Saturday mornings, helped to speed up the wait, and finally, Tom started his three month's work experience at his godfather's company, Robertsons prior to leaving for Nottingham University to study Engineering. In line with his final year at school, Tom was still subdued in his first two years at Uni, but his grades kept him top of his year, and he had started to join in with the discussions at the lectures. Although he was on good terms with his classmates, he hadn't struck up special relationships with any of them, despite a large amount of interest from the few females who had started to break the norm of becoming Engineers. In his final year, one new arrival, an attractive young lady named Helen, set her sights on Tom and she proved quite difficult to ignore.

Helen's parents and friends had tried to put her off a career in Engineering, her parents were concerned that it would be difficult for her to make her mark in what was still a male-dominated profession and she would have to work harder than the men to receive the same treatment and opportunities for promotion, but she was stubborn, and knew that she could match anyone given the chance. She had been interested in engineering since she was old enough to construct intricate constructions with her older brother's Lego and Meccano toy sets and was fascinated when her creations became more complicated when motors, electrical relays and electronics became involved a few years later. Her friends were worried that she might be turning into a lesbian, but she'd had a few boyfriends when she was growing up and she knew which way she liked her bread buttered, and at no time considered wearing comfortable shoes. She was always one of the top of her class in Maths and Physics but even the careers' master had tried to put her off engineering and put forward different options to match her exam performances, such as accountancy, human resources and even teaching, but Helen wouldn't budge from her choice.

Helen was receiving a huge amount of attention from the male students, but she politely turned down their offers of a meal, a few drinks or a visit to the cinema or a night club. She maintained a degree of civility to those who were not so well-mannered, and made other proposals, but like her career in engineering, she had set her sights on Tom. Some of her expectant suiters had noticed the way that she looked at Tom and were getting more and more jealous of him, and even more pissed off with his indifference, but it didn't deter her at all. Entering the name Tom Harbod into a search engine reported a large number of entries relating to the death of his parents, and he was quite obviously unattached, so Tom became her latest project. One evening, a few of Tom's classmates had organised a get-together in the Students' bar, telling Tom that they would be discussing their strategies for the forthcoming assessment. Although Tom still didn't drink alcohol, except for the rare occasion, he could see no reason not to attend. As if by magic, as soon as it became obvious that the topics of discussion about the assessments had finished, Tom's stalker was by his side. Tom had no idea that she had asked two people from Tom's year to arrange the evening, and he was also too polite not to answer her back when she started to talk to him. Tom knew that her name was Helen, but that was about all. One of the younger students, who thought, incorrectly, that he stood a chance with her, tried to join their conversation, and became angry when she continuously ignored him. She looked at Tom for help.

"Tom, could you please ask Clive to leave us alone, there are some things that I would like to speak to you about that only a final year student would know?"
"Don't talk as if I'm not here. If you have something to say, then say it to me."
"I don't have anything to say to you Clive, I just want you to leave me alone."
"The last time I checked, it's a free country, I'll stand where I like."
Tom couldn't see any reason to argue with someone with their own agenda. "If you want to have a discussion with me Helen, we can talk further away from the bar."
Clive was even more pissed off. "I'm not going to be ignored by a fucking zombie."
Tom looked at him blankly, and then turned to Helen. "Come on, let's go."
Clive punched Tom on the jaw, with what he thought was enough power to knock Tom out. Tom continued to look at Clive blankly, which didn't improve Clive's temper at all, and Clive tried to punch him again. Rob would have been proud of Tom's defence as his left arm moved up to block the swinging right fist. Helen flew at Clive to stop him, and Clive made the grave mistake of punching her as well. Tom had been brought up to believe that men shouldn't hit girls, irrespective what they had done wrong, and Clive ended up in a heap on the floor. Helen took charge of the situation immediately.
"I think that we should get out of here now. Follow me."
Tom looked out of the window when the taxi stopped. "What are we doing here?"
"These are my digs, it's the best place for us at the moment."
Helen got out whilst Tom paid for the taxi journey and followed her inside.
"Clive's a dickhead, he'll probably phone the police, accusing you of assault, and you'll spend the rest of

tonight in police custody until it's sorted out. You can sleep in my spare bed tonight. I doubt if the police will come here, but if they do, I'll tell them that you accompanied me here, but I don't know where you are now."
"Oh, okay, if you're sure."
"Would you like a drink?"
"Coffee?"
"Doubtful. Vodka?"
"I don't usually drink vodka."
"You don't usually fight with people in the Students' bar either."
Two large vodka and cokes changed Tom's perception of the evening. Although Helen made most of the conversation, Tom had also added his own contribution, usually about his course work, but Helen was interested in that, as well as being good company, so the night was more enjoyable that he thought it would be. He wasn't really tired and was surprised that it was almost midnight.
"It's time I went to bed, I'm sorry to keep you up this late."
"You can use my toothbrush, if you want. The bedroom's through there, I'll join you when I've cleaned my teeth."
"You said that you had a spare bed."
"I had my fingers crossed."
"I'll sleep on the sofa then."
"You won't. I'm not the sort to invite someone back and not give them a bed for the night. Hurry up and clean your teeth, then you can warm the bed up."

At the following morning lecture, Tom reviewed the previous night, and was surprised that he'd had a fight, drank the most vodka he'd ever consumed in one go, and finished it off with very enjoyable sex. He was still unsure how it had all happened, but people had noticed that there was a trace of a smile on his face. The people who were intrigued about his new demeanour didn't know the full story of what had happened the previous night after he left the students' bar but would have realised that receiving a good blow-job will always bring a smile to someone's face. Evenings, and nights, with Helen, including alcohol and regular sex, became a common occurrence, and when he finished at Uni, he truly meant it when he said that he would keep in touch.

Tom fully expected to go to work for his godfather's Company, Robertsons, when he finished University, but his grandfather was a very persuasive person and he started at Grangers soon after his return. He also renewed his friendship with his great uncle, who still had the same outlook on life that Tom remembered from when he was younger; he was also good company. Thomas was pleased that Tom no longer had the air of indifference that he had when he left for University, but he didn't approve of the drinking habit that he had brought back with him. He told Tom that he disapproved of drinking too much alcohol and that the house would be made secure at midnight each night, and he didn't want his sleep disturbed after that time. The first time that Tom had arrived home after midnight, Thomas had just drawn the bolts on the doors and was about to turn off the houselights and go to bed. Tom could see his grandfather through the keyhole and had banged on the door.
"Gramps, open up, it's only just after twelve o'clock."
Tom heard the bolts being pulled across the door, and the door opened. Tom noticed that his grandfather looked more disappointed than angry.
"Twelve o'clock is plenty late enough to get home from a night out drinking, especially as you are at work tomorrow morning."

"I'm sorry I'm late gramps, but I had to make sure that great uncle Frank got a taxi home, he'd missed the last bus."
"We'll talk about it tomorrow, I need to get some sleep."

Tom quickly settled into working at his grandfather's company and fitted in well with the team that he worked with. True to his word, he also kept in touch with Helen, and met up with her regularly over the next eighteen months but was surprised when Helen phoned him out of the blue at work.
"I'm in Oxford this Friday, did you want to meet for a drink on Friday night?"
"I'll be in the Corn Dolly with my great uncle Frank on Friday night from eight o'clock, if that's OK?"
"I should be there sometime around eight thirty." She would be ready much earlier than that but had learnt that Tom was becoming a little more appreciative if she kept him on his toes.
"OK, see you there."

Tom was walking down Cornmarket Street with his great uncle on Friday evening, when a drunken youth lurched in his direction. "You snobby bastard students are killing this city. You think that you're better than us, well you're not."
Tom was startled at the vitriol incorrectly aimed in his direction, and the punch that followed the words. He looked at his assailant, and another punch made contact. The angry young man was bigger than Tom, but that had never bothered him, on or off the rugby field; Tom didn't want to meet Helen with punch marks and blood on his face. Tom dodged the next punch, and a quick response to the assailant's jaw resulted with the young man on the pavement, and Tom went through the entrance into the Corn Dolly and down the stairs to the bar for a pint. Frank picked up the young man and

checked that he was ok. "If I was you, I'd go home before you get into more trouble."

The bar of the Corn Dolly was always busy on a Friday evening, usually with people a lot younger than Frank, but he liked it that way. The seating was much more comfortable than that in most of the other pubs in Oxford. He also liked the loud music, which was from the late sixties and the early seventies, not the synthetic rubbish currently on Radio One. He loved the raw excitement that the Rolling Stones, the Who and the Kinks brought to the public in the sixties, long after he was no longer a teenager, swiftly followed by Led Zeppelin. Frank's favourite memory was the hot afternoon in 1976 at Knebworth Park, when he saw and heard Lynyrd Skynyrd for the first time, and the crowd's reaction to the guitar frenzy at the end of Freebird. There was a huge wait later that night to see the Stones perform a fantastic live set for over two hours until it was almost light.

Frank always liked to stand at the bar for the first hour or so until his legs became too tired, and they easily found room at the bar for their first pint. Twenty minutes after they arrived, the angry young man stood in the doorway at the bottom of the staircase leading into the Corn Dolly bar, next to a powerful-looking man with facial similarities.

He pointed towards Tom at the bar. "That's him. He punched me to the ground."

The larger brother looked at the young man at the bar. "How many times did you hit him first?"

"I didn't, he attacked me without provocation."

"How many?"

"Twice, but I hardly touched him."

"Go up to him and apologise."

"I can't do that."

"Offer him and his friend a drink, and say that you're sorry, but you thought that he was a student."
"I can't afford it."
"Here, take this fiver, and get me a drink as well."
The assailant walked up to Tom at the bar. "Excuse me, I'm sorry that I hit you, I thought that you were a student. Could I buy you and your friend a drink please?"
Tom was caught off-guard by the stupidity of the situation; he held out his hand and laughed, surprising everyone, including the assailant's big brother.
"When did you start laughing?"
Frank turned to the big man stood next to them. "This is a first for me, as well."
Tom was still smiling when he noticed that it was Dave from the boxing club who was stood next to the angry young man. "Hello Dave, have you moved on from fighting old ladies yet?"
The young man had been confused since he entered the bar, and now someone was taking the piss out of his brother, who was a successful heavyweight boxer.
"Gary, let me introduce to Tom Harbod, you've heard me talk about him. I'm sorry about Gary, but his girlfriend has just dumped him for a student."
Gary looked at Tom in a new light. "I thought that you'd be bigger."
A female voice behind Gary joined the conversation. "That's something you don't often hear about Tom Harbod."
The men at the bar turned to look at the new arrival. "What does a girl have to do around here to get a drink?"
Tom turned to look at Helen and wondered how she had become so attractive in the last few months. Frank had known how pretty she was from the time that they had first met and gave her a big hug. "This night gets better and better. What brings you to Oxford?"

"The train. We still have them oop North."
"Did you come all of this way just to see me?" Frank always tried to chat up every female but knew that he had no chance with Helen whilst Tom was around.
"I wish. No, I had a meeting in Oxford with Robertsons today, so I asked Tom if he was free to meet up afterwards."
After the round of introductions was over, the conversation went back to boxing, and nightlife in Oxford. The brothers left after a couple of drinks, closely followed by Frank, who could see that Tom and Helen needed to be alone. Tom was curious about Helen's visit, amongst other things.
"I'm in my last year at Uni now, and will need a job if I want to carry on in Engineering."
"Why didn't you ask me, we're always looking out for new recruits?"
"I wanted to get a job on merit, and not have people making comments about how I gained employment by shagging the Chairman's grandson."
"Oh, so is it too presumptuous to ask if you're coming back with me to the Chairman's house tonight?"
"I was thinking about it on the way here tonight and decided that my days of climbing trees and breaking into people's houses are over."
Tom was astonished that this upset him so much. Helen saw this and kissed him.
"That doesn't mean that we can't stay in my hotel room. I made sure that the room had a double bed."
Tom phoned his grandfather to tell him that he would be with Helen for the weekend. He took Helen with him to pick up some clothes the following morning and his grandfather easily persuaded Helen to come back for dinner that evening. Tom took the opportunity to show Helen the delights of Oxford in the hope that he could use some of his grandfather's persuasive manner to make her move to Oxford on a permanent basis. On

the Monday morning Tom accompanied Helen to the train station on her way back to Uni, gave her a long hug and kiss before they parted, and then went back to his grandfather's house to get changed for work. His grandfather was the first person to notice that Tom's smile was back.

There are always unexpected events and circumstances that change peoples' lives, and that Friday brought in a number of huge changes to Tom, which he hadn't previously thought about. He would have eventually realised how much he liked being with Helen, and how much he missed her when she left, but he expected to live with his grandfather for the foreseeable future. He didn't see the sense in booking a hotel room every time that Helen came to visit, but if she was no longer in favour of breaking into his bedroom, he would either have to get his grandfather's permission for her to stay with him, which he was still too embarrassed to ask, or he could buy his own place in Oxford. If Helen was offered a job at Robertsons, and Tom couldn't think of any reason why she wouldn't be, she would need a place to stay, so it made sense for them to move in together. Tom and his sister had inherited a large amount from their parents, including shares in Grangers. He'd invested most of the cash, but he could sell some of his Grangers shares to add to his deposit. It didn't take long for Helen to phone Tom with the news that she had been offered a position in Robertsons; when Tom told her that he was thinking of buying a house or a flat in Oxford, and asked her to move in with him when she started work she agreed before he had the time to think that there was ever any chance of the answer ever being 'no'. She would be coming to Oxford to speak to Robertsons the following week, so they could look at prospective properties then. Helen didn't start crying until after she hung up. His uncle Frank offered him a good deal for his shares, and it was a done deal before his grandfather found out and could make a counteroffer to keep the shares in his part of the family. His grandfather didn't show how sad he was on the day that Tom moved out. He knew that Tom had somehow found a way to get into the house after the curfew, and sometimes had female company for the night, who Tom had magicked away before he saw them. Despite his old-fashioned views, he would have been more than pleased if Helen had moved into the house with Tom, especially as Tom's sister had recently married, and had already moved out. Tom's desertion left the old man on his own thinking about the many happy years he'd spent in the big old house, which suddenly became very desolate for the first time since he'd moved in with the only woman that he'd ever loved.

TWO

The plain brown envelope felt as heavy as usual, and he knew that he didn't have to check the contents, as the amount in used notes enclosed inside was always as expected, no more, no less. The thin man seated next to him on the bench picked up the package containing the information to pass to his client's Technical office. The value of the research and development information was considerably more than the amount that he had just paid, and it would keep the business that he was dealing with one step ahead of the opposition, which could be the difference between being awarded a lucrative contract and going bust, with the opposite result for the company providing the information. A smile appeared on the face of the thin man as he disappeared into the gloom surrounding the early morning. The risk of being caught added a buzz to his current boring existence, which was unusual in his line of work.

He watched the thin man leave as he put the cash into his inside jacket pocket. Although he was more awake than the walking dead around him so early in the morning, as they fought off their lack of sleep to make their way to work, he got up slowly from the bench not wishing to draw attention to himself and zipped up his jacket to prevent the money from being stolen. He'd risked everything to obtain the information, but the money it brought him would keep him in the game, and would most likely save him from another severe beating He ambled to the bus stop to catch the next bus to the Company HQ in Cowley. Unlike his recently departed partner in crime, although he had plenty of time for breakfast before he started work, his appetite was diminished by the taste of fear that accompanied his meetings with the thin man. He was always surprised that there were so many people up and about going to work at such a God-awful time in the morning, which seemed to gainsay the reports in the news about the recession currently gripping the country

He glanced down at his watch whilst he waited for the bus to arrive. Although it was not yet seven o'clock, he knew that, by the time that he reached the office it would be busy with people trying to justify their position in the company, in light of the current round of job cuts in progress. He felt a sharp pang of guilt in the knowledge that his actions would have a detrimental effect on the company, but there was no other way out of his current predicament, even the loan sharks would no longer touch him. He was glad that he was earlier than normal as it would give him time to prepare for the 'emergency' meeting called by the Chairman at ten o'clock for some reason or other. He couldn't understand why the old bastard didn't just retire and leave them to it, instead of poking his nose in all the time.

The thin man caught the train back from Oxford to Paddington, arrived at his small office, and checked the information that he'd just received. Pleased with the clarity of the details captured, he put the information into the safe, and made himself a cup of coffee whilst he waited for his two colleagues to arrive. The sign on the office door called them 'Distributers' but anyone checking their company with Companies' House would find no details of their existence. If the sign said 'fraud, blackmail and industrial espionage', which was their actual business, they would quickly find themselves in deep trouble with the law. The office was as untidy as that which anyone would expect of somewhere populated by three grown men, except for the lack of large files of paperwork, which would in their case provide evidence for their arrest. The three men used their own heavily encrypted laptop computers, which they kept with them, or in a very secure place at all times, so apart from an expensive shredder, the office also hid any features which would support the suggestion that the work that they were in was highly lucrative. His two colleagues, when they eventually arrived, had a completely different physical appearance to the thin man. Where he was short and thin, they were tall and muscular, however, for his line of work, he needed to be able to melt into a crowd without anyone showing any interest. He was also an expert in taking photographs of blackmail victims who he had set up with any of the beautiful young ladies, or in some cases young men, who he had added to his list of useful contacts during the last few years, to entice the victims into doing things that they didn't really want anyone else to know that they were up to.

"Morning Stumpy. How did it go with the contact at Grangers?"

Although he was from London, the man spoke with no accent, which was usual for someone who had joined the Army as a boy soldier and worked his way through Special Forces to the rank of Sergeant Major. The newcomers had no idea of the thin man's past, they just thought that he was good at taking photographs of people in incriminating situations, usually in the dark, without the victim knowing, but despite the physical difference between the them, the thin man knew how to talk to soldiers, and was quick to stamp his authority.

"Listen in Steve and listen in good. My name is Tony, not stumpy, or short arse. You need to show some respect. I'm the person who has all the contacts, identifies vulnerable companies, and analyses the companies' workforce. I also do all of the work to set up the blackmail victims and take all of the risks."

"Keep your hair on, it's a term of endearment for fuck's sake."

"Well you might find it endearing, but I don't. Cheap muscle is two a penny in London, if I leave, you'd be back working with the debt collectors and the bookies."
"Yeah, fine, loosen up."
Tony didn't loosen up, but that was as close to an apology that he was going to get. "I got everything that we needed, but I still think that we are getting close to having to find a replacement. He's getting more and more shaky. If we aren't careful, he'll give the game away, if he hasn't already. I told you that two months ago."
"You're supposed to be careful. There's nothing that could lead him to us is there?"
"Of course there isn't, but we don't want to warn off Grangers. It's difficult enough getting the information out without causing Grangers to raise their security even further."
The other associate, almost a carbon copy, and with the same background of the first one, joined in the conversation. "So what do you think that we should do about it?"
Tony looked up in surprise at Graham, his other accomplice, as he very rarely spoke, Steve usually said enough for both of them. "If you'd asked me that ten years ago, I would have said to choose another victim and set up a honey trap, but with all of the crime shows on television these days, they all seem to be more aware of what's going on, and are not so gullible."
Steve was back on Tony's case, expecting a more positive response. "Our client pays us a lot of money when we provide this information; I don't want to lose this income stream just yet. Have a look at your analysis of Grangers' employees and let me know who is next in line for one of your special treats."
Tony turned away and pretended to be looking for something on his laptop, whilst he took a deep breath so as not to show the other two his feelings. He'd told

them time and time again that they rose or fell on his input, but in the eighteen months that he'd worked with them, it was always them who made out that they ran the business, and gave the orders as if they were still in the Army, and he was their lackey. He turned back when he had retained his composure. "I think it's about time that we left Grangers alone. Any more of this and they'll lose so much business that they'll have nothing left for us to take."

"That's Plan B for Grangers. If our client can get another one of their contracts, Grangers' share price will fall low enough for our client to buy enough of the company to take them over. There's a really big bonus when that happens."

"That's not we agreed when we took on this work."

"Well, the client feels differently now, and this is the new way forward."

"What do the controllers say about this?"

"What's it to do with them? They'll get their cut, why should they be bothered what we do?"

"You're a fucking idiot, you need to learn to leave things that you don't understand well alone. The controllers set up this work, and any changes to what they tell us to do will result in risks that they have no intention in taking."

"Well, we've decided to move things on a bit. I've been offered a nice little earner for this extra work."

Tony was getting more and more pissed off with their dangerous decisions, dangerous as in increasing the chance of them being caught, and dangerous that other companies would be warned that their information was being stolen, and they would be more suspicious to any unexpected changes to their business. The biggest danger was that, if anything went badly wrong, the controllers would retire him from the business. Painfully and permanently.

"I didn't agree with that, and I never would have."

"We gathered that, that's why we didn't ask for your comments when the client got in touch with me personally and increased their requirement."

"Steve, I'm warning you for the last time, if you change the agreements that we have with the controllers again without consulting me, I'm off, and you can see how long you last on your own."

"We'll that's your choice, but I've already told the client that we'll get the extra information, so we're going to see this contract through to the finish."

Tony had first-hand knowledge of the people in overall charge of what they did, and had seen with his own eyes what happened to the people who upset them, and intended to have words about the two 'associates' that they'd assigned to him. However, against his better judgement he opened up his computer file on Grangers to find someone else who might be less fragile to provide them with the information required to complete their contract.

The 'old bastard' otherwise known as Thomas Harbod, or the chairman of Grangers, usually spent his evenings working late in the office at Oxford or working or reading at his large home with his two cats, which he much preferred. The previous evening he'd been joined at his house by a fraud investigator named Richard; someone who he had used on a number of occasions, and one who had become a trusted member of his small, but very elite, circle of friends. They were trying to work out a way to discover how vital information, that was losing Grangers business and turnover, was leaving the company. Twice in the last six months Grangers had been underbid for large contracts of work, when they were certain that their price would be the lowest and provide the best end product. Thomas had also noticed that technology very similar to that developed by Grangers was being used by their competitors. Despite his age Thomas kept up to date with modern business innovations and was fully aware of the concept of the 'Global phenomenon' of new technology being produced at the same time in different areas in the world without any link between those introducing it, but he didn't believe in coincidences. He probably wouldn't even have noticed when he was too busy working all hours of the day, but he had, grudgingly, handed over some of his duties during the last few years to prepare both himself and the company for his retirement, and used his spare time to keep abreast of improvements made by his competitors. His grandson, Tom, was the head of Production in Grangers, and was smarter than anyone that he knew, so he'd asked Tom to take their latest development work on a large project that they were about to submit a bid for, and put in some variations that would make it fail, but only when it was at maximum capacity under working conditions. He asked Tom to put in a few miniscule adjustments, which affected other areas, so the design was innovative and looked accurate, and it was impossible to identify the reasons for the failure until a large amount of time and money had been spent. He told Tom that it was important that he told no-one about this work and explained why. It was no longer possible to hack into the company technology design computer, or download the information externally, because the computer had no link to the outside World. Although mobile phones were able to take highly detailed photographs, there were strict rules banning their presence in the Production Department, but it was easy enough to take photographs of the technical documentation by other means, usually by miniature camera, and then download the information to a computer and print them off when there was more time, where they wouldn't get caught. It was also possible to upload the photos to a mobile and send them to a recipient with only a small chance of discovery, but the person collecting the latest information preferred the old, risk-free method. Tom had hidden the original design documents and left the amended papers in the usual secure locker, where anyone in his team would expect them to be. He also hid two very discreet tell-tales to highlight when the papers had been disturbed, with instructions from his grandfather to let him know immediately when the tell-tales had been moved. When Tom reported the movement of the tell-tales two days ago, Thomas had set up the meeting with Richard.

Richard didn't believe in coincidences either. "If you expect your bid to be the lowest, you could put losing a bid for work down to bad luck on one occasion, but for it to happen twice within a short timeframe opposing bidders would need to have inside information to be successful."
"But we're known for providing first class products, this should also be taken into consideration when the contracts are awarded."
"The contract is usually given to the company quoting the lowest cost; a fact astronaut John Glenn often quoted was that he tried not to think that each part of the rocket that was hurtling him through Space was procured at the lowest possible cost. For a company to be certain that it makes the lowest bid, it will need information about the bids from the other companies who have received an invitation to tender a bid for the contract; this will also enable them to undercut the other bids by just enough to win, and keep any losses from the contract to a minimum."
Richard paused for breath. He knew that Thomas understood what he had just said, but then added the part that he knew his friend wouldn't like.
"That information can only come from inside the companies tendering a bid."

Thomas was unimpressed with the implied lack of security in his company. "We increased our internal safety measures when we lost a contract that we expected to win the first time, so if someone is passing on this information they must be in a high position of trust, otherwise they wouldn't have the ability to obtain the detailed information to provide a breakdown of the costs from each department involved in the bid. How are we going to find out who it is?"

Richard took a deep breath, expecting that his next statement would not be well received, but, in his experience, the traitor would not be caught with the evidence. "If someone in the company is being forced to get information out, he will find a way to do it. We need to discover the cause of the deception, not the method."

"How are we going to do that?"

"That usually takes a long time, even with many people scrutinising all of the possible culprits. If they are being blackmailed, have cash or personal problems or are stealing information because they feel that they have a huge grudge against the company, then they will eventually give themselves away by their manner, and by the way that they interact with their colleagues."

"I don't have a long time or an army of investigators to check out the company personnel, and this needs to be resolved now, so what ideas do you have?"

"If we can get all the people who have access to top level information together in a high-pressure environment for long enough, I'm sure that they will drop their guard for a few seconds, which should be long enough to give themselves away." Thomas was still unsure of how this could be achieved.

Richard continued. "I have a friend who runs corporate team building events. Two days of his command tasks and non-stop stress will allow us to identify those who are definitely untroubled by their conscience and should highlight the few we need to take a closer view of."

"But that would be expensive, and there could be about twenty people who would have to take part, maybe more. I have already called a meeting with the senior staff at ten o'clock tomorrow morning to tell them that our profit has reduced again, and to tell them that I expect improvements to be forthcoming within the next few months. How am I going to tell them that, at the same time that I expect them to improve their performance, I am also sending them away from the office for two days?"

"You could tell them that the team building will provide a method of improving the performance of the senior team."

"But you said that the senior team needed to be put into a high-pressure environment, most of them could coast through team building exercises."

"Infer at your meeting tomorrow that any future promotion, or even their jobs, could be lost as a result of underperformance at the team building. It's been successful before."

Thomas wasn't so sure. "And how are we to discover the culprit from the list of possible suspects?"

"I know an accountant who you could recruit into the company for a few weeks who could do this. You could tell your management team that he is an expert in looking at companies currently having problems and finding ways to turn the company back on course. When can the team building event be arranged?"

Thomas moved his two hairy cats from their place on the sofa and took out his work diary, which was full of dates when it would not be possible for the main players to be away from work, and shook his head as he turned the pages, until he found two consecutive days when it might be possible. He showed the diary to Richard, and

Richard phoned his friend to arrange the event, which only took a few minutes, and the date was agreed.
"If you have any ideas how I'm going to sell the idea of the team building to the senior management, without letting them know that we are looking for someone giving away secret information, let me know, because I'm not that devious. I'll need to draw up a list of attendees tonight, so we can re-arrange the workload." Richard smiled. He was used to the old man's lists. He gave Thomas his views on how to inform the company senior staff why they are taking two days away from work at such a critical time for the business, and why it was important that all attendees took the team building seriously, and wished his friend good luck.

At the stroke of ten o'clock the following morning Thomas entered the Company HQ boardroom and looked around at the senior staff and managers already gathered there, most of whom he'd either worked with for tens of years, or he'd been involved in their recruitment. The chairs in the boardroom had been set out in rows facing towards the podium set up for the speech, instead of the usual boardroom style with everyone sat around a table looking inwards at each other, and the large oblong oak table, which was usually in the centre of the room, had been moved to the back. The senior staff and managers took their seats still holding loud conversations, as Thomas stepped up onto the pre-arranged platform facing the audience, making him even higher above them than the usual presenter's position. Despite his age, he was still an imposing figure, and the fire he had as a young man still burned inside him, as his voice boomed out to get their attention.
"Ladies and gentlemen," he began. The position of power as he looked down on them, and his loud, stern voice, silenced the crowd. "We have just produced the

accounts for the last quarter, and our profit for the period is even lower than that of the previous quarter. With that in mind, the company has recruited an expert to look at the business to put it back on course. Unless there is an improvement in our performance we will have to make further savings to enable us to continue in business, and the quickest way for us to make savings is to reduce staff numbers by even more than we are currently planning. No-one's job is safe, that means senior management as well as those on the shop floor. We need to step up our game." He could see that some of the audience wanted to express their view on his statement, but he held up his hand to cut them off and continued. "We have organised a team building event for the senior staff, that means you, ladies and gentlemen, not your nominees. Clear your calendars for the 15th and 16th of next month, this is your top priority. We need to turn the company around, and start performing again, so the consequences of your non-attendance or poor performance at the team building cannot be understated. That's all I have to say at the moment, goodbye."

The stunned silence as he left was replaced by turmoil, and as he walked down the corridor to the exit, Thomas smiled to himself, knowing that they would be in the right frame of mind for their appearance at the team building.

THREE

The coach left Grangers' head office at half past eight in the morning and arrived at the undisclosed team building location just after eleven o'clock. There were two single storey accommodation buildings, a larger two-storey building, and a reception building with a restaurant and bar area, all surrounded by open fields set out with different command tasks. The coach went past the accommodation buildings and parked next to the large building, the doors at the front of the coach opened to allow a fit-looking man in his forties in an expensive suit to enter it. "Right, ladies and gentlemen, collect your belongings and come with me into this building." The thirty passengers followed the man to a classroom on the ground floor of the large building where their names were checked against the list of attendees on the man's slimline, portable laptop computer. As expected, the attendees matched the names on the list and the large name badges on the table at the front of the classroom.
"My name is James, and I will be the main facilitator for the next two days. We'll go through the format for the time that you are with us here after lunch. The first thing that we need to do is to get everyone into the right frame of mind for your short stay with us, so if everyone would follow me please, I'll take you to the first command task. Leave your bags and coats here, they'll be perfectly safe, you can take them to your rooms after lunch. Please make sure that your name badge is securely attached to your clothing and is in full view "
The attendees followed James outside and waited whilst the locked the building. "The accommodation buildings are the single storey buildings that you passed on the way in. Each of you will have your own room, and there is a list showing the room allocations with the room keys in Reception; we'll walk past that on the way to the

command task. We will be doing another command task this afternoon, so it will be a good idea if some of you change your shoes and clothing for something more appropriate after lunch. It's a beautiful day outside, so you should enjoy yourselves in the sunshine."
They stopped briefly outside the Reception building. "You'll be split into three teams for the first command task. Lunch will be ready for you in the main reception building when your team has completed the first task, and your room keys are ready to be picked up from the main desk."
They moved on, and came to a stop next to a single line of white plastic tape on the ground, and were divided into three teams of ten people each, the first team from the first ten people who had arrived at the command task, and so on. On the other side of the tape was a grassed area containing a series of fifteen thick tree stumps, about eighteen inches high, and another line of tape on the other side of the stumps, parallel with the first tape. The stumps were divided into three areas, each series of five stumps forming a zigzag from one line of tape to the other. A member of James's team stood in front of each of the three lines of stumps next to two planks of wood, and each team moved in line with their own series of stumps. James waited until they were all in position, and each adjudicator had put a tick on his attendee list against the name of each person in the team that he was responsible for. He then explained what they had to do to complete the task.
"This is a simple task to get you thinking and working as a team, all you have to do is to get each member of your team from one side of the white tape to the area on the other side of the far white tape, without touching the grass, using only the wooden stumps and these planks of wood. If any team member, or a plank, touches the grass, anyone who hasn't got over the far tape will have to go back to the start. Each team will have an

adjudicator who will ensure that you start again if any of your team touch the grass. Start when you are ready, I'll meet you back in the classroom at one thirty, after you've picked up your room keys. One of my colleagues will be waiting in the unlocked classroom so that you can collect your bags and take them to your rooms. Hopefully you'll have had time for some lunch." James moved away to where he could get a full view of the three teams.

Tom had moved up to the front of the procession, taking in the surroundings whilst holding a discussion about his newly born nephew with his sister's husband Mark, who was also attending the team building, and was in the front of the group when they reached their destination. He looked at the other members of his team, and no-one was forthcoming with any ideas on how to get across the grass. His face lit up with his usual contagious smile and addressed the team.

"OK, let's stand next to the planks to see how many people we can get on each of them." No-one had a better idea what to do. Tom was one of the youngest people at the team building, but he was head of Production and had a reputation for making good decisions. He was also the Chairman's grandson, so they all complied. There was room for five people standing next to each other sideways, or facing from end to end, and the planks were sturdy enough to take the weight of five people quite easily.

"Right, that's simple. The planks will reach to the post closest to them in sequence but are not long enough to miss any stumps out. We can get five people across on the first go, two people will need to return with the planks, leaving three on the other side of the tape. After the next run we'll have another three over the other side, and on the last run we'll bring back the remaining two. Does anyone have a better idea?"

Complete silence, as they looked at one-another and then at the planks and the stumps. Tom also had a reputation of not belittling people when they offered opinions, however stupid they might appear, but the participants in this particular folly had yet to get in tune with the requirements.

"We will need to have the two strongest to carry the planks, someone at the back to pick up the plank from behind and pass it forward after we've all gone across it, and someone at the front to put it onto the next post, without it touching the grass. That'll be you and me then, Mark." Mark nodded in agreement, and Tom continued. "Ok, let's get going. Who's going to be the first three to join us? Remember, lunch is waiting for us, and the first team finished gets first choice of food."

The other teams had started already, but had no plan, and had both fallen off and re-started. Tom's team was going well, until someone in the middle lost their balance and ended up on the grass just before they reached the tape on the other side for the first time. As they made their way back to the start, Tom noticed that none of the other teams had made any progress either and were losing their initial interest in the task. The team closest to the Reception building, which consisted of those who had hung back on the walk to the command task, had two planks between the first three stumps with all of their team members on top of them. Tom's uncle Frank was stood on the stump in the middle shouting at them, "This is like herding cats," but they were stuck in that position, with no way to move the planks from under themselves.

Tom realised that this was going to take a very long time. He called out to his team's umpire. "Are there any rules apart from going over the ground between the white lines using the stumps and planks, and going back to the start if we touch the grass?"

"No, that's all you have to do."
Although the plan seemed good in theory, and would eventually work, it needed a better version, or they would be there for ages, especially if anyone lost their balance again. He looked at Gordon, who had taken the lead for the team next to Tom's. Gordon was the oldest person taking part and was also Tom's second in command as Production Manager. Gordon's team was also back at the start, and Gordon was trying, unsuccessfully, to get his team motivated.
"Gordon!" Tom had a piercing voice when he wanted, and Gordon looked over to him. He walked over to Gordon, beckoning his team to follow him. "This will take ages, and we're beginning to get pissed off." Most people nodded in agreement. "If we use our planks and yours to get across one line of stumps, we can get both teams over in a line in one go, nice and steady so no-one falls off."
Gordon knew that Tom was much cleverer than he was but couldn't see how using four planks could work. "There's too many of us to fit on four planks."
"They want us to think outside the box Gordon, there's twenty of us, we can use three planks to walk on, and each plank can take five people, that's fifteen, a strong person on the tree stump at the front of the line and another on the stump at the end to move the planks forwards, that's seventeen, the three smallest can be carried across pick a back if they're spaced out equally, one on each plank."
Fifteen minutes later, the two teams were eating lunch in a much better frame of mind than they were when they joined forces. James entered comments on his laptop and he and the three adjudicators were left discussing a method they'd never seen before, and whether they should change the rules to prohibit the use of more than two planks per team, and the health and safety aspect of some people carrying team members

on their backs, but rejected the idea, as it would suppress what they called 'sky blue thinking', and they doubted that they would see it again. The last team was too busy arguing with each other to notice what had happened and were even more dismayed when they saw the other two teams walking off laughing. Tom could see Kwame making suggestions on how to complete the task, but he was shouted down by Tom's uncle Frank. After much argument, and no further progress, Frank finally realised that Kwame was right and they could only get five people over each time and later found that they needed a strong person at each end of the line, or they would drop the planks on the grass. Frank put 'his' new plan into action and the last team joined Tom and Gordon's teams in the dining room half an hour later, just as they were leaving to get their room keys.

When they all met up back in the first classroom after lunch most of them had changed their footwear for trainers. They were also in jeans or casual trousers, and woollen pullovers or sweatshirts instead of shirt and tie or blouses. There was an agenda on each table, next to some writing paper, a pen and a small bowl of mints. James was already in the classroom waiting for them, standing in front of a large whiteboard, on which was projected a larger version of the agenda.
"As you can see, we have another command task this afternoon, followed by an open forum on Leadership and Management led by a director of a large British company. Please make sure that you take an active part in the forum as he is an expert in this area. Finally today we have our own version of a psychometric test for you to complete, which is based on two scenarios, one during normal business and one in a high-stress situation, with the extra problem that time is limited. The test is not marked on a 'pass or fail' basis, as there are

many different types and styles of leadership, and a person can change between these types to meet the different situations that they have to resolve. This evening, after dinner, there is a quiz in the bar, which is part of the activities, so your participation is expected. In this classroom after breakfast tomorrow, we will return your test papers, with our interpretations the grading given to each paper. We will also discuss how psychometric tests work, and what characteristics they identify in the person taking the test; if we discuss this before you complete the test this afternoon it may encourage you to provide answers that you think you should put, instead of more realistic ones. This will be followed by a lecture on motivation, before we have the final two command tasks, followed by lunch. The event wash up after lunch usually lasts for about an hour, and will give you the opportunity to discuss amongst yourselves, and with us, your views on the briefings on leadership and motivation, and how they can be applied to make improvements back at work. After that you will be free to leave. We will be sending a report to the Chairman in about a week"

Each of the team members was given a pair of overalls to cover their clothing for the next command task. Details of the teams were listed on the wall; they had been reduced in size to five teams of six, and Tom was fourth on the list of a team that consisted of himself plus three females and two of the shortest men taking part. The afternoon command task was held on the grassed area just outside the classroom. The teams were lined up on one side of a series of walls about three feet high, and were given four long hollow circular iron poles, one of them about two feet longer than the others, three lengths of rope and a large, very heavy plastic container full of water, which had a strong circular carrying handle at the top. Each wall was situated in the centre of a square sand pit, with the grass one metre from the front and back of the wall. James explained what they had to do.

"This task is even simpler than moving people along a series of tree stumps. The task is to get half a bucketful of water using the poles, ropes and the canister. You, the poles or the canister are not allowed to touch the wall or the sand or you will have to dismantle everything and start again, the bucket stays on the other side of the wall, and the water must go over the wall, not around it. When you have made your plan choose one member from each team to stand on the other side of your wall with the empty bucket. Your team member has to get half a bucket full of water back to the classroom, whilst the rest of the team put the poles, ropes and canister back where you found them. We have plenty to do this afternoon, so there will be a cut off time of one hour for those who haven't completed the task by then. Start when you're ready."

Each team instinctively tried the weight of the large container of water, and even the strongest team member could barely lift it. They looked at the poles and the rope and made up either an A-frame or a tripod. When Tom heard the word 'start' he inspected the container and tested its weight, which was much heavier than it should have been, mainly due to the lead weights he could hear clanking about inside when he shook it. Although he could take off the top of the container, the opening was sealed except for a thin slot to allow the water in or out, but not the lead weights. He watched the other teams' members arguing with one another for a minute whilst the remainder of his team watched him making his plan. Tom was smiling again. "Does anyone have any ideas on how to do this? There must be plenty of ways."

Julie broke the silence. "We could build two A-frames and tie the canister to the top of one of the frames by its ring. Then we could tie the frames together at the top and pass one of the bases of the A-frames over the wall to the person on the other side. One of us could climb up the A-frame on our side and push the canister until it is over the wall, and then we could release the rope holding the canister to lower it to the other side."

Tom picked up one of the shorter iron poles and stood it on the ground next to him. The top of the pole was level with the top of his head, equalling his height of six feet. "Good idea, however, the highest point of the poles when they are tied together will need to be directly over the top of the wall, so that we can get the canister over the wall without touching it. The poles are six feet long, so that leaves about five feet six inches when they have been tied together. The bottom of the A-frames will need to be on the grass three feet six inches from the wall on both sides. If the A-frames meet directly above the wall, the line from the top of where the poles meet through the wall to the ground will be at right angles to the ground, so using Pythagoras's theory; five feet six inches squared is thirty and a quarter, three feet six inches squared is twelve and a quarter, leaving the square root of eighteen for the height of the frame above the wall." Julie was also an engineer, and understood the words, but couldn't work out the maths in her head; she would have had problems working it out that quickly with a calculator.

"The square root of eighteen is about four and a quarter feet, minus the height of the wall, which leaves one and a quarter feet. Unfortunately, the canister is eighteen inches from the bottom to the top of the ring, so the poles wouldn't be high enough above the wall for the canister to pass over it without touching. Although that is the obvious method which will be tried by each team, I'm sure that the organisers made the wall just slightly too high on purpose so that way would fail."

Tom was beginning to lose the others' attention, so added some humour into the conversation to get them back again. "If the canister wasn't so heavy, we could throw it over the wall."

His team (there was no doubt that he was the leader of the team), laughed in agreement with this, thinking that Tom had found the simple solution. Unfortunately, he hadn't. The top comes off, but the opening is sealed closed except for a thin slot. The reason why the canister is so heavy is because it is full of lead weights, which are too thick to get through the slot. We could pour some of the water out, but not enough to reduce the weight of the canister enough for us to be able to throw it. So what other options do we have?"

The team members looked around at the other teams trying, and failing, but had no better ideas than those already being used. Tom moved to the middle of his team and quietly explained his plan. Everyone nodded in agreement and John the Accountant went to the other side of the wall with the bucket. Tom's team made a sturdy tripod with the three shorter poles, tied one end of the long pole to the top of the tripod and passed the other end to John on the other side of the wall. Tom took the top off of the container and emptied enough water out to make it easier to lift and hold in position for the short time required to complete the task. He then tied a rope to the ring on the container, throwing the other end of the rope over the top of the tripod. One of his team held the tripod in place, two of them pulled down on the loose end of the rope whilst Tom and Alan, the tallest team members, pushed the container up to the top of the tripod. They moved the top of the container to the end of the free pole and tied the rope to the tripod to keep the container in place. Tom and Alan tipped up the bottom of the container until the water started to flow out of the hole at the top, and enough of the water poured through the centre of the pole over the wall into the bucket until John waved his hand to signal that the bucket was over half full. Tom's team quietly disassembled the tripod, put the poles, ropes and canister back where they found them whilst they watched the other teams, and then walked back to the classroom with the bucket.

The team with Frank made two A-frames, passed one of the A-frames over the wall to their team member with the bucket, just as Julie had said. As expected, the poles weren't high enough for the container to go over the wall, so they tried plan B, which was to stand the A-frames upright, and loosely fasten the third piece of rope to the top of the A-frame on their side. They pushed the rope through the ring on the container and threw the other end of the rope to their team member on the other side of the wall for him to fasten it to the top of his A-frame. The team lifted the container as high as they could whilst Frank pulled his end of the rope over the top of the tripod as tight as he could and tied the end to his A-frame. They then tried, spectacularly unsuccessfully, to slide the container down the rope from their side of the wall to the other. The weight of the container pulled the rope downwards, both A-frames crashed inwards into the wall, and the container fell into the sand.

The way forward used by three other teams was to make a tripod, pass one end of the remaining longer pole over the wall, and tie a piece of rope to the ring of the container to try to control it during its journey over the wall. They put their end of the pole through the ring on the container, and with great difficulty, tried to lift the pole onto the top of the tripod, but the canister was too heavy. Only one team had the strength to succeed in putting the pole on top of the tripod, but their team member on the other side of the wall couldn't hold his end of the pole up high enough for the canister to clear the wall, and the container crashed into the wall. This method failed, even when they tried it a second time.

Tom's team had gone to the classroom without any of the others noticing what they had done. They didn't start laughing until the bucket of water was safely inside. After about thirty minutes, Anna's team joined them. Tom smiled at a very tired looking Anna and looked at the clock on the classroom wall. "You must have almost run out of time. How did you complete the task then?" He received the answer that he expected.
"The problem was the tripod. It wasn't high enough for the container to get over the wall, so we put the end of the fourth pole through the ring of the canister, but when we made the tripod tall enough, it was too heavy, and we couldn't get the end of the fourth pole and the container onto the top of the tripod."
Tom laughed at their problem. "So, unlike the other teams, you placed the tripod far enough from the wall for you to be able to have the three strongest people on the grass between the wall and the tripod for them to lift the pole upwards after the canister had been attached to it."
Anna looked at Tom in awe. "Shit, I said that at the start, but I couldn't convince the others that we wouldn't be able to lift up the pole with the canister on it from behind the tripod. The longest pole was just long enough for three people to stand between the tripod and the wall. After we'd tied one end of the long pole onto the top of the tripod, we swivelled the pole sideways on the tripod to get the other end of the pole through the ring on the container. We then lifted the pole until the canister was higher than the top of the wall, and then moved the pole until it was over the middle of the wall. We had to tie the other two ropes together to make it long enough to control the movement of the canister

from behind the tripod. We then lowered the pole slightly so that the canister started to move down the pole until it reached Terry, on the other side of the wall. The three strongest members of our team were holding the pole in place so the two of us on the rope had great difficulty releasing the rope slowly enough to prevent the canister from flattening Terry as it started to speed up, and the ones holding up the pole and the canister were getting really tired. Luckily we got the canister over the wall before we dropped it. Then Terry had problems lifting up the canister to get the water in the bucket, and most of it went on the grass." Anna paused for breath. "We tired ourselves out trying the same methods as everyone else. The others agreed to try my way whilst we were having a breather. How did you do the task so quickly?"

Julie shrugged and responded with a straight face, "We didn't have the strength in our team to lift the canister and the pole over the wall, so we lifted up the canister on an A-frame using ropes, and poured the water down the centre of the pole into the bucket."

They were still laughing when the other teams joined them in the classroom, having run out of time before completing the task. Not one member of the unsuccessful teams ever thought that they would need to use Pythagoras's theorem after they left school.

Most of the attendees managed to stay awake during the leadership briefing; despite it lasting for over an hour, some of them showed a real interest, and were actively involved with the speaker. Unknown to those listening to the briefing, notes were being taken regarding the attention they paid and their interaction with the speaker. Tom was unusually quiet, but took a few notes during the seminar, and asked questions at the end. He'd heard most of the content many times before whilst studying for his Engineering degree, and unlike his uncle Frank, who always said that he'd forgotten more about leadership than Tom had learnt, Tom had forgotten none of it. The psychometric testing also took over an hour, after which they were allowed to go to their accommodation to have a shower and change into their more casual evening clothes. Each attendee had their own small rectangular room, which consisted of a bed, a wardrobe, a reading table and chair, and a small en-suite bathroom and shower, and although they were basic, they were warm and clean. By the time they had showered and changed, they were more than ready for dinner.

After the attendees had left the classroom, Richard, the fraud investigator, joined James and the other facilitators in the office at the rear of the Training building to discuss what had happened during the day and their thoughts on those taking part. The general consensus was that, if Tom was not part of the family, he would be working for a much larger company, with the opposite feeling about Frank. There were very few leaders, and those that showed the attributes of a strong leader were the younger members of the attendees, but the others weren't so willing to follow them. Some of the attendees were slow coming forward when decisions and leadership were required, and others were quick to make the wrong decisions, but no-one appeared to show any concern that they had things on their minds, such as they were selling the company's future to outside interests, and only Frank had treated his team members with a lack of respect. The facilitators left their notes regarding the attendees with James and went home for the night. Richard was left with James to discuss the day's events further, until Richard was left alone with the psychometric test papers to mark and to match his findings with the comments from the command tasks.

The prices at the bar were more expensive than they were used to, but the company bought the first drink to get them into a good frame of mind for the forthcoming quiz. Everyone expected Kwame and Julie to win easily, as they spent many evenings upsetting customers in the pubs around Oxford by taking their money at the pub quizzes, but the questions were not the usual 'General Knowledge' or 'Celebrity' based ones, and there were many blank faces when the first question was asked.
"Why is it illegal for someone living in Southampton to be buried in Portsmouth?" This was followed by other unusual questions, such as 'What did Winnie the Pooh and Attila the Hun have in common?', 'When does London begin with an 'L' and end with an 'E'?, 'Where is women's hair the curliest?' and, 'After winning the German Grand Prix in 2012, what did Lewis Hamilton say that he wished was longer?'
When the results were revealed, most of those taking part discovered that, despite their answers being based on the urban myth relating to the dispute between the people in Southampton and Portsmouth during a strike at Portsmouth docks in the 1890s when some dockers from Southampton allegedly went to Portsmouth and broke the picket line, the real reason why it was illegal for them to be buried in Portsmouth was because they were still living. The link between Winnie the Pooh and Attila the Hun was not honey, as most people thought, but was because they had the same middle name, London always begins with the letter 'L', and End always begins with the letter 'E', women's hair is curliest in Africa, and Lewis Hamilton said that he wished that the UK National Anthem was longer, because he would have stood on the winner's podium for a longer time being applauded whilst the music was being played. The 'True or False' round was easier, and, they all

agreed that the statement that 'ring doughnuts were not invented to allow waiters to carry more cakes in nudist colonies' was false, and Screwfix was not a dating agency.

James, along with his assistants, had stayed professionally detached from those taking part during the day, but when he appeared in the bar after quiz, he needed to speak to them on an informal basis to gather the more personal information. He already knew the answers to most of the questions that he planned to ask, but wanted to check their reactions to the questions, and how their responses varied from the information provided by the Company Chairman. The first person that he wanted to speak to was Tom, not only for his personal information, but also what Tom thought of his colleagues. As usual, Tom was not difficult to find.

"Hello Tom, congratulations on your win in the quiz, you seem to be having quite a successful day." Tom responded with his regular smile.

"I owe a lot of the quiz success to Rashid; he has a strange brain that can work out the odd things in life."

"You seemed to manage ok with the command tasks today."

"That was mainly logical. If you can match what you have with what you need, and remove the factors preventing you from achieving something, then all that's left is usually the answer."

"How did you get the idea to use the extra planks for the first task?"

"The task could be achieved using only two planks, but it would be done so at such a slow pace that there would always be the problem of people losing their balance and falling off, and having to start all over again. The best way was to get everyone over in one flowing movement. The thing that was stopping us from doing that was the lack of planks. If Frank wasn't too busy shouting at the rest of his team, I would have asked him for his two planks as well, and we could all have walked over in one line without having to take any of the planks with us."

"That's the first time that we've had people sharing planks before. Why didn't you ask another team to share the iron poles for the second task?"

"I didn't need them, although it would have been much easier for those that tried to slide the canister down the pole from a tripod if they'd had another three poles to make a slightly lower tripod on the other side of the wall, then they would be able to secure the longer pole on top of the two tripods with enough height for the canister to clear the wall when they slid it to the person on the other side."

James shook his head in disbelief that Tom had found another way to beat their system. "We'll have to add in the rules that each team can only use their own props. Is there anything else that I should change?"

"I would have liked someone a bit taller and stronger in my team, but someone put me in a team of short people." He looked at James with mock suspicion.

"Caught red-handed, I'm afraid. We thought that we needed to put in a handicap to slow you down. We might have to do the same with Anna tomorrow, but we'd like to see how she interacts with some of the others."

Tom was beginning to like this man much more than he expected. "We're lucky to have Anna, but she has family responsibilities, and the Chairman was keen to keep hold of her when she went off on maternity leave. He treated her well during her pregnancy and kept in constant touch with her during her time off, and then allowed her to work a few days a week to adjust when she returned to work, including working from home, which wasn't very common in those days. Loyalty works both ways, and she's not the sort of person to forget that. Babies are a huge distraction for working mothers, especially single ones, but they grow up quickly and are soon learning their own way in the world at nursery, followed by school. Anna was well worth the wait."

"Anna's a single mother?"

"Yes, she got involved with a bastard called Kevin some years ago, and when she became pregnant, he didn't want anything more to do with her."

The man knew most of this already from her file, and mentally logged the rest because the lack of money required to bring up a child could be a factor if Anna was the person that they were trying to identify. He continued without losing the thread of the conversation.

"You seemed quite quiet during the leadership briefing this afternoon."

"I know I shouldn't say this, but I really have heard most of it before. The main point that I raised at the end is always missed by people from better backgrounds. The concept of people treating anyone without authority as a leader just because they have the skills and the ability to voice them with some degree of confidence works in the USA, but this is England, and position will always take precedence over ability."

"You seem to manage all right."

"I'm the Chairman's grandson. It would be different if I wasn't."

"Is Frank your father?"

"No, I call him my uncle, but he's my grandfather's brother's son. He's a Harbod though, and that proves my point about leadership in England. Frank thinks that he's a leader because of his position in the company, not because of his ability, and people listen to him because of that reason. If Anna was senior management her team would have listened to her on the second command task, and they would have

finished much quicker. You'll probably notice that in a few others tomorrow."
James paid a mental note of Tom's reaction to his question about Frank being his father, despite already knowing otherwise, and Tom's view on leadership. He liked what he'd heard about Tom and was greatly impressed with Tom's qualities and how he interacted with everyone at the team building. He gave Tom his card. "I run this establishment. I'm not trying to steal you from Grangers, but I would like to use you as a consultant now and again, if that's ok? There's a lot of money to be made in this line of work, and we'll make it worth your while. I need to talk to the other attendees, so I'll bid you goodnight, but please keep us in mind."
The next person James spoke to was Frank, but the conversation was much shorter than the one with Tom, mainly because he had a lot of people to talk to that evening, but also because he had so much more to say to Tom than the others, especially Frank, and he wanted to speak to Frank early, before Frank had had too much to drink, as was detailed in his brief.

Eventually the attendees were left alone to talk and drink amongst themselves, with Frank leading the discussions, usually about himself and his family's role in Grangers. Frank went to the bar and shouted back to those remaining, asking them what they wanted to drink. At least half of them responded with an order. The drinks were ferried back to the drinkers, and Frank re-joined them, carrying on from where he left off, until he noticed that Tom did not have a fresh drink.
"What's up with you tonight, I remember when you used to go out to the pub drinking every night, quite often with my father."
Tom recalled his memory of Frank's father, also called Frank in line with the Harbod family tradition for the naming of the first-born son. Frank senior was the older

brother of Thomas Harbod, the Company Chairman, and had retained his thirst and capacity for alcohol until his death well into his eighties. His interest in drinking and females had started as soon as he was allowed in the local pubs, much to the disgust of Tom's great grandfather who regularly told him at the time that he was wasting his young life running around town when he could be working with Thomas on the business with the original owner. Tom's great grandfather was less than amused when Frank senior got a casual acquaintance pregnant after an alcohol fuelled meeting and married beneath him. When Tom's parents were killed, a teenage Tom and his younger sister moved in with their grandfather. When Tom came back from university as a young man, Tom was more like Thomas's brother, Frank senior, than his own father.
"Times were different in those days I was young and had no responsibilities."
"You're still young. What responsibilities do you have now, you don't Have any children? You won't find many places as welcoming as a British pub."
Frank lived his life with the belief that most of things in his life were far more important than his job, unlike Tom, who had gradually acquired his grandfather's love of the business after leaving University, and realised that drinking too much alcohol on a regular basis reduced his performance at work. "I doubt that I would get away with turning up to work unshaven and smelling of alcohol these days."
"How did you get away with it then? Your grandfather was a miserable sod whose world revolved around work and hated people wasting their time and money drinking, and became even worse when a drunken driver caused the death of his wife and your parents."
Tom frowned at the memory. "The doors to the house were locked and bolted at midnight, and although I had my own key, it wouldn't get me in late at night as the

front and back door would be bolted as well as locked. If I wanted to get in after midnight, I would have to bang on the front door and wake him up."
"He must have moaned at you every night then."
"No, if you remember, there's a tree outside my old bedroom window which I could climb up quite easily and get inside without being caught. Some nights, I also brought a female companion home. My grandfather is always up early, so I had to get her out of the house before he was awake, which was quite challenging after a night of drinking and other exploits, especially in the dark."
"But he keeps that big house as tight as a drum. He must have locked all of the doors and windows, including the one in your bedroom, and if you did get in through your bedroom window, you wouldn't have had the time to get to the house alarm to turn it off."
"I'm and engineer, Uncle Frank. I fixed the window so that it can be unlocked from the outside, without it being noticed from the inside, and if I can't disable a burglar alarm, I would have wasted my time training."
This not only brought a large amount of laughter from those present, but also encouraged others to join in the conversation. Rick, Frank's youngest son, was also present at the team building, which surprised some people, and re-enforced Tom's view on people's position and leadership. "I don't understand why you still spend so much time in the pub, Dad. There are many better places to go to now."
"Don't you knock pubs son, that's how I met your mother."
This closed the topic of pubs, and the crowd in the bar, including Tom, gradually dispersed back to their rooms. Tom was surprised to see a light on as he passed the training building, and noticed James inside talking to another man. Tom thought 'I don't think I'll be taking him up on his offer if I have to work 24 hours each day.'

A few diehards stayed in the bar until it closed and reconvened in Frank's room with the bottle of vodka and larger bottle of coke that Frank usually travelled with. It was always good to keep in with the senior management, especially when all you needed was the tooth-glass from your bathroom to share the free vodka.

Although the door was locked, the master key had no problem allowing the attractive young female to enter the room. Tony was crouched in the darkness outside the window with his camera ready to take the incriminating photographs to recruit another member to the conspirators. She locked the door as quietly as possible, but her sounds were drowned out by the loud snores of the man deeply asleep in the bed. She unzipped her dress, and let it fall to the floor, leaving her naked as she slid onto the bed, with him between her and the window. She pulled back the duvet and he came awake with a start when she started to play with him.
"Shhhhh, don't wake the others darling, I'm a present from the management."
The large amount of alcohol consumed allowed his aroused penis to take over the situation, as she climbed on top of him and started to move up and down, whilst Tony took a series of photographs which would be very interesting to the man underneath, and especially to his wife, if he wouldn't do what they wanted him to. Tony was impressed with the quality of the photos produced by his infra-red camera, which negated the use of flash photography, keeping the victim unaware of what was happening as well as greatly reducing the chances of being caught himself. As soon as the target was finished, she quickly put on her dress and joined Tony in the darkness outside, leaving him to drift back to an uninterrupted sleep until he woke up a few hours later

with fragmented remnants of a pleasant memory which he was unsure had actually happened.

The following morning there were two absentees, John the Accountant and Mark, who had both ignored the high cost of the beer, and had later shared the vodka in Frank's room, and drank far more than they should. They both worked on the principle that the major cause of hangovers was waking up, so had gone back to sleep when they should have been getting washed and shaved and remained asleep when they should have been eating breakfast. They wouldn't have been able to face a full English but should have eaten something to jump-start their bodies into action for the day's activities. They entered the classroom, sheepishly carrying a cup of coffee, half an hour after James had started to explain what psychometric tests achieved, and how their grades matched their mental aptitude with their personality and behaviour style. The separate results were passed to the person whose name was on the top of the paper and were not made available to all and sundry. Although most people would have expected Tom's result to show that he was outgoing, with sound judgement and quick at making the correct decisions, they would have been surprised to learn that Frank was a strong leader who was innovative and pushed through change, which highlighted the drawback where the person entering the information selected the option describing how they would like to be, or maybe even, incorrectly thought they were   This encouraged Frank to be even more vociferous during the briefing on motivation, and the first command task which followed.

James led the attendees to the command task and gave them an update from his findings of the day before. "The assessors noticed yesterday that some people's suggestions to solve the command tasks were

disregarded because the people with the good ideas weren't in senior managements posts." This statement was incorrect because it had come from Tom, not the assessors, but those present weren't to know that. "The consequence of this was that the tasks took longer to complete than they should have, or the teams failed to successfully complete these tasks. We are going to stress this as one of the main points raised at the 'Leadership' presentations in the future, and, if nothing else, please take this thought with you for the remainder of the morning, and hopefully, for the remainder of your career in management."
Frank thought that James' perspective was aimed at those who accompanied him the day before, but Tom knew that his remarks to James regarding Anna the night before had been understood and noted.

The make-up of the teams was changed again. The two with hangovers had promptly moved to the side of the area to try to recover, and four teams of seven started the first command task of the day. This task involved making a large, foot high wooden square wall around the attendees, with long planks of wood which had tongue and groove edges and ends which only allowed them to interlink in one way. There were small coded markings on each plank, but they were difficult to see or decipher, and had been ignored by those taking part in the initial run through, except for Rashid. He shouted for everyone to stop whilst they could work out how to use this information. Rick and Sally carried on regardless, thinking that their way, which had no clear strategy, but some activity instead of talking, would complete the task. Rashid went to Tom to speak about the markings.
"Tom, the wall is three planks high, these marks show which corner each of the pieces of wood are located, and whether they are on the first, second or third level.

If everyone takes the pieces of wood with their allocated markings to their own side of the wall, they should all join together. We should be able to complete this task really quickly." He stood in front of Rick and Sally. "Stop what you're doing, all you're achieving is completing one side, and preventing the rest of the team from doing theirs. If we all work together, we can do all of the sides at the same time."

Sally threw her piece of wood to the ground. She was one of the older members of those taking part and had been a member of the management board for some time. Her age and large weight were causing problems with her stamina. The stress and physical requirements of the activities on the first day had taken their toll, and she was now having difficulty keeping up.

"I don't know why I'm here. I'm busy enough at work without been dragged away from my office to waste my time doing these stupid tests."

She stormed off to join the two with hangovers and was quickly joined by another of the 'older' contingent in Frank's team. Rashid looked at Tom, spreading his arms out for moral support, and Tom nodded his head in agreement.

"Don't look at me take over, it's your idea, get on with it." Rashid stood in the centre of the wall and pointed out the markings on the end of each of the pieces of wood. He nominated one team member to each of the corners and allocated each type of marking to each corner, a fact that didn't go down too well with Rick who didn't think that he should be told what to do. Rashid and Tom helped to sort out and distribute the wood. The team quickly identified their pieces of wood, and slotted them together, being the only team to complete the wall in the time allocated for the run through. They were then told to disassemble their walls and change areas with each of the other teams to prevent them from pre-sorting the wood for the proper race.

When the clock started for the proper task, Frank took control of what he deemed to be his team, giving them his initial brief on how he wanted the task to be carried out, followed by his favourite motivational statement, "Let's get moving, this cock won't suck itself." Throughout the task he continued to shout his instructions and what he perceived would keep the team moving. "This is stupid. It's like trying to put together a jigsaw puzzle without the picture on the top of the box." His team were, as usual, the last to finish. The team containing Tom and Rashid finished the construction of their wooden wall in a new record time. Anna's team, which included Kwame and Julie, finished a close second, with the other two teams a long way behind. James made notes in his laptop and moved the teams to the next command task at the side of an oval lake with a small island in the centre.

"I'd like the people who missed out on the last command task to re-join the group please. Frank, Rashid, Anna, Julie, Kwame and Tom please come and stand next to me. Please keep quiet and watch what the others do." He split those remaining into two teams of twelve. Frank felt that his performance during the command tasks had been so good that he had been singled out to demonstrate this to the others. "Maybe this will encourage everyone to push themselves forward for the final command task."

Tom looked over at James to see his raised eyebrows confirming that Frank was well off the mark with his perception of why they had been taken to one side. The other five had taken the lead on the previous tasks, and without their presence others will need to come out of hiding or the last task would never be completed, but Frank had been taken away to allow others to get a chance to speak, and show their leadership qualities without him shouting them down.

The last task should have been simple, all they had to do was get the teams from where they stood on the bank over to the island about thirty metres away with each team using one of the two small wooden boats, the pointy part of each of the boats was tied closely to the bank with its own long rope, which had a small loop at one end and a larger loop at the other. There was a long, double-ended paddle in each boat, held in place by a retaining clip at the front and the back of the boat. They were told that they were not allowed to use anything from the other boat, only one person was allowed in the boat at any one time, and they were not allowed to touch the water with any part of their body. They could see another, longer rope on the island, but it was wrapped around a thick post which stood in the ground just out of reach from the water's edge. The reason why the task was not simple was because the metre-high bank at the landing part of the island had been cut away downwards for a further metre below the water level, making the water deep right up to the edge of the island. There were footholds cut into the bank on the island but nothing to hold onto. Another, as yet unknown reason why the task was so difficult was that the rope on the boat was a metre short. Both of the teams put the small loop of the rope onto the clip at the back of their boat and untied the other end from the front. John the Accountant decided that he needed to make up for his hangover-related late start, jumped into his team's boat and frantically rowed to the island. Both teams discovered too late that the rope was just too short for them to disembark onto dry land. John stood at the front of his boat trying to propel himself as close as possible to the island to have a chance of jumping the difference, but his forward motion was matched with an equal backward force on the boat, making the distance far too long. He lost his balance and ended up in the lake and was quickly rescued by two of the facilitators. Mary in the other boat was not going to make the same mistake as John and looked back for direction from the others. Rick was still laughing at John's unexpected bath and stopped for long enough to shout "Jump!" to Mary at the top of his voice.

"No chance," was the response, and she continued to hover around the front of the boat.

Rick took his belt off of his trousers, and put it back on outside of his overalls, pushed through the crowd and grabbed the large loop at his end of the rope. Although he was now talking to the people on the bank next to him, Rick was still shouting. "Hold onto my belt." He leant forward and the front of the boat moved a little closer to the edge of the island. "Jump!" he shouted again. Mary sat down in the boat and started to cry. Rick pulled the boat back to the bank. "Get out you useless cow and let someone in who'll do as they're told."

No-one moved forward, Rick had noticed that Mike had hung back during the command tasks so Rick grabbed hold of him and pushed him into the boat. "This is easy, I'm the one doing the dangerous part by leaning out over the water to put you close enough to the island for you to step out of the boat onto dry land. Go over there and show them how it's done."

The other team had pulled their boat back and also had another volunteer paddling back to the island, whilst John had gone back to his room to have a shower, dry himself off, and put some dry clothes on. Rick's team's boat had reached the island, but Mike would not jump from the boat despite the shouting from Rick, and no-one else was offering any other advice. Mike stood at the front end of the boat but couldn't quite reach the footholds and wouldn't go any further. Rick eventually became frustrated by the inaction and yanked back on

the rope, resulting in Mike ending up in the water.
James went to the two teams on the edge of the lake.
"I think that it would be a good idea if you tried a better way to complete the task, as this one obviously isn't working. Does anyone have any ideas?" After two minutes of muttering, no other solutions were provided. James looked at the six people that he'd pulled from the task. "What are they doing wrong?"
Frank gave his view, which was consistent with everything else that he had done previously. "They're not trying hard enough, and they don't have a leader like me telling what to do. They're all over the place like a disorganised mob, it's just madness."
"Would anyone like to expand on Frank's answer?"
Tom gave his best diplomatic answer, although Frank wouldn't have understood a sarcastic one. "Frank is absolutely correct. Einstein's definition of insanity is doing the same thing over and over again and expecting a different result. They can see that the rope isn't long enough, but they're trying the same method each time without looking for another option."
James looked at the others. "And is there another option that would be successful?"
Tom looked at the other five and waited for a response, but none came, so he gave them his thoughts. "There has to be a way to do this task or we wouldn't have been asked to do it, the only time I've heard of a task with no way to achieve it was in Star Trek, and Captain Kirk succeeded by cheating. An Engineer would use a functional analysis approach and look at things differently. People look for something that they think will enable them to resolve a problem, so, when the problem requires you to undo a nut, they try desperately to get a spanner not to find any available method that will enable them to undo the nut. If you can't find a spanner, you need to work out another way to undo the nut, not to keep looking for a spanner. The task is to get someone

in the boat onto the island and get the empty boat back again and repeat the process until everyone is on the island. The problem that they have is that the person in the boat can't get onto to the island if the others are holding onto a rope which isn't long enough." He then looked at the others, but they were still quiet.

Eventually Julie said, "But they don't have anything else."

Rashid finally moved to the correct wavelength, "Ok, if using the rope is stopping them from reaching the island, they have to use what they have for a different purpose. They can extend the length of the rope by putting the paddle into the clip at the end of the boat with the long part sticking out over the back of the boat. Putting the other end of the paddle through the smaller loop on the rope should make it long enough."

Frank looked at Rashid in disgust with his simplistic answer. "Even I could see that, but the rules were that you aren't allowed to touch the water, so they wouldn't be able to paddle across."

Rachid didn't allow Frank's bullying tone to put him off. "They can take off the top of the seat and use that as a paddle. When they get onto the island, they can get the other rope and tie it to the front of the boat, and the team pulls the boat back to the bank, another person gets in the boat and the team pulls the boat quickly from the bank to the island and back again."

Tom was impressed with Rashid's idea, but had his own view. "Although that might work, it would take a long time to get over to the island using the seat as a paddle, instead of the paddle itself. And the person on the boat would have problems getting onto the island. It would be quicker and easier if the first person used the paddle to get to the island, threw the large loop of the rope over the post holding the second rope like a lasso. There has to be a reason for the rope to have a large loop. The person in the boat could then secure the boat in place using the first rope and use the rope and the footholds to get onto the island and collect the other rope. He could then tie the rope from the island to the post at one end and the front of the boat with the other end, holding the boat in place until he gets back in it. He could then take the first rope off of the post and put it in the boat and paddle back to this side of the island, connect the first rope and the paddle to the back of the boat and pull on the rope at the front of the boat to get back to the island. Each person on the boat could pull the boat over to the island in turn, and those on this bank could pull the boat back again until everyone is on the island. Once you have people on the island, it wouldn't take much time to pull the boat back and forth."

James addressed the crowd. "Both of those methods have been used before, not very often, and both are successful. What would you have done if the rope on the island was also too short?"
Anna was starting to catch up. "I'd paddle over to the island, lasso the post to get onto the island, bring the other rope back, and tie the two ropes together attach one end of the rope to the back of the boat and the other end would be held by those on this bank. Each person in the boat could paddle the boat to the island, climb onto the jetty, and the others on the bank here could pull it back with the rope."
"Correct. There would now be enough rope on the boat to secure the boat to the post on the island for the first person to get onto the island for the second time, after that, there would be someone on the island to assist the person inside the boat. The first rope was a red herring, and most teams that participate in this task look no further than using it instead of trying to find another solution which had a greater chance of meeting the objectives set. We'll end the task now, and meet up in the classroom at one thirty, after lunch."

The teams were demoralised after their poor showing during the last task, and a great deal of spin was employed by James during the wash up to focus on the successes of the two days, how to assess the factors that caused failures, and take advantage of them, to send the attendees home feeling good about their efforts of the two days.

FOUR

Richard had written his report on the Team Building and returned it in person the following Saturday evening to Thomas. Richard liked working for Thomas, he was now getting close to his fiftieth birthday and was starting to feel his age, but the first time that he met Thomas, Richard was surprised how healthy and alert the much older man was, and immediately felt better about himself. Everywhere Richard looked he was surrounded by youngsters, who were trying to take his place. Richard was tall and still fit and strong, which was necessary when he had the occasional altercation with people who disagreed with him. A friend of a friend of Thomas has recommended Richard when Thomas noticed that one of their designs had been reported in the business papers with the heading 'Is this the way that Grangers is now doing business' with a negative write-up about how their machinery affected Global warming. The write up was incorrect, but could be conceived to be truthful, and they noticed a reduction in orders for their latest car. Grangers' management couldn't identify who the culprit was, so they hired an investigator who spent four weeks with the same result, by which time some of Grangers' other business sensitive information was reported in the media. Richard went through his normal list of checks for a week to find out how the information had left the company, and who was responsible for it, and could find nothing. There was no way that the newspaper reporter would divulge the source of the information; if he ever did, he would soon be out of a job. Some of the married employees were having affairs, others were meeting prostitutes, and there was an increase in people being reported as gay, in line with the current trend of it no longer being anyone else's business, some were taking illegal drugs and two had gambling debts, but nothing that Richard's team found would be enough for them to release the information to the press. When he met up with Thomas at Thomas's house after a week, he had nothing to report.

"My associates have checked everyone on your list who had access to the information, and there is no-one who could have been coerced into providing the information against their will."

The old man was visibly upset that he had been failed again. "I was told that you would sort this out. This is a personal attack on everything that I've done in my life."

"That's what I was going to say next."

This didn't do anything to improve the old man's mood. "So you can only tell me what I already know."

"No, what I was going to say was that by taking away every possible reason that someone could be forced to do this, it only leaves a person with a personal grudge against you."

"What have I ever done to upset anyone so much that they would try to blacken my character?"

"Is there anyone on your list who has been badly treated by Grangers, or had a friend or relative who could hold a grudge?"

"Not at all, I know most of them. The management team has vouched for the ones that I don't know in person."

Richard gave Thomas a report that he'd been working on throughout the previous night. "This report shows the parents and grandparents of everyone on your list. Is there anyone in the report who you recognise?"

Thomas looked at the report for a minute until he looked up at Richard. His finger was fixed on one of the names of the grandparents. "I know that name. John Jones! I know Andy Clark, he's a nice young man. I didn't know that Johnnie Jones was his grandfather. Johnnie Jones was one of the original workers when I joined Grangers, I told them that they had to change the way in which they manufactured their cars or they would be bankrupt, he said that I didn't know what I was talking about, and that he could make a good profit setting up on his own using the old methods. I didn't realise that the two were related as he's the father of Andy's mother, so they have different surnames."

"What happened to the man's business after he left Grangers?"

"He went bust within a year. He lost everything he owned to pay back the money he'd borrowed. Mr Granger offered him a job when he heard that he had problems, but he said that he wouldn't work in the same company as me. I never heard from him again."

"Is there anyone on the list that you recognise?"

Thomas looked at the rest of the names on the list and shook his head. "No, he's the only one. It felt good when I was proved right, but I was still sad that they went under. There were three of them who left Grangers when we changed our business strategy, two of them realised that they had made a huge mistake and cut their losses early, one of them went to work for another garage, and one of them came back to Grangers. Johnny was too pig-headed to admit that he was wrong and threw good money after bad"

"What do you want me to do about this? I can get the newspaper to release an apology for their reports, or are you friends with the editor?"

"If the editor was a friend of mine, do you think that he would have allowed this rubbish to be printed?"

"Sometimes people will print anything if they think that it will sell more papers."

"None of the editors that I know would."

Richard was back to the same question. "So do you want me to speak to the editor?"

Thomas couldn't believe that Richard had enough leverage to obtain an apology from the paper. "Is that possible?"

"I believe so. I'll get them to write an apology in the paper and tell them to report that you have asked for them to make a donation of £100,000 to a charity. Do you have any preferences?"

"We've always supported Oxfam because it's our local charity."

"Ok, what are you going to do with the person releasing the information?"

"Let me see." Thomas opened his telephone contacts book and dialled a number.

"Hello Glenn, it's Thomas Harbod. How are you enjoying retirement?"

"Fine thanks, I should have done it year's ago, but you kept asking me to stay on."

"That's because you were a good worker and a good friend."

"Are you so stretched that you want me to come back to work?"

"No thanks Glenn, you enjoy your retirement, you deserve it. Are you still in touch with Johnnie Jones's family?"

"Not since his funeral, why do you ask?"

"Do you know his grandchildren?"

"Yes, he had about six. One of them works for you."

"Andy Clark?"

"Yes, that's right. He's a nice lad. He drinks in my local pub I see him quite often."

"Could I pop over later and speak to you please? There's a favour that I'd like you to do for me."

"No problem, I'm free all day, I'm retired remember."

"Ok Glenn, I'll see you at six o'clock."

"I look forward to it. See you later Thomas."

Thomas put the phone down.

"Glenn is an old friend of Johnnie's and will tell Andy exactly what happened. That should end the matter. If he agrees to stop, I will forget that it happened."

"I could never do that. If anyone working for me ever thought that they could get away with something like that, they would be given a strong physical persuader to make them change their mind."
"We'll see what he says. I'll get back to you in two days' time regarding what happens next."

Glenn met up with Andy in the pub the following evening. Although he was relieved to get lucky on his first try, the old man was able to look surprised to meet his friend's grandson.
"Hello Andy, I haven't seen you for ages, how's your new job?"
"New job?"
"At Grangers."
"I've been there for three years now. I'm glad that grandad doesn't know that I'm working there, he hated Grangers, and detested Mr Harbod."
"Really?"
"Defo, he blamed them for losing all of his money and he was lucky not to lose his house!"
Glenn had heard Johnnie persistently moan about Thomas Harbod, and how he 'wrecked his life', but he had first-hand experience of who was to blame.
"That's not exactly the truth. Let me buy you a beer and tell you what actually happened."
They moved to a table further away from the bar and sat down with their pints. Andy had always liked Glenn, and his grandfather had always said good things about him, so he allowed him his few words.
"The first time that I met Thomas Harbod, Grangers was just a very small company, which was on the verge of running out of money. Thomas came up with a plan to save Grangers, and he and his father put money into the company to pay off its debts. There were only six workers at Grangers in those days, Mr Granger called a meeting and Thomas told us that the only way for

Grangers to survive was to change the way that we were making our cars to cut costs and Johnnie disagreed with him. Your grandfather said that he could do a better job at making cars than Grangers and got up and left the meeting. Johnnie was one of the best mechanics that I ever knew and was always telling us that we could make our fortune making and selling our own cars, so another two of us at the meeting, including myself, left with him."

Andy nodded. "That's what grandad told me."

"Your grandad really was an excellent mechanic, and kept telling us that workers like us would never get rich working for someone else, but Grangers already had a workshop set up to make the cars, plus a full order book, cars already designed, contracts with suppliers for the parts, and a good name. We had nothing. We had to pay over the odds for everything that we bought, and we had to pay for all of our car parts and supplies when they were delivered. We didn't start to produce cars until we'd been in business for six months but still hadn't sold one single car."

"That's because Grangers reduced the price of their cars so no-one would buy the ones that my grandfather made."

"Grangers reduced the price of their cars because they were able to make them cheaper and quicker using the new production methods introduced by Thomas Harbod. They still couldn't make enough cars to meet the large increase in demand. We couldn't make our cars for the price that Grangers was selling them for, and their cars were better than ours so no-one would pay more for our cars and we ran out of money."

"My grandfather carried on and started to sell cars."

"The cars were sold at less than the price it cost to make them just to bring in some money. None of us could afford to keep losing money. Not only had we lost all of our savings, we'd also taken out a loan from the bank, and had to pay that back. We had to go back to working for someone else to pay for the rent, feed our families and pay off the loan. Your grandfather was too stubborn to give up and lost far more money than we did."

"He did ok in the end."

"That's because Mr Granger helped him."

"What?"

"Mr Granger offered him a job."

"My grandfather could have got a job with anyone. He wanted to work for himself."

"That's right, but your grandfather almost lost his house because he wouldn't stop what he was doing and continued to lose money. Not many of us owned their own house in the 1950s but your grandmother had inherited her family home, and your grandfather had put up the house as security to obtain another loan. He would have lost the house if Mr Granger hadn't helped him."

"I don't know what you're talking about."

"Mr Granger said that he would help to pay off some of the loan but your grandfather turned him down flat, so he gave your grandfather an interest-free loan, and told him that he didn't have to start to pay him back until he was back on his feet again."

"He never told me that. That would explain why he always complained about Grangers but never had a bad word to say about Mr Granger. He blamed Thomas Harbod for everything that had gone wrong."

"Mr Granger told your grandfather that he should work for himself but would make much more money setting up his own company to repair cars rather than making them. There were lots of cars on the road by this time and they were breaking down on a regular basis, Mr Granger convinced your grandfather that he should use his skill as an experienced mechanic to make his business a success."

"It was a success, but he told me it was all down to his hard work, despite everything that Thomas Harbod did to try to hold him back."

"Grangers continued to send a large amount of work his way after Mr Granger died, which would have been agreed by Thomas."

"He never told me that."

"He probably didn't want to tell you that, but Thomas is not a man to hold a grudge, despite what your grandfather used to say about him."

Andy went quiet. Glenn caught up on some drinking time, as he'd spent the last ten minutes talking, whilst waiting for the young man to realise what he'd done.

"I've fucked up, haven't I?"

Glenn smiled. He'd expected this outcome since Thomas had spoken to him at his house.

"Can you tell me exactly what happened?"

It was Andy's turn to take a long drink of his beer before continuing.

"About a month ago a man started talking to me in here. It was late on a Friday night, and I'd had a few too many, and he bought me a pint and a large vodka and coke. He told me that he used to live in the area and mentioned the names of the people who he used to drink with. My grandfather's name was one of those mentioned. He also said what a shit Thomas Harbod was, and I became interested, and I told him a few things that my grandfather had told me."

"Was this man as old as your grandfather would have been?"

"No, he was about fifty, in smart clothes, and looked fit for his age. His hands and fingernails were clean, nothing like my grandfather's were, even after he retired his hands were still gnarled and dirty."

"Would you recognise him if you saw him again?"

"Definitely."

"Why?"

"For one, he was really tall, and he had a full head of dark hair, most people I know have started to lose their hair or go grey at his age."
"Anything else?"
"Not really. His face was quite pale, and he had a small scar underneath his left eye, which most people probably might not have noticed."
"Ok, thanks. What happened then?"
"He told me that Grangers were cutting costs and were doing things that were dangerous for the environment. I told him that wasn't the way that Grangers did their business, and he said that was exactly what they wanted everyone to think."
"Did he ask you to do anything for him?"
"He asked me if I could get a drawing of any of the latest projects that we were working on. I had access to some information, but it wasn't very detailed or protected so I gave him a copy of one the following week."
"Did he pay you for it?"
"Certainly not. He said that he was looking for any information that would make Thomas Harbod look bad, and I thought that my grandfather would approve if I helped him. Am I going to get the sack?"
"I doubt it lad. Thomas isn't as bad as your grandfather told you, you'll be ok as long as you don't tell too many people what you did, and you don't do it again."

Glenn phoned Thomas when he got home from the pub, the phone call lasted a good five minutes, mainly due to Thomas taking notes, and asking Glenn to repeat a few things.
"Thank you for doing this for me Glenn, was the £10 enough for the drinks?"
"Yes thanks, and it was good to catch up with Andy anyway. It's always good to speak to young people these days, they have a far different view on life than we used to."

Thomas phoned Richard with the details of the conversation. No matter what time he phoned Richard, he always seemed to be awake and alert. Richard was most interested in the description that Andy gave of the man who spoke to him.
"It was good that your young man noticed the scar. I know the person who gave him that. I'll call the editor and arrange a meeting with him tomorrow to discuss what you've just told me."
"Will he meet you at such short notice?"
"That will not be a problem at all. I know people who have quite a lot of influence over others who are well-placed and influential. I think that we may be able put this episode to some advantage."
"Thank you, Richard, goodnight. I'll speak to you tomorrow."

The following lunchtime Richard and the editor met up in Sainsbury's car park, out of the view of the closed-circuit cameras. Despite the lack of rain, Richard's face was kept out of view by his umbrella as he walked over to the car. They discussed the problem regarding the statements in the paper about Grangers and Thomas Harbod, and the editor's face went from pale to white as Richard described how much shit the paper was in.
"Okay, okay, what do you want me to do?"
"Surprise me."
"We can print an apology and pay Mr Harbod a substantial amount to put right his wounded feelings."
"You can do a lot better than that."
"How?"
"You could publish a whole article in the paper stating how beneficial for the environment that the work that Grangers is carrying out will be."
"And the stuff that we've put in over the last few weeks?"

"I'm sure you'll be able to put a spin on that."
"Who is going to talk to us from Grangers to give us that sort of information after what we've just done?"
"Thomas Harbod would be a good place to start."

Richard and Thomas had become good friends after that. The type of work that he carried out for Thomas stayed within legal limits, but sometimes only just, and the word went around that Richard was more than competent in resolving sensitive problems usually by making it look like the problems were due to misunderstandings. This side of Richard's business had started to become a regular occurrence compared with his previous line of more illicit practices. He hadn't decreased his unlawful work, but had managed to keep below the police radar, mainly due to his regular presence at Fraud seminars, and his contact with the police when he was assisting businesses who had suffered at the hands of industrial espionage.

Unlike most divorcees, Richard hadn't taken too long to get back on his feet after he kicked his wife out. Luckily she only knew about his legal business, so the financial pay off was much lower than it should have been, but it still made him angry when someone told the old joke that hurricanes were named after women, because when a wife left, she did actually take her husband's house and car with her. It never once occurred to him that his ex-wife was uninterested in his speeches on how to detect fraud at business conferences, and she blamed him for leaving her alone too much too often so that when she was chatted up by the man called Kevin at one of them, she found it hard to resist. Richard sometimes used the conferences to recruit new people to his circle, for both the legal and dishonest work, but usually for a combination of both. He had considered asking Peter Stevenson to work with him when they first met at a conference, but the people checking on Peter reported that he was lacking the backbone to carry out the scarier side of the business. What Richard wanted was a cross between Peter, who was not only very intelligent, but had plenty of both business and common sense and his bastard friend Kevin Stevens, whose morals were so low that he had disappeared with Richard's wife at the conference when he was too busy to notice. He did get his own back on Kevin years later at the request of Peter and was surprised to discover that Peter may have some hidden talents in nastiness and backbone after all!

Richard added a new member to his team when he was introduced to a young management accountant named Jerry after he'd given his usual fraud presentation at a conference. Jerry was just the sort of person he was looking for; another bright young man, about the same height and build as Richard and with the same outlook on people. Richard always had people wanting to talk to him after his presentations, usually from people interested in his work, and sometimes from people who wanted to add the fact that they had spoken to the presenters at the conference when they reported back to their office. Jerry wanted to talk to Richard for another reason and waited until the crowd had dispersed before talking to him.

"How do you expect to find the person stealing information from your company if he has an IQ greater than three dustbin lids, and doesn't want to get caught?"

"My presentation mainly deals with ways to prevent a company from hiring people who could be subjected to blackmail to make them release sensitive information. It is difficult to find the person responsible if they are bright enough to cover their tracks when they've done something wrong, but if we are asked to find a culprit, what my team usually do is try to create a shortlist of suspects and analyse why those on the list might be open to blackmail."

"That sort of work looks interesting in the films, but most of the groundwork must be time-confusing and boring surely?"

"It can be boring, but I've had cases which have proved to be quite dangerous, with both the person being blackmailed and the person requesting the information trying to keep their identities a secret, and they can use extreme violence to put my team off of their work. However, when we are successful, it can be highly rewarding, especially financially."

"The people depicted in films doing that sort of work all look as if they can't afford a decent set of clothes."

"They're the ones who aren't too successful in my line of work. Are you having problems in your company?"

"Not that I know of, it's just something that I've always been interested in, but I could never understand why everyone thinks that it's so important."

"Ok, in a nutshell, most companies can live with losing one contract now and then, but being shielded from fraud gets important when a lack of internal security results in them losing more than one contract within a short timeframe especially if they needed the contracts to keep them in business. I'm not saying that this is a regular occurrence in British companies, but there are a large number of overseas companies buying British companies these days. Some large organisations find other companies whose business and customer list would be greatly beneficial to add to their own. If they can prevent the target company from winning a few contracts, the target company's declining profit, or loss in some cases, will result in the reduction of money available to pay dividends to their shareholders. The share price will also reduce. Shareholders, such as large company pension funds who need the dividend payments to pay their pensioners, will sell their shares in those companies when this happens. The share price of the targeted company will reduce further. This enables the aggressive company to buy the shares being sold for a price much lower than their true value. If they can buy enough shares, they could get a controlling interest in the target company. Are you ok with this so far?"

Jerry nodded his head, "Yes, carry on."

"Sometimes the aggressive company will make a loss due to them putting in a bid for contracts so low that they will lose money fulfilling. Then they hope that it won't take too long for the profit that they make either from the company that they've bought into, or increase in the price they get when they sell the target company shares is larger than the loss they made on the contracts that they reduced their prices to obtain. If the company is too far gone, they could make money by selling off the land and the assets held by the company that they've bought into."

Richard paused for breath, giving Jerry a chance to ask a question. "I understand all of that, but where does your involvement start?"

"The information for this to happen usually comes from inside the target company. It's my job to either prevent it from happening or to find the person responsible for leaking the information and put a stop to it."

"Can't you report the aggressive company to the authorities?"

"It's not always that easy to prove, but I sometimes help to do that as well."

"Is that where it gets dangerous?"

"Usually."

A young couple who'd been round the buffet twice and wanted to kill time before they sloped off decided that a few minutes talking to Richard would be a good idea, so Richard and Jerry swopped business cards and parted company.

Richard asked for a report on Jerry, including a list of his usual pubs and clubs and 'bumped' into him a few times in the following months until they became friends.
Richard even liked Jerry's sense of humour, despite his distasteful comments, especially on marriage.
"You can say what you like, but everyone gets married sooner or later."
Jerry would always have a quick response to most topics. "Not me, I've seen too many of my friends who were all happy and had lots of money and friends and then they met a special someone and got engaged, followed by an expensive wedding and honeymoon followed by a change of lifestyle, not going out drinking with their friends any more, and then they split up with their wives and were taken to the cleaners."
"Everyone gets married eventually."
"Everyone but me. I won't get married, but to fit in with everyone else, I might find someone I don't like and buy them a house."
Richard started to give Jerry work the following week.

As usual, Richard and Thomas met at Thomas's house but Richard wanted their business to be completed early in the day otherwise Thomas would have insisted that he joined him for dinner which would not have finished until late, and Richard had other fish to fry that night.
"No-one at the team building showed up as a direct suspect, however, we have graded the attendees, showing those who we think are definitely innocent of subterfuge, those who are probably innocent, and the 'probables' and 'possibles' who need more attention."
"I hope that my grandson isn't one of the suspects."
"Absolutely not. He is one of the best attendees they've ever had and showed a strong bond with his fellow management team members. The team building

manager was so impressed that he asked Tom to help them out in his spare time."

"Thank God for that. I don't think that I would be able to carry on if that was possible."

"We also think that Rashid, Julie, Anna, Kwame and Gordon wouldn't be involved either. Anna, as a single parent with the usual problems of extra living costs and only one income fitted the criteria in most places of someone who could be coerced into providing sensitive information for money, but her performance, character and her relationship with the other attendees proved otherwise." Richard gave Thomas the report. "As well as those already mentioned, the report contains a list of those who we think that it is doubtful that they are involved in corporate misconduct, plus a list of the attendees that did not get involved enough in the team building, but mainly because they were out of their depth. We feel that the people on this list are also not involved in anything untoward, but if this was a process to provide a list of personnel that you might like to let go, to improve the overall performance of the company, you might like to consider their future."

"Most of my personnel are loyal and hardworking, just because they are not dynamic, and can't do command tasks, doesn't mean that they can't do their jobs."

Richard didn't agree with the old man's perspective that senior management didn't have to be dynamic or be able to carry out tasks outside of their normal remit but didn't want to discuss that with Thomas and continued with his report. "The final list contains the people that we consider who need closer scrutiny, they are Rick, Sarah, Mike, Mark, John the accountant, Linda and Frank."

"Frank? My nephew Frank? You can't be serious!"

"I'm afraid we are. Although Frank has a substantial amount of Grangers shares, he treated the other team members with no respect whatsoever. He had little idea of how to resolve the problems, but thought himself to be superior to them, and spent most of his time shouting out useless commands. He has a strong, very misplaced sense of his own worth and importance, and no doubt feels that he is not in as high a position in Grangers as he should be. This assessment was reinforced by the results of his psychometric tests."

"Are you sure that Mark should be on the list? He's married to my granddaughter."

"He showed no real interest in the team building, and he also didn't get involved with the others when they were trying to work out what they needed to do. He had far too much to drink in the bar for someone concerned about their future with the company, and seemed more subdued the following day that a hangover would normally cause, especially as the day progressed, when the effect of the alcohol should have worn off."

"He's probably tired at the moment. My granddaughter is currently on maternity leave from Grangers, otherwise she would have been at the team building. The baby is obviously disturbing his sleep which is to be expected, I know that I suffered from a huge lack of sleep when my son was born. He probably used the night as a chance to let his hair down."

"We know who Mark is married to, and about their new baby, and took this into consideration. We felt that there was something else affecting his performance that requires further analysis."

Thomas had problems with the analysis from the team building. "Rick is also a member of the family, making it half of those on your list."

Rick was the first person on Richard's list for a number of good reasons, and Richard had asked his associate Jerry to carry out a full check on Rick, and find out what he could on Frank in the remaining time available before reporting back on the Friday night before Richard visited Thomas with his findings from the Team Building.

Richard had many associates in the network who could provide answers with enough information within a few days to let them know if a more detailed scrutiny was required and Jerry had helped him in this side of the business for some time.

Unlike his father and his father's father, Rick had somehow managed to marry someone with more money than he had, mainly due to his affluent family name. After the wedding it didn't take Rick's wife long to find out what he was really like and made regular barbed comments on what he was doing wrong.
"Why do you spend so much more money than you earn going out drinking every night? It's not doing your bank balance any good and must have a detrimental effect on your performance at work. Unless you curb your enthusiasm for alcohol, you'll never be considered for promotion."
She never ever let him know that she knew about his involvement with other women, but he'd managed to keep secret of how much he was losing at the casino and various forms of racing and other sports, some of them illegal. She warned him more than a few times that she would leave him if he didn't change his ways, taking her money with her. At first Rick cut down on his drinking after her rants but didn't take long to revert back to doing what he wanted. He became even more bitter every time she reminded him that she was much richer than he would ever be, until he reached the stage that he would visualise how good his life would be if she was no longer around, but her money was. He was beginning to hate her more than he loathed his cousin Tom. Everywhere he went he heard "Tom this" and "Tom that", even his own grandfather preferred Tom's company. Whenever his grandfather came over to visit, if he wasn't talking about Tom, it would be about one of his favourite rock stars, which could be almost as

boring. Rick had recently started to appreciate the story of a singer named Sandy Denny, who he'd never heard of, who sang in a group that he'd also never heard of, but the favourite part of the story was how she suffered from depression, and died by throwing herself down the stairs at home. How Rick wished that his miserable wife would follow in her footsteps. Sometimes his imagination would leave him with the hope that his wife would crash the car on one of her regular white-knuckle drives on the M40 into London She thought better of going through a divorce, because she knew that her mother would be distraught at having to face her friends when they found out about her daughter's failed marriage, the members of her mother's circle of friends were expected to put up with most of their husbands' indiscretions. Rick's wife's lack of interest in bed resulted in Rick increasing his alcohol intake which coincided with an increase in interest to females elsewhere, including using his position in the company to try to make untoward proposals to two women in his team, which his manager, Gordon had to warn him about.
"You do realise that I'm a Harbod, and all that goes with it?"
"Your father might support you if I said that you should be sacked, but the Chairman is also a Harbod, and he would be disgusted by the way that you treated the female staff, you would be dismissed without a reference. This sort of behaviour is not tolerated in Grangers."
Rick was angry when he left Gordon's office, and vowed to get his own back on the two frigid cows who'd reported him.

Growing up, there were plenty of girls who wanted to go out with him, but he always thought that this was because of his own opinion of his good looks and personality, and nothing to do with the social standing that came with the Harbod name. Rick was no intellectual, and barely managed to scrape the results required to get a place at university to study engineering. He was jealous of Tom who always got what he wanted without trying, all the way through school and university, even getting better jobs in Grangers.

Richard didn't show Thomas Jerry's report on Rick, but it made interesting reading. Jerry received details of Rick's drinking, womanising, gambling and fighting, none of which he was particularly good at. Rick had a low tolerance to drink but was not put off by this. He was also a mean drunk, not a happy one like his own grandfather who spent more time with Tom than he did with Rick, another factor in Rick's growing dislike of Tom. There were reports of Rick arguing and starting fights from an early age, most of which he lost, and which were still taking place despite most people becoming more easy-going as they approached middle age. The more he drank, the more derogatory comments he made about people around him usually ending up with Rick going home with a few more bruises than he went out with.

There is only so much money a person can spend on alcohol in a pub, despite Rick having to buy more than his normal round of drinks to ensure that he didn't drink alone every night, and Jerry discovered that the majority of Rick's outgoings were down to his losing at gambling; the casinos, horses, dogs, boxing, football, Rick was losing money hand over fist at all of them, and people were starting to press him for payment of the money he owed them. The amount he was paid for his company shares only kept the pressure off for a short while, and his long-suffering wife had noticed the reduction in their bank balance, which now included the payments for the loans he'd taken out to clear the money he owed. He had an occasional big win, but never learnt to stop when the going was good, and lost the winnings straight away, always blaming bad luck or other factors when he did so. Jerry also noticed a name on Richard's 'interesting people' list who cropped up on three occasions with a link to Rick. Jerry had no idea who Kevin Stevens was, but included his name on the report to Richard, with the intention to dig a bit further himself after he'd completed the report on Rick and his father. Jerry was also told that Rick used to buy Kevin most of his drinks when they were together because Kevin gave him a certain amount of protection when Rick had pissed people off enough for them to want to punch him. There was much less reported about Frank, who had started to look and act his age. Frank had a circle of male friends, usually of his own age group, all of them white, who spent most of the weekend evenings in the local pubs, or in his social club watching the football. Frank didn't consider himself a racist, or any type of 'ist' and he often commented that he had friends who were black, but no-one ever told him that Labradors didn't count. There was no more than a reported passing interest in Frank chasing after women, he had a favourite lady of the night who he would visit on rare occasions, but no mention of any interest in men or boys. He also took his wife out for a meal once or twice a month, Indian, Italian or steak and chips, but they didn't talk to each other a great deal, and never argued in public.

Thomas could not believe what he was being told, especially the brief, watered-down version of the report on Rick, and changed the subject. "So what's the way forward from here?"

"The business analyst starts on Monday and will report to Tom. I met with him yesterday, and gave him a full brief on Grangers, and the findings from the Team Building exercise." This was one of Richard's white lies as he didn't want Thomas to know that the business analyst coming in to check out Grangers was the same person who had provided the report on Rick's way of life. "Everyone has been notified about him coming in to save the company, and are they expecting him to ask questions regarding the business. There should be no problems if he's accompanied by Tom, as the management and workforce trust Tom as a person and respect his position in Grangers. He has two weeks to look at your procedures and speak to everyone in a high enough position in Grangers, to discover how the information is being obtained and passed on. He can link his findings with those with the ability to access the information, whilst I will investigate the details of the people on the list of suspects."

"Two weeks isn't long enough to do all that."

"It will have to be. He has a large amount of experience in this sort of work and knows what he's doing. Any longer than that, and people will start to get suspicious, and dry up. He's been told only to report to the two of us. I'll carry out the analysis work with him in the evenings and we'll probably need a few days after that to consolidate our findings."

"Is there anything that I can do to help?"

"The share price is holding steady at the moment, despite the drop in profit, but another profit warning, or bad publicity about losing another contract could put it into free-fall."

"Why would we report that we missed out on a contract?"

"You wouldn't, but it only takes a quick phone call to the financial press from someone trying to manipulate the

markets, and the comments will avalanche. The outcome could be disastrous."
"But how would another company do that, it would make them look bad as well?"
"It won't be another company actually making the comments; it would be 'attributable information' from someone who deals in buying and selling stocks and shares. I'll put a few feelers out to see if I can find out who's showing an untoward interest in Grangers' shares. Meanwhile, you need to do something to reduce the damage of any further bad news. A charm offensive could work."
Thomas was confused. "A charm offensive?"
"Give an interview to a major newspaper. Use your old-fashioned charm to tell everyone how Grangers was set up, and what a nice people and environmental-friendly company this is. If you're going to be talked about, tell the people good things to balance the adverse comments."

Tom was already waiting in reception when the business analyst arranged by his grandfather, arrived on the dot at nine o'clock on Monday morning. Thomas had given Tom the low-down on the visitor from what Richard had told him. He was a management accountant with strong business knowledge and had asked Tom to treat him in the same way that he would deal with any member of the board, as the answers that he provided would be hugely beneficial to Grangers. Despite his smart appearance, and shiny shoes, he wasn't wearing the usual 'power suit' that Tom had expected, he was also much younger than Tom expected him to be. Tom also thought that he was much more at ease with himself than someone would be who had come to tell everyone news of plague and pestilence that would soon devour Grangers.

"Good morning, I'm Tom, I've been sent to meet you and take you around the company. Do you want a coffee?"

He shook Tom's hand with a firm hold and smiled. "People call me Jerry, and no thanks to the coffee, I've already had a cup of tea this morning. If I have too much caffeine, I won't get my afternoon nap."

Tom was smiling already. It wasn't that often that he encountered an amusing accountant. They went to Tom's office to discuss the business, and the plan of Jerry's meetings with the other managers and important members of staff.

"How long have you been Head of Production?"

"About two years. I took over when the old one retired."

"Were there many applicants for the post when it became vacant?"

"A few. Why do you ask?"

"I wondered if there was anyone who was upset that you got the job instead of them. You are quite young for the post, and you have family connections."

"A couple of the older team members thought that as well, but they accepted my promotion soon enough. You seem young to have the reputation that my grandfather told me about."

"I have years of experience."

"What?"

"Some people think that they have thirty years' experience but have only done the same year thirty times. I've had a considerable variety of jobs in many different areas of business, not just finance and accounting. When you hear 'management accountant' don't focus on the word 'accountant' like most people do; I'm more productive with beans than just counting them."

"I'll try to remember not to call you a bean counter then."

Jerry went back to his list of questions and seemed to show a larger than expected interest in the security of the Research and Development work, which was Tom's main responsibility.

"How many people have access to the R&D information within the company?"

"All of the engineers and the design team have access to their own projects, and information for the other projects isn't restricted to anyone inside the Production team. Why is this relevant to Grangers losing money?"

Jerry didn't expect to be asked difficult questions; that was his job. He was quick witted enough to provide a plausible answer, "You're right, it isn't, but you could be incurring extra expense if R&D information was restricted to a few team members, resulting in duplication of effort."

Tom wasn't truly convinced of the answer but tried to hide his concern for now.

"Is there anyone outside of the Production team who could gain access to the R&D information?"

"It's doubtful that anyone would want to. The chairman shows an interest sometimes, and I give a presentation to the board now and again, but I don't go into too much detail. The blueprints are locked in cabinets each night, and the cabinet keys are locked in the key press. The doors are locked when we leave work, and the door keys and the key press keys are kept in Security and booked out by the first person in work each morning. Anyone wanting the keys outside normal working hours would also have to book them out, Security is very strict about that."

"Does that happen very often?"

"Not by anyone outside of the team, and if we are working late, there would be more than one of us, and I would be there."

"How are you sure of this?"

"I check and sign-off the security sheets each week, so I would notice if anyone had booked out the keys at an unusual time."

"Couldn't the security guards get in without anyone knowing?"
"Of course they could, but they would have to know which cabinet held the information that they were looking for, and which file held the designs and details of the project. We also have close circuit television in the corridor at all times. I also check that every week."
Jerry decided to move his attention to other areas before raising too much suspicion but was already too late.
"The chairman should have already given you the list of people that I want to talk to, and they should already have been warned off to expect me. I would like to speak to the accountant first, mainly to look at the breakdown of costings for each project, especially those that Grangers put in a bid for but was unsuccessful. He should be expecting our visit at ten."
Tom picked up the phone and called John the accountant. "John, are you ready for the visit from our visitor?"
"Yes, come on over. I'll see you in a few minutes."
They arrived at the accounts main office and were immediately offered the inevitable cup of tea or coffee, which was turned down. Jerry was impressed by the tidiness of the office. He'd heard that John had problems dealing with the more stressful parts of his work, but everything looked in order.
"You probably know why I'm here, so I won't waste your time and mine by going through another long introduction. This won't take too long, I have a good idea of what goes on here, but I would like to look at how the details of a bid for a large contract are collected, approved and retained. Do you have the details of the last unsuccessful bid ready for me to look at?"

John opened the file on the table next to his computer. "I have a hard copy here, and I can also show you the details on my computer."

Jerry looked through the reports in the file for twenty minutes, taking notes, whilst Tom and John decided that they wanted a coffee after all, and John put the kettle on and prepared the cups.

Jerry closed the file and looked at John's face for any suggestion of guilt. The small trace of concern showing could either be due to his detection of small mistakes within the folder, or might be due to something dishonest. He tried to lighten the mood to prevent John from becoming too defensive.

"I've met you before, haven't I?"

John was delighted with this question, as he might as well be the invisible man as far as most people were concerned. "I attended one of your presentations last year about how to turn around a company that had lost its way and was running out of money."

"I remember. You asked me why no-one notices that it's all going pear shaped until it's too late. It's all conjecture you know. Most chairmen of companies that fail are in denial that their business is about to go tits up until it's too late to save it. The main factor that saves companies is having a set of procedures that identify and report the performance measurements that are the early indicators where parts of the business are not doing as well as they should be. The next factor is believing what they see, and acting on it, not just expecting the problem to sort itself out. Grangers has reported a reduction in profit for the last two quarters, if nothing is introduced to change that, the next quarter's report will probably show a loss, and the company will start to have problems generating enough cash to pay its creditors. That's why I'm visiting all relevant areas of the business."

Jerry had achieved the exact opposite of lightening the mood, but now had the full attention of John and Tom. There was a stunned silence, so Jerry went back to his list of questions that he had written down whilst reading through the report that John had given him, plus the questions that he had already prepared, mainly based on access and security within the accounts department. These took an hour to answer, and Tom was even more worried.

More often than not, Tom would visit his grandfather for dinner on Monday night, and had happily accepted the invitation without the knowledge that, this time, there was an ulterior motive for them to meet. He'd moved back into his grandfather's house when he returned from university, and it always felt like home to him, but he needed his own space when his relationship with his girlfriend, Helen, moved from casual to what he considered to be serious. Helen had grown to love Tom's grandfather and his old-fashioned manners and courtesy. She became a regular member of the Monday night dinners with Thomas and was included in the deep conversations relating to business, engineering and the world. Her sharp mind reminded Thomas of his greatly missed departed wife and Helen had become trusted enough to be included when the discussions related to Grangers and the projects that they were bidding for.

Tom had always enjoyed the old man's company, even more so when he wasn't being criticised for his drinking and staying out late, activities which were uncommon before he went to university; he didn't want to tell his grandfather that it was Helen who led him astray. Tom had resorted back to his old boring lifestyle when Helen moved in with him, which coincided with his current drinking partner finally feeling his age and a mild stroke resulted in him no longer being available. Tom took great pleasure in the good food and the high quality of wine at his grandfather's house, and it was also a good way to catch up on what was happening in the parts of the business where he wasn't directly involved. Tom also wanted to use the meeting to mention his feeling that some of the questions that Jerry was asking had no relevance to turning the company around and were more in line with checking the security of the information and procedures within Grangers. Malcolm, the chairman of Robertsons, was already in the drawing room. Robertsons was a large company that should have been a rival with Grangers, but Malcolm had been a good friend of Tom's father during their time at university, and later in business, and was also Tom's godfather. Thomas had already informed Malcolm that Helen was going to be there, so the only person surprised at Malcolm and Helen being there at the same time was Tom himself. The two chairmen had joined forces on several projects for a long time, trusted each other implicitly, and had become strong friends. His grandfather's friend Richard was also there and joined them for dinner. Although Tom had met Richard briefly a few times before, he'd never held a conversation with him, and was unsure of his connection to his grandfather. He'd never taken that much notice of Richard before, but when they shook hands Tom had a strange feeling about Richard that wouldn't go away. Tom knew that he could speak his mind safely to Malcolm and Helen but wasn't so sure about Richard.

Tom's sister Lucy, had moved out to live with her husband, Mark, when they got married, and Richard noted that his report had been listened to, he knew that they were usual attendees at the Monday night dinners but had not been invited to this one. Although there were only the five of them for dinner, Thomas still used the large dining room, with the plush chairs, large antique polished table, expensive china plates and silver cutlery. He could see no reason to do otherwise. They sat at one end of the long table to make conversation easier, and after the usual chatter during the meal, and talk about what was happening in the world, and how it affected certain parts of the business, the housekeeper cleared the plates away, and the port came out to accompany the cheese board. Thomas raised the matter of the business analyst's visit.

"How did your day go today? I'm sorry that I had to ask you to act as host to Jerry on his tour of the company, but everyone would have been much more open in their dealings with him if you were there with him."

Tom looked towards Richard without answering. Thomas noticed the glance, and smiled at his grandson's attention to security, despite them having knocked back several glasses of wine. "It's ok, Richard helps me with the security aspects of Grangers. You can say what you want."

"Jerry's not here to improve the company's performance, is he?"

"We expected you to notice that, but I didn't want to say anything to you until you'd introduced him to everyone, so that you would be your normal self."

"We? Who's we?"

"Richard and I."

Tom looked at Richard to check his reaction to the statement, but there was none. "Ok Gramps, what's really happening?"

"Some of our important information is finding its way to some of our competitors, but you know that already. Richard and Jerry are helping me to find out how; and who's involved. Malcolm has the same suspicions that it's also happening at Robertsons. We want to know who is giving away our information, and how it's happening, but more important than that, we want to know why it's happening, and who the main beneficiary of the information is, especially if it isn't the company being awarded the projects that we and Malcolm have lost."

Tom looked at Richard again, this time with a much harder stare, and the strange feeling was explained by a picture in his memory. "You were talking to James in the training building late at night at the team building! I saw you through the window on my way back from the bar."

Richard thought that he hadn't been seen but couldn't deny it. "Yes, I was. The team building was my idea, and I set it up. I marked the psychometric test papers and spoke to James at the end of both days to get his views on everyone's performance and demeanour. He was very impressed with you."

Tom was saddened that he hadn't been consulted in their actions. "Why didn't you tell me what was happening at the team building? Don't you trust me?"

Thomas didn't expect Tom to react like this and used his warm tone as he tried to appease him. "I didn't want to put extra pressure on you during the team building. We're telling you everything now, that's why I invited you here tonight to discuss it."

Tom had the same view on the way forward as the other three men, but was more forthright; "So what are we going to do about it?"

FIVE

Whilst Tom was showing the accountant around the company on Monday morning, his grandfather was on the phone to the *Daily Telegraph*. They'd been trying to get an interview with him for years, so the door that he was pushing against was already wide open.
"We have one of our interviewers free on Thursday, can she come and visit you then?"
Thomas wanted more time to prepare but decided that if the main subject was Grangers, then he should already know enough to keep the interviewer busy for a few hours. He also wanted to get it over with as soon as he possibly could.
"Can you come to my house at two in the afternoon? I have a meeting at work in the morning but can clear my calendar after that." His business calendar was much quieter than it used to be, but it still had more entries than his social calendar.

At his great age, one day in Thomas's life was very much like any other, and Thursday arrived before he'd given the interview any conscious thought or preparation. He was surprised that the interviewer was so young, but these days, anyone under thirty looked as if they should still be at school. She was slim and pretty and dressed in a very business-like grey skirt suit, and he put her at ease as soon as he had ushered her into the drawing room and poured her a cup of tea from the china tea pot which he normally used. The cameraman was left free to go around the ground floor of the house and the gardens, whilst the young lady set up her recorder and took out her interview notes.
"I'm ready when you are Mr Harbod. What I'd like is your story of how Granger's started in business, with any people-related stories, as the company grew into what it is today."

Thomas was impressed with her professional manner, and, as expected, his old-fashioned charm took over when he started his story.

Every generation will tell you that their lives were very different, and far more difficult than the ones that followed, but in our case, they really were. The world changed out of all recognition after the Second World War, as did peoples' aspirations, but it took a few years for the improvements to take place. Instead of being lifted, food and fuel rationing remained until 1950, except for meat and a few other items, which ended in 1954. There wasn't much money around for the first few years, and the people who had been used to surviving on bread and potatoes during the war were happy to sell off some, or all, of their meat ration to pay for other things, and had no problems dealing with the black marketeers who enabled this situation, with the police usually turning a blind eye as long it wasn't stolen goods that were being sold; which was particularly common for manufactured goods where the contents of a whole delivery lorry could be stolen or misplaced and sold off cheaply, hence the saying 'it fell off the back of a lorry'. The availability of work and money increased as Britain, assisted by money from America, built its way out of the depression that had caused so much poverty before the war began. Television started up again after the war, and although there was only one channel, the BBC, broadcasting news, westerns and soap operas in black and white, and which closed about eleven o'clock each night to the National anthem, it was much better than the radio. Sales of televisions were sky high in 1953 when people wanted to see the coronation of the young Queen Elizabeth in their own homes, and television started to change peoples' lives by providing a reason for families to stay at home instead of going to the pub every night for their entertainment. Expectations grew in line with the prosperity of the Country, the standard of living finally started to improve from 1950, and unemployment virtually disappeared. Technical improvements and mass production of televisions, household goods and cars made them available, and the reduction in controls on hire purchase agreements meant that more and more people were able to buy things that they wouldn't have dreamt about whilst they were fighting in the trenches. People were beginning to feel good about life. We also had National Service for all young men, where the only ways to get out of spending two years of being shouted at was either to fail a medical examination which consisted of a lady doctor holding onto your testicles whilst you coughed, or by working in an apprenticeship. Although National Service provided Britain with a supply of trained and well-disciplined young men, I chose the apprenticeship option, in the motor car industry. I left school at the age of fourteen, which was normal at the time, with the basic grounding in English and arithmetic and went to night school to improve my education, especially to learn about business and finance, which they didn't teach at school until a long time after I'd left.

The first time that I met Michael Granger was when I was about 22 years old. I was still single and living at home, which was unusual, as people got married a lot earlier in those days, which was probably due to the lack of contraception more than any other reason. A good percentage of those who did get married in the fifties lived with one set of their parents or the other until they had saved for a deposit for a house or had enough children to qualify for a council house which were becoming widely available. I spent most of my spare time studying, unlike my elder brother Frank, who also lived at home, but liked to spend his time at the local pubs, or out chasing women, or both. I liked to go out to the pictures, and occasionally the theatre, which were much better than the television, and still are, and I sometimes went with my father to see the wrestling, but I rarely went to the pub because there were better things to spend your money on than alcohol, and the pubs were always full of cigarette smoke. Unlike most people of that time, I didn't smoke, all of my family and friends did, I just didn't for some reason. One Saturday night, my father said that we should all go to the pub. My elder brother was already out, and it took about an hour for my mother to get ready, but we were in the lounge bar by eight o'clock. My parents were on their second cigarette when Mr Granger came in. He was a few years younger than my father and was the owner of the local car manufacturing company. My father knew him during the war, and they remained good friends. My father regularly told me about how Mr Granger helped keep the Army vehicles going when no-one else could, and how he started up his business when the war was over. People were able to set up businesses much easier after the war. Motor cars were becoming a regular sight, and Mr Granger was kept busy repairing them. He also wanted to make a higher quality model than the cheap mass-produced ones, and started a small workshop making cars to order, which he gradually expanded as he became more successful.

My father introduced me to Mr Granger, but I already knew who he was from my business course, where he was regularly mentioned, almost as much as William Morris and Henry Ford. We didn't know what an entrepreneur was in those days, but Mr Granger was definitely the first one that I ever met. He and his wife joined us at our table, and he bought us a round of drinks, not showing off that he had money, it was just his way. I didn't know until later that he was starting to have money problems and was keeping up appearances for the sake of his wife and family, and also the reputation of his company. His wife and my mother must also have been friends, as they started talking about this and that, not the usual polite conversation between people who don't know each other. My father asked Mr Granger how the business was going, and he really came to life. It was the thing that he most liked to talk about.

"Things are going well, thanks. The Order Book is full, but there is quite a long waiting time until the cars are ready as it takes a long time to manufacture them, and we can only make a maximum of six cars at any one time. The cars are costly to make because each car is built to order from a choice of ten models, but the customers seem to like that, as it makes each car special in its own way. There is an assembly area for each of the cars, and the six members of the production team are highly skilled, with each worker responsible for their own car from start to finish."

I wouldn't usually have had the nerve to ask him questions, but I was intrigued how he managed to make a living using old-fashioned methods. "I'm surprised that you haven't changed to a 'production line' method. Your company must be really well organised to chop and change production from one model to the next, and still make a profit."

"What we do brings in the customers. We make unique, high quality cars built to the customers' specifications."

"The quality of the product shouldn't decrease just because it's made on a production line. A company's manufacturing capacity using the old production methods is much lower, and the extra time required to make the cars could result in a cashflow problem."

Mr Granger went silent for a few seconds, thinking about my comments, and was dragged back to reality by his wife, "Come on, you've had your pint, if we don't

leave for the restaurant now, we'll lose our table, and all of the food will be gone."
"Goodnight Frank, watch out for that son of yours, he's too bloody clever by half. He'll have our jobs if we're not careful."
An hour later my parents and I were joined by my brother, who had obviously been unsuccessful in his search for female company that night, and the topic of conversation jumped around from football and horse racing to girls and drink, and the earlier discussion was washed away by the beers we consumed.

On Monday evening my father was surprised when Mr Granger phoned us at home and was even more surprised when he asked to speak to me. I was doing some course work in the kitchen, and was pleased to be dragged away from compiling a pretend business plan for a non-existent 'widget' manufacturing company to receive an even more surprising invitation to Sunday lunch at Mr Granger's house for the forthcoming weekend.

I wanted to make a good impression, so wore my best, and only, suit, hoping that my nerves didn't let me down making my hands shake so much that I spilt gravy down my front. I arrived a polite five minutes early, with a bunch of flowers for Mr Granger's wife. He took the flowers from me and ushered me into the dining room.
"Sit down next to me lad, we have a few things to talk about. I hope that you don't mind singing for your supper."
I had no interest in singing and would have preferred to have sat in his office with a sandwich if we were going to discuss business matters, but, as far I as I knew, this was not a formal meeting. Two women entered the room carrying plates and bowls of food. I stood up when they came into the room, as my mother had

always told me to do. Mrs Granger looked accusingly at her husband. "What are you doing in here, the foods not on the table yet."

"Can you bring each of us a glass of beer please? Sit down lad, the lunch will be ready soon." Mrs Granger tutted in disgust, and went out to bring in more food, but returned with the glasses of beer. Eventually, the two women joined us at the table. The younger female was a slimmer version of Mr Granger's wife and looked unimpressed that the usual Sunday lunch was being interrupted by someone that she'd never met before, or had any prior warning of. She was wearing slacks and a loose-fitting sweater and no makeup but was still an attractive young woman. It was plainly obvious that Mr Granger was fond of his daughter.

"You probably don't remember Thomas, he's Frank Harbod's son. My daughter Mary works for Grangers and is keen to be part of the running of the business."

"If I was a boy, I'd be a manager by now."

"No you wouldn't." He turned to me and winked. "If I had a son, I'd be able to cuff him around the ear when he was cheeky."

Mary turned her attention to her food in mock disgust, and Mr Granger turned his attention back to me. "I was interested in what you had to say about the use of production lines instead of the assembly bays that we use for each car, but before you do, let me tell you about the business. Grangers has always made its own engines, which are faster and more reliable than those in the cheaper cars sold to the general public. When we expanded, many years ago, I bought a machine which made even better engines and produced them much faster than before, but unfortunately, it got old and was continuously breaking down. I managed to keep it going for a while, but eventually had to buy a replacement. The interest payments for the machine are taking up most of the profit we make, the loan is due to be paid soon, and there won't be enough money in the company to pay it."

This was news to his daughter, who stopped eating, and sat open-mouthed, waiting for me to respond.

"How many different engines do you use in your cars?"

"Three."

"And how many different car bodies do you have?"

"Ten; we have a different car body for each model." Mr Granger answered this as if it was the major rule of the motor car business that you weren't allowed to use the same body shape for different sized engines.

"Do you have any best-selling models?"

"We have two cars that sell more than the rest of the total of all of the other cars, but all of the models are popular, and each of the models has differences built in, as requested by the customer, that's our main selling point."

"What sort of differences?"

"We have a large choice of colour for each of the cars, and the interior fittings such as seats, seat covers, dashboards, steering wheels, gear sticks, lots of things."

"Do the two best sellers use the same engine?"

"No, but they use the two larger ones. The best seller has the largest engine, but the three models that have the smallest engines fitted are very popular."

"Which cars do you make the most profit from?"

"We don't keep that sort of information. Why does that matter?"

"It would be a good idea to get the top three most popular choices for each of the fittings, and cross-check the different fittings with the amount they cost, to discover which of the popular ones cost the least, so that they can be fitted as standard. The supplier will charge you less when you increase the order quantities, and you'll probably get them quicker."

Mr Granger shook his head. "We don't have that sort of information either."

His daughter, anxious to be part of the conversation interrupted, "I could get that information, but it would take me a few days."

Lunch had now become inconsequential and was forgotten, whilst I continued. "That is only a small part of the current problem. The world is changing, and everyone expects that sales of cars will carry on increasing for a long time, unless we have another war. But there is a much larger choice for car drivers than there used to be, and there is also a large increase in the number of women driving, meaning that certain cars will need to be produced and marketed especially for them, instead of being treated as an extension to a man's……. I went bright red, remembering that I was in mixed company, and couldn't complete the analogy. Luckily, Mary knew the correct word.

"Ego."

"Um yes, ego. The problem is that production of cars will also increase to a point where supply could be greater than demand, increasing the choice for those buying the cars especially when we start to receive cars from abroad. This also usually results in a reduction in price. For a business to succeed when this happens, it will need to provide something that the customer wants, at a price that he is willing to pay, at the same time as providing a large enough profit to pay the bills with some left over to keep the business ahead of the others. This is usually achieved by keeping costs as low as possible, as well as buying materials for less, production costs will be reduced by spending a lot less time to make the cars. The best way to do this is on a production line."

None of this was really news to Mr Granger or his daughter, but it went against the way that they did things. "There's nothing new about production lines, Morris Garages have used them since before the war, so has Henry Ford. The cars that roll off production lines like sausages are cheap and unreliable."

"They don't have to be, they're the most efficient way to reduce costs and you could retain your high performance and reliability. If you sell cars at a profit of £50 each, then making savings of £1,000 is the same as selling an extra twenty cars."

Mr Granger shook his fork at me. "We keep a close eye on our costs."

"I'm sure that you do, but cheap, mass-produced cars manufactured by the Government-owned companies are subsidised, to enable their prices to be within the reach of the common man, whilst providing employment to the public. A private company needs to be run more efficiently than they are."

Mr Granger felt that his management skills were being belittled. "Are you telling me that my company is being run poorly?"

"No, that's not what I'm saying at all. You're running a business against unfair competition, and the only way to beat them is to exploit new production methods and change and improve as soon as new technology allows you to. The subsidised companies don't do this, because they don't have to."

"I've made a good living for the last ten years, why should I change now?"

Mr Granger's wife banged the table with the handle of the knife, managing to get the attention of the two men. "I haven't spent two hours cooking this meal for you two to spend the whole lunchtime arguing instead of eating it."

I went red with embarrassment, and Mr Granger apologised after being castigated for his bad manners. "I'm sorry dear, we shouldn't be discussing work at the dinner table. We've exhausted the subject for now, but I would like to talk about this another time."

His daughter, as usual, wanted the last word. "I'd like to be present the next time that this is discussed Daddy; this is as much my future we're talking about as yours.

I've always said that it takes us too long to make each car, and if we have to change the way we do things to stay in business, then we need to listen to what Thomas has to say."

We finished lunch, moved to the drawing room and had another glass of beer whilst the conversation changed to Formula One racing, and whether Stirling Moss was a better driver than Juan Fangio. Mr Granger was a really nice, interesting man, but I wanted to get home to look at some relevant information before the next meeting. If I hadn't got up to go home then, I would have probably still been there until the following Sunday.

My father was interested in what was discussed with Mr Granger when I got home, but I wanted to think about it, and make a few notes, so I said that I would like to sleep on it and we would talk about it the following night, so whilst my mother washed the dishes after dinner the next day, I brought my notes to the dining table.

"The main problem is that Grangers produces ten different models, each with different features, and each of the cars have a large choice of modifications and fittings, as requested by the customer, to make them unique. There's nothing wrong with the cars themselves, but they take a long time to produce, which increases the production cost, and time is also lost changing from the manufacture of one model to another. The profit margin for each is only small, otherwise the price would be too high, and they wouldn't be able to sell them."

"Is there any way that they could reduce their production costs, or increase turnover?"

"Not as much as they need to if they carry on with their current production and marketing strategy. If they only made the cars that use the two larger engines, time and money would be saved from the setting up costs of the machinery. It would be cheaper if they only made two models, based on their two best sellers, as the company that supplies their car bodies would be able to concentrate on two set ups instead on ten different body shapes, reducing the supplier's costs. They would also save money if the cars had standard fittings. They would make enough profit to keep them going for some time, but to increase their turnover enough to prevent the company from suffering from the same problems again in the near future, they also need to manufacture their cars on a production line instead of assembly areas for each car. This would speed up production and allow Mr Granger to employ lower skilled workers on lower rates of pay concentrating on their own certain area of manufacture instead of skilled mechanics each making a whole car. Unfortunately, they don't have the money to put this in place. Mr Granger doesn't want to change, as he has been successful until now with his old business model."

"Is that all?" My father was joking, as he thought that they were the only issues. He was a successful businessman himself, and understood the problems caused by the rapid changes that were happening in post-war England. The war had caused huge advances in technology to keep up with those of the enemy, these advances had moved into normal business, and the same problems applied to all of those who didn't move with the times.

"The big problem is that there is a large loan that they need to repay soon, and they don't have the money to pay it."

My father exhaled sharply. "Anything else?"

"No, that's it... They need a large injection of cash to pay off the loan and set up the production lines. Then they need to concentrate on the top two best-selling models, built to the most popular standard, and stop adding costly fixtures and fittings to make the cars different."

"But that's how he said that he gets his customers."

"The cars would still be better than those sold by the other companies, he could promote the fact that they are high performance, good value quality cars, and more reliable. Where some potential customers might be lost, many more would be attracted due to the decrease in price, increasing the demand, sales and profit. When they've done that, they can add extra models in the future, and keep improving the design and performance."
"Are you going to tell him this?"
"There's no real point. I think that his daughter would accept the changes required, but it's doubtful that he would."
"You underestimate him. Your argument sounds good to me, so he'll understand what's needed, and if it will save his company, he'll listen to what you're saying."
"But he also needs money to set up the production line and pay off the bank loan."
"I have money saved up that could be invested in the company, if you think that the changes will be successful."
"What would you get out of it?"
"If he takes you on as a partner, I'm willing to put money in."
"But that's your money, for when you retire."
"Don't you think that I'll get it back? I was expecting this to be an investment."
"In that case, I have some money that I've been saving for a deposit for my own house that I could add."
"If he hasn't phoned us by Wednesday, I'll phone him."

As my father expected, Mr Granger phoned the following night, and my father discussed what we had talked about previously. The result was another Sunday lunch at Mr Granger's house, this time for the whole of my family, which we accepted, except for my brother, who was busy doing other things. This time we ate

dinner before discussing business, and then moved to the drawing room whilst Mrs Granger and my mother cleared away the plates and did the washing up. Mr Granger's daughter joined us and was not too pleased when her father offered me the job of Production Manager, and a share of the business, in exchange for my father's and my investment.
"But you already have a job."
"I can give them a week's notice. We will all need to work closely together for this to succeed."

I didn't know this until her mother told me much later, but on the third Sunday, Mary came down from her room for the family lunch wearing makeup, a pretty dress and nylon stockings. Her mother also told me, in strict confidence, that Mary spent a lot of time and effort brushing her hair. She looked at the three place settings at the dining table and was visibly upset.
"Is no-one else joining us for lunch today? It's been quite a social gathering lately."
"No, it's just us today."
Mary picked at her food for a few minutes, and then left the table, stating that she had a headache. Mr Granger carried on with his meal, not taking any notice of his daughter's departure. He put down his knife and fork on his empty plate, and looked over at the full plate opposite him, and then at his wife's plate, which had also hardly been touched.
"I hope she's feeling better tomorrow, we have an important meeting with the production team."
Mary's Mother looked at Mr Granger and shook her head in disbelief. "You really have no understanding of the world outside your cars, do you?" He didn't.

The meeting with the production team to discuss the change in production strategy didn't go as well as I had hoped. Mr Granger's daughter met me at the entrance

to the workshop and I followed her inside the cold, dark building, where the main lighting was around the assembly bays. The noise was deafening as the workers constructed their cars, and the noise level hardly reduced when we went up the unsteady stairs to her father's office and closed the door. The meeting room, next to the office, also doubled as the staff tea room, and was dirty and untidy, with the workers clothes which they had exchanged for their overalls, either hanging up on clothes pegs on the wall, or thrown across the backs of the chairs. I carried in chairs for Mr Granger, Mary and myself from the office whilst Mr Granger went downstairs to collect the production team, who downed tools and followed him upstairs. Mr Granger introduced me to the team as an expert in the future ways of manufacturing, who would be managing the change in production methods. He informed them that Grangers would soon cease to exist as they were not making enough cash to pay the bills, and explained the changes required. The most experienced member of the team did not believe this. There was no production manager at that time, and he was not happy with the information that a much younger person was being brought in to do this. If the company needed a production manager, then he was a far better choice. He stated that the plan to replace skilled workers with machines and paying those left in the company barely enough for them and their families to live on was not the way to reward their years of hard work and loyalty.
"I can't believe why anyone would listen to a snot-nosed kid with no experience of real business. Grangers sells cars because of its reputation for distinctive, made to order, high value goods, not mass-produced rubbish, and it will go bust within months of losing its reputation."
I kept quiet at the meeting, as Mr Granger had asked me to, but he had listened to my father and me after the Sunday lunch get-together, and he knew that the only

way to save his beloved company was to put into effect the changes that we recommended.

"We're not reducing the quality of the cars that we make, we're just using a different method to make more of them, and make them quicker and cheaper, so that the company can survive."

"I can make the same cars that we push out here myself, and make a tidy profit, so if that's the future of this company, I'm off. Is anyone joining me?"

Two others left with him, but the other three remained, and it was agreed that the changes would be made straight away.

After the meeting, Mr Granger, his daughter and myself went back to his office, and we talked about the enforced change in the plan, due to the decrease in skilled workers. Mr Granger's concerns started to weaken his resolve.

"Grangers will have a hard time fulfilling its orders. I was counting on the income from those to keep us going whilst we set up the new production line."

Mary was still confident that the change would work. "It looks like we'll have to move quicker than we planned then, Daddy."

"How are we going to replace the three skilled workers who have just left?"

Mary looked at her father and me and shook her head. "Are you too important to make the cars that we sell now? And I thought that Thomas knew all about working on an assembly line, or has he been overselling his abilities? I can take more involvement in the running of the company to free you two up to work on the shop floor until the first production line is set up, and we have recruited new staff. We also have to agree the design of the two new models, change our production set up and stop taking orders for the old models."

"I won't be able to take orders for the cars if I'm working downstairs."

"Don't worry about that Daddy, I know what to do, I do most of that already, you just don't seem to have noticed. I'll need to move into this office until we're back to normal. You'll be too busy working downstairs to need this office anyway, you'll also need to work for the next few weekends to produce the last few small engines to clear the orders for the cars that use them, then we can start to re-arrange the workshop floor to put in the first of the two production lines."

As well as working seven days a week for the first month, Mr Granger, Mary and I worked nights on the design of the new models; the two car bodies remained close to their original shape of the two best-selling old models, but now looked much more streamlined and somehow exciting. Not only had Mary accepted the change in Grangers, she had also manoeuvred herself into a more strategic role within it, and she became the Sales and Marketing Manager, despite having done so unofficially for the previous year. She also designed the plans for the interim set up of the workshop floor, so that the first production line could be put in place to make the new model which we expected to be the best seller of the two, and the layout with the two production lines, which we hoped to be ready soon after the order book for the older models was cleared. Oddly enough, under her re-arranged floor plan, with the first production line in place we still had enough room for four assembly areas to clear the order book of the older models, until that part of the workshop floor could be cleared for the second production line. Whilst the first production line was being set up, I carried on working on the old models, and Mr Granger was freed up to recruit the new staff. With the first production line and the four assembly areas operational, production had doubled, and the workshop was now much better organised, tidier, cleaner and much quieter.

Mary also produced a marketing plan to price and promote the new cars. She tried everything she knew to make the public aware of the availability of our '*breath taking*' new car, which still had the Granger '*high performance and reliability*', at an '*affordable*' price. We needed to sell the new cars as quickly as possible, before the money we had invested in the new cars ran out. When the first batch of the new cars was produced, Mary arranged a visit from the *Oxford Mail* to promote the new car. The local paper picked up on the fact that the Sales and Marketing manager of a car production company was a woman in a very much man's world, and made this the main topic of its report, which was picked up by other papers and the story went nationwide. The story of Mary and the new car also went out with the news feature before the main films at the cinema, which helped no end, and the orders flew in.

Mary had a 'make-over'; I don't think that they had a word for it in those days, in preparation for the national newspaper report in the *Daily Mail*, and the accompanying photograph of her famously standing next to the shiny new red car, which Mary jokingly nicknamed 'The Ego', that was fresh off of the modern production line. A large framed copy of the photograph, which showed more of her legs and cleavage than she'd intended or would normally have allowed, is still hung up in our main boardroom. She took her mirror from out of her handbag and had a quick look at herself before the newspaper arrived.
"I can't understand why I have to wear makeup and a girlie dress, people should be more interested that I am

moving women forward in the world of business, and leave the fluttering of eyelids stuff to the fashion models"
"They're also interested in the fact that you are young and pretty, and that sells more papers than a story about cars."
"You need to get your eyes tested."
"What? You are one of the prettiest girls that I know."
"You're just saying that."
"No, I'm not, anyone can see that."
"If you think that I'm pretty, why haven't you asked me out?"
"I thought that someone as nice as you would have better people than me to ask her out." Mary walked to the office door, opened it, and looked up and down the corridor.
"Nope, I don't see any long queues. Ask me out; you might be surprised."
"But I never go out anywhere, I wouldn't know where to go, and I wouldn't be able to hold a conversation."
"You could take me for a meal, and you could talk about work. You might find that I would be very interested in that."
"Oh!"
"Well?"
"Well what?"
"Are you going to ask me out, or not?"
"What?"
"Good God, you're useless! I'm going to book a table at Crawford's for Saturday night; if you're not there by seven thirty, don't bother to talk to me again."
Thomas smiled at the memory of her storming off. "She was so beautiful when she was angry."

Less than a year later the production team members who had left discovered that, despite being a 'snot-nosed kid', I was telling them the truth, and they had gone out of business. One of them asked for his old job back, but we had moved on from the requirement for any more skilled workers and could only offer him semi-skilled rates. He came back a month later and accepted the job. We became more successful than I ever imagined, and luckily, Mr Granger lived long enough to be part of the success. I still called him Mr Granger, even after he became my father in law, it always seemed the right thing to do at the start, and became a joke between us, even though he had become the best friend that I ever had, except for Mary of course. We were both heart-broken when he died, far too young, but he had achieved everything that he had set out to do, and more. Mary always had her heart set on being the first female chairman in Oxford, she never understood the grammatical problem of achieving her aim, but when her father died, she told me that she would leave Grangers if I didn't take over as Company Chairman. I had inherited my father's shares in the business, but it was nowhere near as many as Mary now owned. We had grown in size by this time out of all proportion and expectations, and the Management Board consisted of much more than her, her father and me, but the appointment was unanimous. Mary worked even harder to make sure that the company didn't suffer under my chairmanship and pushed us through even greater change, with moves into aerospace and heavy industry including large Government contracts. We had planned to retire, but when she died in the same car accident as our son and daughter in law, there was no other successor from the family or from the board ready to take over as Chairman, and I needed something to do to take my mind away from my grief.

The young girl turned off the recorder, trying her hardest to retain her composure after the moving end to the old man's story.

SIX

Kevin very rarely received visitors, and those who did were people who expected something in return, everyone else having disowned him. Susan would have loved to have spoken to Kevin to let him know that she had finally got her own back on him but didn't want him to start looking for Peter again. The private investigator who Kevin had employed when he first went to prison couldn't understand why Kevin wanted to speak to him again. The case was cut and dried, the evidence showed that Kevin was guilty, despite the police not finding Peter's body, so what did Kevin want now? It had better be worth his while.
Kevin's manner had improved when he took over as the Finance Director, but he had slipped back to his old self.
"Do you have any news for me Paul?"
Paul looked blank-faced at Kevin.
"Hello? Peter Stevenson? Have you found him yet?"
Paul was still none the wiser.
"Have you been looking for him at all?"
"There's no trail to follow, he disappeared completely. Everyone expects that his body will turn up eventually."
"That's bollocks, he's still alive. What about his wife? That little shit used to follow her round like a puppy. Peter won't be too far away from her, especially now that he has a son. Where is she now?"
"I don't know."
"What do you mean, you don't fucking know."
"I did everything that you asked me to, I checked all of the CCTV cameras at the hospital when Peter's son was born, if he was going to turn up, he would have turned up then. I thought that we had finished our business."
"What? What do you think that I paid you for?"
"You haven't paid me anything for the last year."

"Well I'm going to pay you now if that's what it takes. I want you to find out what happened to Peter's wife. If you find her, you'll find him. Come back in three days and give me some good news for a change."

Kevin was in a better mood after the meeting three days later.
"Did you find her?"
"No, but I know where she is."
"Go on."
"She's living in the Outer Hebrides."
"What the fuck is she doing there?"
"I have no idea. She is renting out her house in Oxford and moved there with her son a couple of months ago. She has a hair dressing and beauty business, visiting people's houses."
"He'll be there. She'll come down to stay with her parents for Christmas with her son. Go and have a look around her house in the Outer Hebrides. You'll either find him or evidence of him being there."
"This will cost you a lot of money."
"Don't worry about money, I have more than enough to pay for this, I've got fuck all to spend it on in here. I'll get five hundred pounds transferred to your account for a starter. If you do this properly, I'll be out in a week, and there will be a nice bonus for you."

Richard had kept an eye on Kevin for personal and business reasons, and the prison guards were happy to receive payment to report when Kevin had visitors, and what was discussed. He wanted Kevin to stay in prison for being the twat who ruined his marriage, and he also didn't want any questions being asked about Peter's new identity that he'd set up, which would become a possibility if Peter was found alive. The details of the two meetings were passed to him just after they happened, and he relayed the news to Peter. Peter was waiting for the call after Kevin's second meeting with the private investigator; there were only three people who knew his mobile number, Susan and Richard were two of them.

"Hello Richard, what's happening?"

"You need to get out of the house and take any evidence of you ever being there with you. Kevin's investigator is on his way. If I were him, I wouldn't want to leave my details by flying there, so I expect him to drive up to Scotland and catch a ferry over to the islands tomorrow."

Peter had travelled 'light' when he left home over a year ago, so it wouldn't take long to pack up his stuff. He had started an internet business providing accounting assistance under his new name, so no longer needed suits and the accompanying shirts, ties and shiny shoes. Most of his 'stuff' was on the laptop, and he was packed and ready to go long before the taxi came to take Susan to Benbecula airport the following morning. He'd also set up a few tell-tales to let him know which parts of the house any interloper had looked at. Susan stared at Peter's suitcases at the bottom of the stairs when she came back from her latest visit, wondering what she'd done wrong.

"Don't worry, there won't be any problems, but I have to make myself scarce for a few days whilst you're visiting your parents for Christmas. Kevin knows that you are living here and someone's coming up to try to find me, and Kevin won't be happy with both of us if I get caught."

"Where are you going?"

"I've spoken to Doug; I'm going to stay with him whilst you're away. He knows most of the story, so won't give the game away. If you could drive me to his house tomorrow morning before it gets light, I should get there without being seen."

They spent a final night together before parting for what could be the last time. Peter's sex life had improved since his 'death' but Susan ensured that they always took precautions these days. A pregnancy would arouse too many suspicions, and Kevin would definitely get to hear about it, especially if he was still actively looking for Peter.

Susan dropped off Peter, his two suitcases and his laptop at Doug's house in the cold, windy darkness that was eight o'clock on a December morning in the Outer Hebrides. Peter kissed Susan and his son goodbye and could taste Susan's tears as he watched the car disappear in the distance before walking slowly into Doug's house. Susan was still crying when she returned home, parked her car in the garage and locked the garage door, but spending time with her baby cheered her up, and she was back to her normal happy self when the taxi arrived to take her and her baby to the airport. The lunchtime flight took her to Glasgow airport, and her father was at Heathrow to meet her and his grandson less than two hours later.

Doug was always a good host, but Peter knew that he would be too distracted to be suitable company for an hour or so, so he told Doug that he had he needed to send out the Companies House information to his clients and went to his room upstairs. He had advertised his services in two accounting magazines and had already taken on the duties of providing sound advice and guidance plus their bookkeeping duties to ten single director companies, and the list was slowly growing each month. He reduced his monthly charge for the first year and was certain that the service he provided would keep most or all of his clients after that. The accounting year for most of his clients ran from April until the end of March the following year. This meant that they had to complete their annual accounts and pay their corporation tax by the first day of January, nine months and one day after their end of their accounting year. Peter could never understand the stupidity of some of the HMRC policies and this was the worst, expecting people to pay their corporation tax whilst most of them were on holiday and the banks were closed. He had collected all of the information that he required to complete each of the companies' accounting returns and had spent the previous four weeks filling in the Companies House returns for all of them. He opened his laptop and e-mailed the year-end accounts details to each of his clients for them to save on their computers and print off. He also informed them how much corporation tax they needed to pay and wished them a Happy Christmas and a prosperous New Year. They already knew how much time and money he'd saved them.

This was the first time that he'd been alone since Susan had re-joined him. Peter had spent a large amount of time on his own after his disappearance, but he hadn't had the time to think about it since Susan arrived. The first few months after he arrived in the Outer Hebrides was the loneliest time in Peter's life. He'd arranged his rental of a house on North Uist by phone two days before disappearing and drove straight to Scotland on the night he supposedly died. The only contact that he had with his previous existence was when Susan phoned him using the pay as you go mobile phones that Richard had provided him with, Peter kept one and he gave the other to Susan.

The house was a long way away from the more populated areas of Benbecula and South Uist, and he ventured out to the local shop to pick up the food he needed to keep him going early in the morning once a week. He still didn't drink and could live quite easily without mixing with crowds of people, so he thought that it was virtually impossible that he would meet anyone that he knew whilst he was in hiding and was as shocked as Doug when they met outside the shop two months after his arrival.

"I thought that you were dead, it was even on the television news."

Peter went white and almost collapsed. From the few times he'd spoken to Doug, he knew that he needed to explain everything to him without lying. "Can we go somewhere to talk, there is a lot I have to tell you. I'm renting a house just up the road."

Doug followed Peter's car to the damp, cold two-bedroom house, and parked off the road. He opened up the back of his car and his dog, Krieger, jumped out and ran to smell Peter. There were no dog biscuits in Peter's pocket like there were the last time they met. Peter unlocked the heavy front door, and they went inside. It didn't take long for the kettle to boil, and for Peter to make two cups of tea. Once Peter had turned on the calor gas heater the house became a little more hospitable. Krieger had investigated the living room and the small, sparse kitchen before curling up on the carpet close to the heater.

"As you can see, the reports of my death have been greatly exaggerated."

"Does Susan know that you're here? We sent her a letter of condolence, and we shared a few letters afterwards, and she didn't mention that you were still alive."

"I told her not to let anyone in on the secret, even her parents don't know that I'm still alive, so don't be too hard on her."

"But, why are you hiding here?"

"Do you have a spare hour, it could take some time? There's a lot to tell you. You know that I'm alive, so telling you the whole story won't do any harm, just keep it to yourself."

"Be my guest."

"When we arrived home after our holiday here two years ago, everything changed, and none of it was good, except for Susan getting pregnant. My parents died, my dog died, my boss died, and Kevin, you've heard me talk about him, became the new boss."

Doug thought that Peter faking his own death was a bit over-the-top. "But why did you make it look like this Kevin person had killed you?"

"I still don't really know. I've often wondered what my life would have been like if I'd carried on at work with Kevin as the boss, but it became unbearable straight away, and would have only got worse. And Kevin would have ruined the company, and the livelihoods of my friends who worked there"

"Couldn't you just move to another job?"

"In hindsight, that would have been relatively easy, but it wouldn't have saved the company."

"So what happened?"

"I've thought about this for the last two months as well, and still don't know. I never seemed to be in control of the situation. Susan came up with some strange ideas, and every time she asked me if I could do something to fake my death, get Kevin blamed for it, and then get a new identity and disappear without trace, I found that I knew a way to do them. I still can't understand how I allowed myself to be talked into it, and why Susan was so keen for it to happen."

"She must have given you a reason."

"Not really, she did say that Kevin should have been punished for the way he treated his former girlfriend Chris, especially after he disowned her when she became pregnant and had his child. But Susan hardly knew Chris."

"Why did you choose the Outer Hebrides as a place to hide away?"

"This was the first place I thought of when I needed somewhere to disappear. If I stayed on the mainland, someone could have recognised me from the television coverage, and if I'd gone overseas, it would have been noticed when Susan left the country."

Doug looked around the drab kitchen. "She's not joining you here is she?"

"We'll see what happens when our child is old enough to travel. The next few years wasn't something that we discussed when I was setting up Kevin for my murder. And Susan didn't find out that she was pregnant until just before I left, and everything was already in place. I never really expected to go through with it."

Doug looked at the inside of the house. "This is no place for a young lady and a small child to live."

"Oh no, she'll have a much nicer place than this one, and it will be in one of the more populated areas, with a shop or two."

"What are you doing whilst you're on your own?"

"I have some box sets that I've wanted to watch for the last few years, and a few books."

"I can lend you some DVDs and books if you want. Which authors do you read?"

"I don't really have a favourite, I usually read factual books, not fiction."

"But if you're on your own, you should read a few fiction books to help you escape from reality for a while. I'll bring you some of mine?"

"Ok, thanks."

"I'll come and see you tomorrow and bring you a few things to make your stay a bit more comfortable. When do you expect Susan to join you?"

"Hopefully in less than a year's time, as soon as the child is old enough to travel this far."

"What are you going to tell your child about who you are when he or she is old enough to start asking questions about what happened to their father?"
"I have no idea. It's something that I'll have to discuss with Susan when she gets here."

Doug arrived with a large box of goodies the following day. Krieger went straight into the kitchen and curled up next to the heater. Doug put the box onto the kitchen table and went back outside.
"Back in a sec." Doug returned with another box containing dog food, dog biscuits and Krieger's lead and bowls.
"What's that for?"
"We thought that you could do with the company, and Krieger will enjoy the extra exercise."
There was also a bag of newspapers. "We get the Daily Telegraph every day. They're a few days out of date, but I'd have only thrown them out anyway, and they will keep you in touch with the mainland news."
"How much do I owe you?"
"Nothing."
"If you don't take any money, I won't take the things that you bought me."
"Ok, £10 should cover what I had to pay for. I also have some spare wet weather clothes and boots in the car. You can come and visit us whenever you want dinner with some human company, no-one ever comes by our house as it's off the main road."
Peter was lost for words and struggled to stop himself from crying.
"Do you have any ideas what you're going to do whilst you're waiting for Susan to join you?"
Peter could always talk about his work. "I'm going to start my own company doing the books for small companies. I chose this house because there is good mobile phone cover here, and the house has wi-fi, so I

could do that via e-mail without having to meet the customers. I won't make much money, but it will keep me occupied."

Susan wasn't able to inform Peter of the birth of his son until she had a few minutes to slip off to the toilet an hour later.
"Hello darling, you have a son."
Peter started crying immediately. "What is he like? Is he healthy?"
"He's fine. He looks just like you."
"Have you decided on a name yet?"
Susan had known what she was going to call her child as soon as she had been told that she was having a boy, but she didn't want to tempt fate. "I think that we should call him Maxwell after your father, Max for short, and Geoffrey after mine."
Peter was so choked up that he had problems talking. "I have to go back to the maternity ward now, I'll speak to you tomorrow. I love you."
"I love you to. Give my love to Maxwell Geoffrey."

For the next few months every day was like the previous one until Susan phoned Peter to tell him that she was ready to book a flight to Benbecula and re-unite the family.
"Where do you want to live whilst you're here?"
"What do you suggest?"
"Lochboisdaile or Daliburgh have shops and facilities, and are close to the ferry, but so do Balivanich and Creagorry, and they are close to the airport. They're also close to Doug, who has been a good friend."
"Ok, I'll see what I can get."

Susan paid the deposit and the first month's rent for a house in Creagorry, close to the Co-op, and booked her flight and a taxi to meet her at Benbecula airport. The taxi was waiting for her when she arrived at the airport and drove her to the Estate Agents where she picked up the keys for the house, and then drove her to the house in Creagorry which would be her new address until she and Peter decided what they wanted to do. She unpacked part of her suitcase, fed Max and waited for Doug to come and collect her. Susan agreed with Peter that it was too risky to show up at the airport in case Kevin was having her followed so Doug had been waiting in his car further up the close from her house for half an hour before Susan arrived in the taxi and he watched the taxi driver follow her into the house with her luggage. After twenty minutes, no other traffic had entered or left the close, so he moved his car nearer to the house, took out the push chair from the boot and carried it to the front door and pressed the doorbell. Susan put the push chair in the front porch and carried Max to Doug's car. Doug was tried to act casual as he looked in all directions to see if anyone was taking an interest in Susan as he drove the few miles to his house where a very nervous Peter was waiting to see his son for the first time. Peter had put on a stone in weight, his hair was much longer than it used to be and he had grown a beard mainly so that Susan didn't have to buy men's stuff; it also changed his appearance. He didn't ask Susan if a beard suited him, especially in the same way that Kevin had many years ago! Susan wanted to get back to her new house to get her son settled in his bed but couldn't refuse the offer of a hot meal before Doug drove them to Creagorry. Peter couldn't eat, and just sat at the table looking at Susan and his son.

No-one showed any unusual interest in Susan and the baby after she moved into the house, people always make a fuss with babies, but they didn't recognise Susan from the news after Peter's death because the only photos shown were those of Peter and Kevin.

Within two months of her arrival Peter had moved into the house in Creagorry. Peter was sad that he was unable to keep Krieger with him and remembered how wretched he felt when Jaeger died as he watched Doug take Krieger away in the car after he dropped Peter off.

Contrary to Richard's warning, Paul didn't travel to the Outer Hebrides on the day after his second meeting with Kevin. He thought that it would be better to see what Susan was like during her visit to her parents in Oxford before checking the empty house in the Hebrides. There was also the chance that she might meet up with Peter in or around Oxford. Paul also wanted to speak to Susan after her return to the Hebrides, and he could think of plenty of other things that he would prefer to do than make the horrible and long journey twice, or wait around being bored shitless in the Outer Hebrides until she returned from her parents' house. Wasting a week in the cold, windy desolation of the Outer Hebrides looking for someone that he, along with everyone apart from Kevin, expected to be dead when he could be in London over Christmas was not an option that he wanted in his life. Kevin didn't know that Paul was still in London but that didn't make him any less angry when Paul phoned him to tell him, quite truthfully, that he hadn't found any trace of Peter.
"You couldn't find skid marks in a tramp's underpants."
"You're the one who's sure that he's here, it's not my fault that he isn't. If he's here, I'll find him, I'm still asking questions, but I want to keep it low-key unless you want him to go back into hiding. His wife is away as expected, so he might be elsewhere whilst she's away. I'll let you know when I find him, otherwise I'll report in the day after Susan gets back here."
Kevin hung up in disgust.

When Paul finally arrived in the Outer Hebrides two days later, he booked into the Dark Island hotel, collected his room key, and took his suitcase to his room. It was easy to find Susan's flight details, she would fly back tomorrow afternoon in time for the New Year. Paul didn't expect to find Peter, but the reaction from Susan when he spoke to her could give the game away if he was still alive. He had picked up a map of the Islands from the hotel reception, he opened it on the bed and looked at the local area. He already knew the address of the house that Susan was renting, and the name of the company renting the property. He'd shown the photo of Peter and Susan in a shop and at the ferry office at Lochboisdale, but no-one recognised either of them. He made the Co-op in Creagorry his first visit when he reached Benbecula and parked his car in the car park on the side of the shop, which called itself a supermarket, and went inside. There was a middle-aged woman next to the sparse fruit and vegetables area who Paul thought would be a good person to start with. He walked up to her and took out the photo of Peter and Susan.

"Hello, could you help me please? My friends from England are staying in the area, but I've lost their address. Have you seen them?"

He was greeted by the same sing-song voice as the lady in the hotel. "I've seen the lady quite often, but not the man. She has a young child with her when she does her shopping."

"Every time?"

"Yes. She comes in here a few times a week, but I don't know where she lives."

"What does she usually buy?"

"Och the normal stuff. She buys lots of fruit and vegetables, low calorie meals, baby food, tea and coffee and gin and tonic water."

"How many people does it look like she's buying for?"

"Only her and her baby. She doesn't eat very much." Paul didn't expect to get her address, but the information that the shop woman hadn't seen Peter, and that Susan was always accompanied by her young son was interesting, but not good news for Kevin. After going to the Co-op, Paul went to the shop in Balivanich, who had seen her, but only once every week or two, and didn't buy much apart from the occasional low calorie meal and fruit and veg. Peter had told Susan not to buy too much in one place or anyone checking would get suspicious. Peter had also asked Doug to get some provisions for them on a regular basis such as tea and gin whenever Susan's supply was getting low. He still didn't drink alcohol but drank plenty of tea and orange juice.

It was already getting dark as Paul moved to part two of his plan. He drove round to Susan's house, there were no lights on. He parked the car further up the close where he could see any movements both inside and around the house. After an hour he walked to the side of the house and unlocked the back door. He was surprised that the door wasn't bolted shut but he could have opened the front door just as easily, he preferred the lower risk option of being out of sight. He put stretchy plastic covers over his shoes and went slowly from room to room by torchlight looking for anything that would have shown that Peter was living there. Kevin had told him to look for accountancy magazines, "I have no idea what other clues he'll leave because he's never been interested in anything normal. He's never had any hobbies, just his work. He doesn't even like football. Or porn!"

There was a distinct lack of anything male throughout the house, and the bathroom was empty of any of the six items used by men, as opposed to the two hundred or so items used by women. The adult clothes in the bedroom were all female ones. There was no food in the kitchen that would be considered to be male-related, mainly low calorie or slimming food, or that suitable for a small child. The car which Susan had bought in the Islands was parked inside the locked garage, with nothing of interest inside or in the boot. He gave up looking after an hour and went back to the hotel.

The following morning Paul drove to Benbecula airport and waited for the lunchtime flight from Glasgow to arrive. He watched as the small passenger plane approached and landed. A few minutes later Susan climbed down the staircase carrying her son and a small bag. Paul wrote on his notes that there was no-one to meet her at the airport. Compared to the large airports, it didn't take long for the luggage to be unloaded from the plane, and the taxi driver carried her luggage to the car outside. Peter's text had told her to go straight home, and Paul followed the taxi a long distance behind to Susan's house in Creagorry, the flat ground made it easy to keep the taxi in sight, and he knew where she was going. Peter and Doug had witnessed all this from the airport car park and had followed Paul's car as far as the Co-op, where they parked in the bottom corner.

The taxi pulled up outside Susan's house, and Paul drove past and parked further up the close. He watched Susan carry her son inside her house and the taxi driver followed her with her two suitcases. The taxi drove off and Paul watched the house for any movement inside, he knew that the fridge was empty, so she would shortly need to go to the shop for food and milk, and as expected, Susan left the house with Max in a pushchair twenty minutes after she had got home. With any luck he could be home the following day. He knew where she was going so he gave her a head start before driving to the Co-op and parking up outside.

Paul went inside the shop to keep an eye on her progress and went to the exit when she reached the tills. He was waiting outside when she came out five minutes later.

"It's Susan isn't it? You're Dawn's daughter."

Susan had no idea who the man was, but her manners wouldn't allow her to ignore him. "Yes I am. Do I know you?"

"You don't, but I know who you are. Could I speak to you for a minute please?"

"I'm sorry, I want to get my son back inside the house before he gets cold."

Paul showed her his fake reporter's ID. "Please come and sit in my car. It will only take a minute and will be better if you speak to me here."

Susan wasn't as good an actor as Peter, but it was easy to see that she didn't want to speak to the man. "I'd rather not. I have to get my son back home."

"I work for a national newspaper. If you don't talk to me, then there will be a hell of a lot more reporters looking for you this week." He opened the back door of the car.

Susan sighed. She put the pushchair behind the car out of the wind and sat in the back of the car with her son. Paul turned on his recorder.

"Can you confirm that you are Susan Stevenson?"

"Yes"

"Why are you living in the Outer Hebrides?"

"To get away from people like you, continuously pestering me."

"Why?"

"Because the newspapers think that they can make a story out my husband's murder, despite the fact that the police have found his killer and put him in prison, where he belongs."

"Did you expect that no-one would find you here?"

"Yes, I did. How did you find me?"

"From your flight booking. We have a list of names of people that are interesting to us, and yours appeared. Why did you choose to live in the Outer Hebrides?"
"It's just somewhere that I saw in a TV programme some years ago, and I thought that it was quiet, and no-one would bother me here."
"What are you hiding from?"
"People asking me questions about my husband's death. I decided to come here for two years until people were no longer interested in me."
"Why do you think that people still think that your husband is still alive?"
"They don't. Everyone knows that he's dead. That's why his killer is in prison."
"Have you been offered money for your story about the disappearance of your husband?"
"Yes, a number of times. I'm not interested."
"People would be interested to read why you feel it necessary to hide away from the world, and how you've changed your whole lifestyle. We would be willing to pay for your exclusive story, you might find that the money will come in handy now that you're on your own."
"I'm fine for money thank you, I have a good business here. I just want people to leave me alone."
"Thank you very much. I'll tell the newspaper that there is no story here, and you should be left in peace. Have a good New Year."
Susan put her son in the push chair and went home. Paul switched off his tape recorder as he watched her disappear into the close on the other side of the road, and then drove back to the hotel.

Peter had a huge problem staying in the car whilst he and Doug watched the discussion between Susan and the private investigator inside the car in the Co-op car park. If Doug wasn't with him, he would have probably given the game away.

"He's not going to hurt Susan, and she knows what to expect, so just stay put." The discussion didn't take long. "If everything goes to plan, he will probably leave tomorrow."
Peter knew that Doug was right. "Susan knows what to do. I texted her earlier and told her to drive to Neilly's shop at midday tomorrow and stay in the car park for five minutes to see if she'd been followed, then to drive to the airport, turn around and come to your house if it's clear."
Peter was still worried, even after he watched Susan walk home without being followed.

Paul went to his hotel room and listened to the recording of his discussion with Susan. Her answers sounded truthful, and his view that Peter wouldn't turn up alive was as strong as when he visited Kevin in prison.

Peter and Doug watched Paul drive away from the Co-op towards the Dark Island hotel. They waited for five minutes then drove to the hotel, Paul's car was parked in the car park at the front of the hotel when they arrived. Peter drove Doug's car back to Creagorry and dropped Doug off, Doug walked to Susan's house and Susan let him in through the back door. Peter drove Doug's car back to the hotel and parked in the dark corner of the hotel car park where a had a good view of Paul's car.

Susan finally stopped shaking when she went inside her house. Luckily, she'd held Max close to her body, so the man didn't notice her shaking. She used her own mobile to phone her mother after Max had been fed, as Kevin had told her to do on her secret mobile phone whilst she was waiting to board her flight at Heathrow.

Paul had dinner, paid the hotel bill, and packed his bag. Peter watched Paul walk to his car two hours later carrying a suitcase and a laptop computer, and drive off towards Susan's house, as expected. Paul drove quietly back to Susan's house, turning off his headlights when he drove into the close. He parked further up the road from Susan's house with a good view of the house. Doug had moved a chair close to the window and stayed out of sight behind the curtains in the dark front bedroom as he watched Paul park his car half-way up the road.

Lights went on upstairs as Susan put Max to be bed, and Paul could see her silhouette as she came back downstairs again, and he could make out the blue light from the television. Within half an hour Paul received details of the phone call that Susan had made to her mother earlier.
"If you're going to be pestered by reporters up there, you might as well come home."
"The reporter said that I wouldn't be troubled from now on. I've just started to increase my customers, and I like the solitude here and running my own business, so I'll wait for two weeks to see if I get pestered again."
It had been easy for Paul's contact to monitor Susan's mobile, and the phone conversation would be included in Paul's report to Kevin, and in his price for the work carried out. Paul and his accomplice didn't expect that Susan was the sort of person who would have another phone which she used to keep in constant touch with Peter.

Doug watched as Paul got out of his car an hour after arriving and walk up and down the close checking to see if there was anyone inside any of the other parked cars, as Richard had warned Peter might happen. Paul then went back to his car, despite his certainty that

Peter would be a 'no show', Paul remained parked up until it was time to leave for the ferry; he had nothing else to do and could catch up on lost sleep on the nine-hour ferry journey back to Oban the following morning. He had no problems with staying awake and was happy that the more tired he was, the easier it would be to sleep during the rough journey back to the mainland on the ferry, especially if the wind was even stronger than the usual hurricane strength. Doug had kept constantly in touch with Peter by text, and Peter collected Doug ten minutes after Paul had driven away. They went to Lochboisdale and saw Paul's car at Caledonian MacBrayne's car park waiting for the ferry to arrive. It was still dark when the cars, including Paul's, started to drive onto the ferry, and Peter watched with relief as the ferry sailed away.

Peter almost wore out Doug's living room carpet waiting for Susan to arrive. At ten to twelve he changed his route and went upstairs to watch the coast road from the front bedroom of Doug's house. At five to twelve he saw Susan's car come into view go past the Muir of Aird turning on the way to Neilly's shop in Balivanich. There were no cars in view behind her. Fifteen minutes later he watched Susan's car pull into Doug's drive, and she parked it out of sight in the garage. Again, there was no sight of any other cars following her. She couldn't wait for Peter to come downstairs, she gave Max to Doug and rushed upstairs to hug Peter. Five minutes later Peter was certain that no other cars were coming down the narrow road to Doug's house and they went downstairs.
Doug was the first person to talk about the previous day. "What was the investigator like? Did he believe you?"
"I think so. He said that he was a reporter from a national newspaper, but he wasn't like the ones that

used to keep asking me questions. He said that I wouldn't be bothered again."

Two days later Paul was back visiting Kevin in prison.
"What do you mean 'there's no sign of Peter'?"
"There just isn't. I spoke to a large number of people in the Outer Hebrides. Most of them had seen Susan, but no-one recognised Peter from the photo. They said that she was always with her baby but there was never anyone else with her." He felt that he had to spell it out to Kevin, "She was always with her baby because there was no-one else to leave the baby with when she went to the shops."
Kevin was not impressed. "Yeah, ok, that doesn't mean that he's not there."
"I staked out the house that Susan is living in for three days and nights and searched the house whilst she went home to her mother. No-one has seen Kevin in the Outer Hebrides and there's no evidence of him ever being in the house as well."
"How can I believe that you have done anything, when you've been away for two weeks and found nothing?"
"Believe this." Paul played Kevin the recording of his discussion with Susan and the phone call between Susan and her mother. "The police have closed the case on Peter's murder and his wife's body language shows that she believes that he is dead. It doesn't do your chances of early release any good that you keep saying that you've been framed when you're the only person who thinks that Peter is still alive."
"I'm the only person who's right. I'm not giving you any more money until you find Peter."
"I've just wasted my Christmas staying on a cold, wet and windy island miles from anywhere, looking for someone who has obviously snuffed it. I've travelled to the other end of the country and back and had to pay for fuel, an expensive return ferry journey and a hotel room

whilst trying to find evidence that he still exists." He gave Kevin the breakdown of his expenses plus his daily rate. "Pay up, or I'll put the word out and no-one will help you again."

Kevin didn't even bother looking at the figures. "I'll give you a quarter of my compensation when you find Peter and they have to release me."

"A quarter of nothing is nothing. Pay what you owe me or you're on your own."

"Pretend that you're a penguin and shove your bill up your arse."

"Don't tell me that I didn't warn you."

Paul left the prison, Richard passed the details of the meeting to Peter as soon as he was informed of Kevin's visitor, and a huge weight was lifted from Peter.

SEVEN

Steve was annoyed, and when Steve was annoyed, he made bad decisions. Despite being in dangerous situations in the Army, he'd always managed to force his way through, but the people who controlled the sort of work in which he was employed were not the usual types that he was used to dealing with; deadly, no morals, untrustworthy, cunning, he was used to all that, but these bastards were clever as well. And they wanted things done, or there would be '*consequences*'. He was getting increasingly more and more pissed off with Tony's attitude; he was far too cautious, the latest job had dragged on too much, and their work had taken far too long already. There was a huge bonus waiting for them when this job was finished, but Tony had become frosty and unhelpful since they told him of the change to the plan of action with Grangers, especially as it could ultimately cause the company's demise, so Steve decided to set up his own meeting with Tony's contact, without telling Tony. The details of Tony's contacts were protected by entry codes but Steve and Graham had Tony's list of contacts and the details of the codes from the good old days, when Tony used to share information with them, so the message that he wanted an update was sent to the contact's mobile, and Steve waited out of sight until the contact arrived. Steve already knew about the Chairman's 'doom and gloom' speech to the senior staff, but he expected something more useful from the senior team's comments about the company at the team building event.

Even though it was still dark, the contact could see quite plainly that the man who sat down next to him on the bench at the usual meeting place was not the thin man, but someone much taller and muscular, and looked a great deal more dangerous. He'd brought no incriminating information with him but still felt that he was being watched on a constant basis since he'd handed over the last batch, and thought that he was going to be arrested, or worse, if that was possible. He was about to try to escape, which was probably futile, but at least he would be trying something instead of waiting for the attack, which could possibly be fatal. A sharp pain changed his mind as Steve gripped his arm. Steve whispered loud enough for him to hear the instructions clearly, but anyone else close by would have been oblivious to their conversation. "Our friend couldn't make it today."

"You must have me mistaken for someone else. I'm just waiting for a bus."

Steve showed him a copy of one of the photographs that the contact had been trying to keep from his wife and family. "I don't think so."

Steve gave the man a copy of a large gambling bill. "This might be your lucky day. We've just purchased this from a friend. All we need is some information from the team building, if you can tell me anything that we might be interested in, you can consider this debt cleared. If the information is good enough, I could consider our business concluded in full and we'll destroy the photos as well."

Blind panic was mixed with huge relief that he would finally be free of the unwritten contract with these people, as he racked his brain to think of something to say. "It was just a load of old bollocks. We were made to do stupid tasks for the two days, whilst the organisers took notes on what we did."

"There must have been people there who were particularly good, or those who showed no interest at all?"

He paused. "Everyone thought that Tom was the star of the show, but they always do, saying that Grangers would be in trouble if he wasn't there. Some of them were their normal obnoxious selves, and a few others didn't want to be there, or couldn't be bothered to join in."

Steve made a mental note of this. "Was there anything interesting that you heard, whilst you were there?"

"No."

The grip on his arm tightened. "Try harder."

"The only thing of interest was the conversation at the bar late on the first night."

Steve woke up from his state of boredom. "Go on."

"Tom was asked how he managed to live with his grandfather's strict regime of locking the doors at midnight each night, and Tom said that he had set up his bedroom window at his grandfather's house so that he could unlock it and open it from the outside, and he'd also de-activated the burglar alarm for the window."

"It's a big house, which one was his bedroom?"

"Tom didn't say exactly which one it was." Steve increased the pressure again and the pain in his arm was excruciating. He racked his brain to make the pain go away. "He did say that he used to climb a tree to get to his bedroom."

"We'll check it out. If what you say is correct, then our business is finished, and we'll delete the originals. If not, then you'll be in deep shit." Steve got up and walked into the darkness as silently as he'd arrived, pleased with the outcome of the discussion. He hoped that his next task of setting up another stooge at Grangers would be this quick and easy.

Two nights later, Steve waited hidden behind the bushes in the old man's grounds with full view of the front door of the house. The good thing about winter was that it got darker earlier, and he'd been able to move into position without being seen long before any expected movements into and out of the house. The bad thing was that it had started to get bitterly cold, Steve had become used to the cold from the annual Army exercises in Norway each January and February; it didn't mean that he liked it though. As well as helping to keep his identity secret, the black balaclava and leather gloves also gave him some protection against the weather. As expected, the housekeeper left at nine o'clock, and no-one had entered the house that evening, leaving the old man alone. The lights started to go out around the house at ten thirty, and, at ten forty-five the inside of the house was in complete darkness. Steve had looked at the details of the house and grounds via Google Earth and found only one tree which could be used to reach a first-floor bedroom. He also knew from their records that there was no dog to be let out last thing at night to sniff him out and alert everybody in the area of his presence. Steve had raised one of his bushy eyebrows when he was told this; alone or not, if he lived in a house as large and secluded as this one, he would have at least two large dogs to provide an alarm and protection. These thoughts kept Steve's mind occupied, and away from the discomfort of the ever-decreasing temperature until it was time for him to make his move. He never considered that Thomas Harbod would have liked the company and security of dogs, but the old man was away from the house too often to provide dogs with the company that they needed, and his cats could look after themselves until the housekeeper visited them each day that Thomas was away. Moving from the bushes, up the tree and into the house was second nature to Steve, and, within a few minutes he was inside the house with no alarm raised. He crept silently down the long staircase to the main hall, his pencil torch providing just enough light as he inspected the paintings hanging on the wall. He reached one that fitted the requirement and took the painting of Thomas's wife from the wall. It was on old painting of an attractive, happy young woman standing next to her light aircraft at Kidlington airport. Steve knew, that if there was anything that would take the old man's attention away from his work, this would be it, not only would he be concerned that someone had been able to break into his house so easily, he would also miss the painting of his dearly departed wife. He took off the back of the picture frame, pulled out the painting, and rolled it up. Although he was as careful as usual when he replaced the picture frame on the wall, the hook holding the painting on the wall had been there for many years, and had become loose, resulting in a large clattering noise as the picture frame hit the floor. Thomas was out of his bedroom in a flash, swiftly followed by his cats, and the upstairs of the house was bathed in light. Steve was blinded for a few seconds, allowing Thomas to get to the top of the stairs and see him before he had chance to move.

"Get out of my house." Despite his years, he'd never been afraid of confrontation, and moved swiftly to tackle the intruder, unfortunately, he was not yet fully awake, and his feet became tangled up with his cats. He lost his footing at the top of the stairs and crashed to the bottom of the stairs and lay there in deathly silence. Steve showed more concern for the old man than the cats, who had gone back to the warm bed. He went over to the old man to check whether he was still alive, his mind racing at the unexpected change of events. The balaclava ensured that his face was hidden from view, so if the old man was still alive, he had to make the decision whether he should he phone for an ambulance or finish off the job started by the cats and the staircase. The decision was taken from him, and the old man's dead eyes and the unusual position of his head indicated that assistance was no longer required in this World. Re-assessing the situation, Steve replaced the painting in the battered picture frame, put it back on the floor next to the hook, and left the house through the window which he'd entered.

Tony had read the news of Thomas's death and had no idea that it was linked to the unexpected text from Richard, who was, to put it mildly, an old business acquaintance, and one of the few people that he actually trusted. The coded message requesting an urgent meeting. It was a simple code, but anyone who obtained access to the message would expect the time to be 2.15, not meeting place 2 at 3 p.m. Tony had just replied ok to the message when he heard the stamp of heavy shoes coming up the stairs to his office. He didn't expect any visitors that afternoon, especially from the plain clothes police, but it was much better than having an unexpected visit from some of the people that moved in the same circles as he did, especially those who cut off parts of your body before they started asking questions, just to get your attention, and to put you in the right frame of mind to provide answers quickly, and without the clear mind to offer up plausible sounding explanations.
"Hello Tony, I think that we are overdue a few words, don't you?" Tony knew his visitors by sight, and by reputation, as you would for any member of the perceived enemy, but he didn't think that they knew him well enough to call him by his first name, or where his office was, and was sure that no-one had ever followed him here. He tried to act innocently, which was one of his best attributes, despite usually being guilty of something or other, but they seemed to be confident that he would speak to them.
"Is it with regard to a consignment that we are moving for you, sir?" Tony used his 'customer service' voice and looked down at his computer. "What's your company name?"

"HM Plod and Son. We'd like you to accompany us to the station." He gave his business card to Tony, and Tony went to the window to get a better view of the name and details on the card, pulling up the blind to let more light into the room.

"Which station? Is there something that we are moving by train for you?"

The plain clothed policeman remained calm. "Just stop the play acting and speak to us. You're not on our radar at the moment, but if we have to put you under caution, the details will be available to anyone interested in you."

Tony's standing in his profession was based on him keeping out of trouble with the police. "If there's something that I can help you with, what difference does it make whether I tell you here or at the police station?"

"I know that you have a low opinion of the police, and think that we can't solve a crime unless someone tells us who did it, or we beat a confession out of a suspect irrespective of whether they are guilty or not, but you might be surprised at the progress that we've made in the past few years."

Tony doubted that they'd made any progress since they'd learnt to blow a whistle but thought it best not to share this view openly with them.

The policeman took a photograph out of the inside pocket of his jacket and went over to Tony at the window. "This picture was taken one street away from the residence of Thomas Harbod about thirty minutes after he died." It was lucky that Tony could keep a straight face, even when the surprise was this big. The photograph was grainy, and the lack of detail was not helped by the lack of light when the picture was taken, but Tony could easily see that the man in the photo was his colleague Steve.

The policeman ran out of patience. "Well?"

Tony looked up from the photo to the policeman. "Well what?"

"Who is the man in the photo?"
"I thought that you were going to tell me."
"Your name has been mentioned by two different people when we've shown them this picture, and it's taken me a lot of effort to track you here. Don't think for one minute that we don't know who you are or what you do, and when we get hold of concrete evidence against you, you'll be locked away for a long time. For now, we're more interested in the death of Thomas Harbod, and why this man was outside his house."
This was interesting. The cause of Thomas Harbod's death was stated in the newspaper as a heart attack after falling down his stairs at home late at night, and being as he was eighty four, Tony didn't think that it was suspicious, so why should the police? And what was Steve doing there? He managed to retain his poker face, but his mind was working overtime; if Steve had anything to do with Thomas's death, they could all be in deep trouble.
"Are you talking about Thomas Harbod, the chairman of Grangers?"
"Yes."
"But he was about ninety; I'd be more than happy if I lived to that age. Who'd be suspicious about that?"
"Let's just say that we are and leave it at that. We want to know who the man in the picture is, and why he was there at the time of death. Have another look, a good one this time, your future wellbeing could depend on it."
Tony looked again. "The picture is so poor that it could be anyone. Actually, it looks a bit like you; I hope that you have a good alibi."
"You know how to reach me. Trust me; you're missing out on a big, big chance to earn some brownie points. When we come after your lot, you'll need all the friends that you can find."
Tony watched them walk down the street from his office window and made a quick decision that he needed a

new office, and a new team, but first he wanted to know how and why Steve was involved in the death of Thomas Harbod. The last problem would be resolved shortly, as Steve was already late for their meeting.

There was a good reason for Steve being late in the office. He was in the local pub having his own meeting with Graham to discuss Grangers without Tony, who would have put the brakes on their work. His personal security was well drilled, and as he turned into the street, he looked up to check the office window when it came into view and noticed the warning sign in the office window. Steve grabbed Graham's arm and pulled him back gently, so as not to bring any attention to them, just in case there were others waiting for them outside the building. He knew that Tony was not in any bother, because the blind was fully up; if Tony wanted them to come to his assistance, but also wanted them to arrive prepared, and quietly, then the blind would have been only half way up the window. They didn't have a warning sign if the person inside the room couldn't get to the window, but that would have probably meant that they were beyond help. Steve and Graham stayed out of sight until the police had walked away from the office building, and gave them a few more minutes, in case the visitors remembered something else that they needed to discuss and caught them on their return visit. Tony was not best pleased with them when they finally arrived, but they had become used to that now.
"I've just had the filth in here with a picture of you taken outside Thomas Harbod's house on the night that he died."
"So what."
"What the fuck were you doing there?"
Steve shrugged, "Everyone's gotta be somewhere."
Tony was not impressed. "Did you kill him?"

Steve didn't care what Tony thought anymore. If he wanted to, he could get rid of Tony and feed him to his friend's pigs, and no-one would take any notice; he'd already reported the problems that Tony was starting to cause with their work at Grangers, so could expect no repercussions from the hierarchy.

"I just made an informal late-night call, and he fell down the stairs and broke his neck. What sort of gratitude was that?"

"The police are showing an interest in his death, and they have linked it to us. Maybe you'd like to explain that to me?"

"I have no idea what their problem is. There's no reason why his death should be suspicious, the newspapers said that he was an old man who had a heart attack for fucks sake. Why would anyone think that we had anything to do with him, and even if they did, there's nothing to link any presence of me inside his house, or grounds."

"If the police start looking at the information that we've stolen from Grangers, they will start to find lots of reasons why we're involved with his death. I told you to leave Grangers' alone, and you just didn't fucking listen?"

Graham kept quiet, as he usually did whilst Tony was having his rant, but Steve couldn't give a shit anymore.

"When we teamed up with you, I was told that you were the best in the business, but now it looks like you've lost your bottle."

"Well, I suggest you find someone who hasn't, because I want nothing more to do with you."

Tony went to the window to check the street, and, despite his concentration being badly reduced by Steve's attitude, he noticed the same man waiting in the shop doorway from the time earlier when he pulled up the blind. He moved back over to the hidden safe, opened it up, and took out a small canvass bag containing a large bundle of banknotes, leaving the safe empty. He threw half of the cash onto the table. "Consider this your severance payment. I'm busy now, trying to save our necks, but that's us finished,"

Tony picked up his laptop and the bag containing the rest of the money, and left Steve and Graham staring open-mouthed at the large amount of cash on the table. He made a quick detour on the way to the exit of the building to another office that he rented, unknown to the others. As usual, the corridor was empty, and there were no hidden cameras watching him as he unscrewed the fire alarm button from the wall and retrieved a set of five keys from his secret compartment behind it. The office door had frosted glass, so that no-one could see what was on the other side. He unlocked the door to reveal a small room, which was empty except for a modest office table and chair, and four robust steel cabinets, all of which were clean and locked so that no-one could tell which one of them had been opened most recently. Apart from clandestine storage, the room was never used, and no questions were asked due to the long-term one-off payment for the rent that Tony had forked out two years ago. He unlocked the closest cupboard and took out a casual jacket, exchanging it for his suit jacket, he took out a belt attached to a long thin bag and clipped it around his waist and filled the bag with the contents from his suit jacket, along with a quick disguise kit, a pay as you go smartphone and the cash that he'd taken from the safe upstairs. There was another stack of cash in one of the other cupboard drawers that he could get later if he needed it. He zipped up his jacket and locked his laptop, suit jacket and the empty bag inside the cupboard. He didn't want to get picked up with the information on the laptop, especially the pictures and audio recording taken during his first meeting with Steve when they were given the job of obtaining sensitive business information from Grangers and Robertsons. Tony was a good judge of bad character and was highly suspicious of the man they were dealing with, the task manager inside his head had been given another assignment 'to check out the person in front of him and obtain a method of protection if things went wrong.' This information was also held on the computer and could be vital for his survival.

Tony could come back for his other possessions when it was safer to do so; his main priority was to meet up with Richard without being followed, or worse still, captured, and it would be easier to disappear from anyone tailing him if he didn't have his bag and laptop in full sight. Tony checked the bus times on his mobile and saw that the next bus was due in a few minutes. The buses ran quite close to their timetable, and he could see the bus lane and the two stops further up on his side of the road, so when the bus left the stop before his he could leave the building with enough time to jump on the bus just before it left his stop, easily out of reach of the man waiting for him. The corridor was still quiet when Tony locked the office door and put the keys back into their hiding place, he went to the main entrance and walked quickly out of the building as the bus approached his stop.

The man in the doorway moved out to follow Tony as he appeared in the street, and Tony stepped aboard the bus before the man got close to him, praising the God of technology who provided the Oyster Card, reducing the time at the bus stops where the few passengers without bus passes would take an age to pay for their fare. The sight of the disappearing bus was usually enough to put people off their chase, but although Tony made it look as if he didn't notice the people trying to apprehend him, he saw the man following him wave to a car further down the street. Another man in front of the bus but on the other side of the road, sprinted past the bus in the opposite direction to join Tony's pursuant, and the car stopped to pick them up. The cacophony of car horns from the drivers held up for a few 'precious' seconds were ignored, and the car was only a few vehicles behind the bus when it left the next stop. The bus lane allowed the bus to extend the lead on the following car, and Tony jumped off at the next stop after the bus went around a corner, out of sight of his pursuers. The car came back into view whilst Tony was still on the pavement, and the two passengers jumped out and ran full pelt after him. Although they were both some way behind him, the covert chase had changed to an obvious hunt, so Tony took refuge in the large Marks and Spencers, and raced upstairs to the changing rooms in the men's clothing area before they could see where he'd gone. He had time to turn his coat inside out, and the black coat was now light blue. The wig in his disguise kit changed his short grey hair to a much longer brown colour, and the thick beard altered his appearance enough for him to escape unrecognised without a full scrutiny. The amount he spent to get a proper looking beard, which stuck quickly and realistically to his face, instead of a 'joke' version used at parties, proved excellent value for money, considering the high price that he put on the softer parts of his body, which were at risk of being agonisingly detached if he was caught. Tony was out of the changing room within less than a minute and noticed the first pursuer climbing the stairs that he had used to go up as he casually went down the stairs on the other side of the store. The second man, stationed at the main entrance was looking for a clean shaven, grey haired man in a dark coloured jacket, and Tony looked in the other direction as he went through the exit so that he didn't make eye contact with him, as he left the store, with the pursuers inside, whilst Tony walked briskly to the pre-arranged meeting, arriving out of breath, and out of sight in the upstairs part of the McDonalds.

Richard was already there, alone, and with a coffee for each of them. "Nice beard."
Tony took a gulp of his coffee, wishing that it had a large slug of whisky inside. His heart beat came back to normal, as did his instincts, and he carried out a full check of his surroundings for anyone, or anything suspicious amongst the crowd of young girls giggling and talking about boys, and single fathers filling up their allocated time to spend with their estranged children. They were well out of earshot from the others in the room.
"I had unwanted company waiting for me outside the office which required more than the usual effort to escape."
"Police?"
"Hah, no these were professionals, I was lucky to get away." Tony's 'luck' depended upon his regular practise of eluding people that he didn't want to talk to, and the different methods that he had in place for doing so.
"If they want you that much, they'll catch up with you sooner or later."
"I'll just have to make that later then, won't I, or better still, change their minds so that they no longer need to speak to me."
"Any idea who it was who tried to pick you up?"
"Most probably the company that I'm doing some work for at the moment, or people that they hired."
"Not the controllers then?"
"It's possible, but if they wanted me, I would have expected them to have got Steve and Graham to hold me until they collected me."

"They'll probably be speaking to Steve and Graham as well and didn't want them to warn you off."
Tony considered Richard's idea, and agreed with it; the controllers would still view himself, Steve and Graham as being part of the same team,
"If the controllers tried to grab me, they must have a good reason. They must want me alive otherwise they'd have sent Jason to get rid of me."
Richard smiled. He knew exactly how capable Jason was.
Tony continued, "And if they want me alive and only want to talk to me, why didn't they send me a meeting request?"
"Like I did, you mean?"
Tony was surprised that he wasn't surprised at anything that had happened that afternoon, and it all started to make some sort of sense.
"Thomas Harbod?"
"Correct."
"He was an old man who had a heart attack; why is everyone so interested in his death?"
"Thomas was a good friend of mine. He was very fit for his age, looked after himself, and should have lasted for a good few more years. He was also trying to save his business from an attack from another company, which I think that you know something about."
"What makes you think that I'm involved?"
"Because when I checked the film from the camera in the street where Thomas lived, I saw that one of your associates was in the area when Thomas died. I got someone from the board of Grangers to remind the police of the camera, in case they hadn't got around to checking it."
"So that's how the police knew. The Old Bill called on me this afternoon asking me about the photo of Steve. Did you tell the controllers as well?"

"Not likely, I stay well away from them. They would have been informed from one of their numerous sources within the police."

"I asked Steve if he had anything to do with Thomas's death, and he said he didn't, and that it was an accident, which was the same as the report in the paper, but without the reference to someone else being in the house." Tony paused to collect his thoughts. "Why did you want to meet with me?"

"The death of Thomas Harbod has made Grangers very vulnerable to a takeover. The financial reports have been poor for the last year, and Thomas's death left Grangers with no-one in charge, resulting in a drop in the share price, which could get worse."

"Why haven't they chosen a new Chairman yet?"

"The board of directors had a meeting, and nothing was properly resolved. Thomas's grandson Tom is the obvious choice, Thomas told me a few weeks ago that he had started to give Tom more of his responsibilities, and expected Tom to take over as Chairman when he retired in the next year or so, but some of the board thought that he was too young and inexperienced. Frank Harbod made a lot of noise, telling everyone that he has the knowledge, leadership skills and experience needed to run the company, and should be a shoe-in, but Frank's view of his own worth is very different to everyone else's."

"Did they tell him that?"

"Certainly not, he owns a large chunk of the family shares, which he's added to in the last few years. The board told him that they needed him to concentrate on his department, even though his work is managed by two of the younger members of his team."

"If they don't do something about that soon, the share price will get even lower."

"Tom told them that at the meeting, so they asked Tom to be the temporary Chairman until they can sort something more permanent. There will be a press release shortly; Tom said that they should make the position appear more than a short-term measure and add some spin to the media to make it sound as if the company was moving forward. One of the ideas was to borrow the deputy chairman from Robertsons's to work with Tom, the problem is that Robertsons are also having problems."

Tony looked a bit sheepish. "I know."

"Is that down to your team as well?"

"Both for the same client. I told Steve to lay off, but he won't listen anymore."

"What do you think will happen now?"

"I don't think that the share price of either company is low enough for a takeover yet, but one or both of them will be soon, unless they find a way to improve their business. If you were so close to Thomas Harbod, I can't understand why you didn't see this happening."

"We did, some time ago, both at Grangers and at Robertsons."

"Why didn't you do something about it?"

"We did, no-one's noticed yet; but your client should start having problems soon, hopefully before they have the opportunity to buy out Grangers."

Tony drank the remaining part of his coffee and went quiet for a while. "I wondered about that. I collected some information from the Grangers contact not long ago which was similar to the stuff that I picked up from the same source a few months earlier."

Richard nodded. "Technical data?"

"Yes, it was. I couldn't understand it at the time, but something must have gone wrong, and their technical department must have been checking it."

"Hopefully it cost them a lot of money plus time lost that has held up the production of the prototype for the work that they stole from Grangers."

"I warned them that they were taking too much, and people would get suspicious." The reason for the afternoon's chase finally hit Tony. "Shit, the death of Thomas Harbod was just a coincidence; they were after me because the information was no good."

Richard smiled. "I hope that it was worse than no good. My colleagues heard about the technical problems, we expected that the problems with the prototype were because of the data stolen from Grangers and could prevent them from taking over Grangers. I wouldn't rule out the death of Thomas Harbod as being the reason why people are trying to get hold of you though."

As far as Tony knew, Richard had no direct connection to the company which he was providing information to, or the controllers. "How do you know what I've been doing?"

"It's our business to know the main players in business throughout the country, and where we might make money when things go wrong."

"Yes, I know, but the work that I carry out is always done on a need-to-know basis. I only get in touch with you when I need information about a certain person, or some new identities."

"What will you do now?"

"I'll lie low for a couple of days; then get in touch with the controllers and tell them what really happened."

"You can stay at my place if you like; I have plenty of room, and it's secure."

"No thanks, I have another place in town that no-one knows about."

"Won't you be missed?"

"Not really, I've already paid off Steve and Graham and told them that I want nothing more to do with them, so they won't expect any requests in their social calendars from me. I have no close ties or dependants. In this game, it doesn't pay to be married with children, they can be too much of a liability."

"What will happen with the work with your client if you're not involved?"

"The client won't know about me ending my association with Steve and Graham, or the link to Thomas Harbod's death yet, so Steve and Graham will probably carry on without me for a while."

"Do you still have any contacts within Grangers to supply you with information?"

"Not anymore. I told the controllers that the person that I was dealing with is in danger of being blown, I didn't realise that Grangers had been aware of this for some time." This was only part of the truth, as Tony also had someone passing them financial information, but, hopefully, Richard only suspected that they had one contact.

"Don't you have anyone to take his place?"

"I did take some photos at the team building exercise, but they are safe from Steve, and won't be used."

"Are Steve and Graham able to set up someone that they can blackmail?"

"Well, they know what I do, and how I do it, so they could try. Steve also has the list of Grangers' personnel that we put together when we started the job. How did you find out the identity of the last contact that we had?"

"We didn't. We were certain that information was being passed on from Grangers, so Thomas just made a few changes to the figures and asked Tom to modify the designs. Tom's a very clever young man, the plans looked good, and the faults that he put in place wouldn't cause any problems until the prototype was put through its strenuous testing regime. Thomas was still sharp, despite his age, and made the costings report given to the board for the last project appear believable, but the real price for the work that Grangers submitted was much lower and we won the contract. Unlike the other bids that Grangers made that were underbid, they will be able to make a small amount of profit from this work."

"Why are you telling me this? I could tell the client what you just told me and clear my name."
"I thought that you'd finished with your current partners and client."
"I have, but I still need to cool things off with the controllers."
"You don't want to upset my crowd as well as the controllers; you'd spend all of your time worrying about who is going to put you out of circulation. It's not so easy to hide from my team, just remember, it was them that set you up with all of your false identities."
Tony took out a pen and wrote a series of numbers on the paper napkin he'd received with his coffee. He passed the napkin to Richard and stood up to leave.
"This is my new mobile number, I had to leave my old phone on the bus. Don't worry, there's nothing of interest on it, I tried to jump off the bus without them seeing me and if they were tracking me using my phone signal, they would have carried on following the bus. Keep in touch."

EIGHT

Board meetings at Grangers were being held on virtually a daily basis. Tom was doing well as acting Company Chairman, but he wasn't given the same authority as his grandfather had, and decisions were being made by committee, so were watered down from what was actually required, and were taking too long to make. He knew what was needed to be done but didn't know if he had the support from the board to move the company forward. He started the conversation at the meeting to find out where he stood.

"The share price is down today, and unless the lack of a permanent chairman is resolved shortly, there will be a run on the share price, and we will be taken over."

Frank, as usual, was the first voice to be heard.

"This is nothing new to what I've been saying since the chairman died. The share price will carry on its downward trend until the business world is informed that a person in which they have confidence in is made the chairman, and we need to do this last week."

Tom had expected this and had already spoken to three people on the board who he knew supported him, and who he could trust.

The first person that Tom had spoken to, made his comments before Frank could say anything more, or to push himself forward for the chairman's role. "I agree, we've already waited far too long to appoint a new chairman."

This was closely followed by Tom's second friend.

"What Frank says is absolutely correct. The share price held firm when it was announced that Tom was taking over as interim chairman, but the delay in confirming his position has created some confusion resulting in another reduction of the share price."

The third accomplice added the coup de grace. "Thank you, Frank for your forthright views on what is required.

If we agree that Tom takes over as chairman today it will end the confusion and stop the share price from getting worse."

Frank was shell-shocked at the turn of events and watched in disbelief as the vote on the appointment of Tom as chairman was unanimous, as he was forced to go with the remaining members of the board or look stupid. Tom was prepared for the vote and its outcome. "Thank you very much. I feel that I owe it to my grandfather and you all to accept your generous offer for the good and benefit of the company. I expect that you have no problems with Gordon taking over from me as Head of Production, if I can persuade him to accept the post and carry on working, despite being due for retirement in six months' time." There were nods of approval and no comments against the idea. "If there is nothing else for today's meeting, Alan please prepare a press report, but could you please give me an hour before this is made public. There are a few people that I need to speak to."

The first, and most important point of call was Gordon who was still in the Production Manager's office. Tom had moved into the Chairman's office when his grandfather died for obvious business reasons, but he was still Head of Production. Jerry had stayed at Grangers and was working with Tom full time looking for new contracts, which eased Tom's workload, but running the whole company should be Tom's priority. When the board meeting finished, Tom had phoned his p.a. and asked her to have some coffee and posh biscuits ready in the Head of Production's office. Tom had spoken to Gordon earlier telling him that he would like a meeting with him after the board meeting to discuss the way forward. Gordon looked up from his computer when Tom knocked on his office door.

"Gordon, could I get you a coffee? There's something that we need to talk about."
Gordon followed Tom to Tom's office and Tom poured the coffees.
"You might like to sit down; I need to ask an incredibly big favour from you." Tom hoped that his friend was still loyal to the company, despite the death of the Chairman, "Could you defer your retirement,"
"I thought that under the current circumstances you would be reducing staff numbers, so natural wastage such as retirements would be an easy way to do so."
"Jerry and I are looking at ways to increase the workload, and we have one project that we managed to win that will be starting soon. You're still young and active and would make a really good Head of Production."
"What?" That was a surprise!
"You should have been given the post five years ago when I was appointed, and many people would have left the company instead of working for someone as young and inexperienced as me. I turned down the job when I was offered it, but my grandfather was very persuasive."
"I know, he spoke to me about you taking over Production as well." This was news to Tom. "He also persuaded me to carry on as Production Manager. I knew him for nearly fifty years, so it was impossible to turn him down."
"You didn't have to be as supportive as you have been."
"I did, I owed it to your grandfather and to the company, and later to you. I thought at the time that Grangers would be better off with you as Head of Production, and you've proven me correct. Why do you think that I would want to be Head of Production now?"
"Because we need people like you at the moment, as we are still close to being taken over, and I can't let that happen."

"Why do we need a new Head of Production? Are you leaving?"
"In a way, I'm taking over as Chairman. I wanted to let you know first."
"I can't understand why they didn't make that decision when the old man died. When do I start?"
"With immediate effect."
"Will I be able to recruit my replacement?"
"Of course."
"I intend to recruit internally, unless you want Helen to apply for the post."
"She wouldn't dream of working for me. I've asked her enough times and she's made that quite clear. Do you want any help in the interviews?"
"No, I don't think so, if you're involved people will think that the choice was yours, not mine."
"That's bollocks, you've always been your own man. I have to get on now, as all hell will break loose when the press release goes out. Good luck as Head of Production."

The next people that Tom had to talk to were Jerry and Richard, to work out their involvement in Grangers with Tom officially in charge. Gordon left the office and gave his first order to his new p.a. "Please inform the Production team that I have an important announcement to make to them on the main shop floor at twelve o'clock today."
The messages were passed to all team leaders, and there was a noisy hum of expectation waiting for Gordon when he entered the shop floor.
"As you should have heard by now, Tom Harbod has been installed as the new Chairman, and has left the post of Head of Production. He has asked me to take over his duties, so we need a new Production Manager, and Tom has asked me to recruit my replacement. I intend to recruit internally, so if any of you are interested

in the post, send me your CV, either via e-mail or hard copy by close of play tomorrow, and I'll be carrying out interviews next Monday."

Gordon was pleasantly surprised with the three people who sent him their CV. Jim's CV was nowhere near as good as the other two, but Gordon didn't want to start his new post by upsetting one of his workers, so he arranged interviews for all three. He knew them well enough not to have to carry out psychometric tests or such like, an interview would be more than sufficient. He also wanted two independent members on the interview panel, Frank and Sally were members of the board, and high up enough in the food chain for people to think that the choice of Production Manager was their own, not one forced upon them. Gordon would give the applicants a debrief the day after the interviews, by which time the interview panel would have made their decision. He would use the debrief to discuss the shortfalls in Jim's CV and give him some suggestions where it could be improved.

The best CV and interview were from Rachid. By the time of the interviews, everyone knew that Gordon was moving to become the Head of Production, so there was no confusion in the new formation of the production team. The main questions at the interviews came from Gordon.

"Good morning Rachid, what do you think that you will bring to the new team management?"

"The old team of you and Tom was as effective and efficient as any team could be. The main reason for this was that one of the leaders was older, fully experienced and had a strong knowledge of what was required, the younger member was top of his field and wanted to push forward new ideas, some of them untested, but with great potential. The structure of the management team should ensure that all aspects of engineering are considered when breaking new ground and the inherent risks are investigated before a decision was made without delays due to constant arguments and checking and rechecking of the requirements. Although I could never claim to be as clever as Tom, I would like to think that I would bring my own desire to move our engineering into the future."

"If you would like to bring in new ideas faster, do you think that you would be better placed as Head of Production instead of Production Manager?"

"The way that the previous team worked made no difference on who was in what post. The team would have been as good with either one in either of the two posts. My view is that Grangers will need to concentrate more on the environment-friendly projects to remain successful. I would like to think that I could bring new ideas to the company in line with the improvements to technology whether I was in either post."

"If it doesn't matter who was in which of the top production posts, why do you think that Tom was given the post of Head of Production when he was?"

"My personal view is that Tom is a Harbod and was expected to be the future of the Grangers. Being Head of Production gave him a place on the board and with it, a better preparation to take over as Chairman than if he had been Production Manager."

Gordon had held this belief before Tom was made Head of Production, and it was good to hear that this view was not his alone, and that Rachid was bright enough to understand the politics within the company.

The other two interviewees used the common clichés, such as promising to give 110% or do the work of two and a half men but failed to provide specific examples of how their promotion would benefit Grangers. When the interviews were finished, and the three interviewers were left in the office, Gordon put his notes for all of the applicants on the table. He looked at the notes made by the other two and despite the fact that he had asked the most questions, he could see that he'd written far more comments than the other two had.

"Thank you for helping me with the interviews today. Do you have a clear idea of who should be offered the post, or do you want to discuss it first, or even spend an hour or so alone whilst you make up your mind?"

Sally already knew who she preferred. "I have no problem making my choice now. Rachid was head and shoulders above the other two. He also has the correct demeanour; the rest of the team respect him and will be happy with him as their manager."

Frank, as usual, was not so sure. "Don't you think that there may be a race problem if you give Rachid the job?"

Tom shook his head. "Frank, all of our engineers can't be Scottish."

"That's not what I meant."

"I know that, and your comments have no place in our company. Do you agree that Rachid is the best person for the post?"

"I tried to get Rick to apply for this post, he would have been a much better choice. He is also a Harbod but he chose not to apply."

"So, do you agree that Rachid is the best person for the position out of the applicants?"

"I suppose so."

"And you don't want to take some time to confirm your answer?"

This was the second time in the last few days that Frank didn't get himself or his son into a better position in the company. "I suppose not."

"Good. I'd like to thank both of you for your help in this matter. Please sign the bottom of your interview notes, I'll put them in the interview file and give them to HR."

NINE

The day after Tony stormed off, Steve sat in the office for thirty minutes before he finally believed that Tony had really left them. Tony was always in early, and always told them if he was going to be elsewhere, mainly as a method of self-preservation; if he was supposed to be in the office, and wasn't, there would probably be a sinister reason for his non-appearance, that had nothing to do with him being left-handed. Tony had told them some time ago that if he didn't turn up, and he had the chance, he would let Steve and Graham know where to start looking for him, or his body, and would also let them know who they needed to avoid. Steve's contact had been in touch the night before, and when Graham appeared an hour later, Steve had already set up a plan of action to move their work forward. Graham saw no reason to get up early and work his way through the rush hour traffic on the off chance that Tony had changed his mind. He was surprised that Steve was hard at work
"I didn't expect to see you here."
Steve looked up from the sheet of paper on the desk. "Why not, there's work to be done, and if Tony doesn't want to do it, there's more money in it for us. Grab a coffee, there's a few things we need to discuss."
The working budget had recently been refreshed by Tony's unexpected input, so Graham helped himself to a cup of decent coffee and a few chocolate hobnobs and joined Steve at the desk.
"Grangers' share price is still holding up, despite the death of the chairman. This must be due to his grandson, Tom Harbod. The contact that I spoke to said that Tom had taken over as chairman of Grangers, and the shareholders have shown confidence in him, so we need to take him out of circulation for a while."

"How do you propose to do that?"
"Nothing we haven't done before. Look at this."
Graham moved around next to Steve and looked at the laptop screen, which displayed a street map of Oxford.
"We get him to meet up with us in this pub and jump him in the alley on the way to the pub, and break a few of his bones."
"Just the two of us?"
"Fuck me Graham, of course it'll be just the two of us. You're not getting squeamish, are you? Are you saying that the two of us couldn't handle one person? Well? Are you wimping out on me as well as Tony?"
"No, but there are two ways to get to the pub, one alley goes down from the High street, and another from this street here."
Steve looked at the screen. "Yeah, ok, I'll get someone to watch the lower entrance as well. We'll have him trapped, and I'll give him the good news."
"We're not used to taking chances like this. Tony would never allow it."
"What chance? We'll jump him in the alley, give him a couple of taps where it hurts, and put him in hospital for a few days. We can tip off a few people in the press that he was attacked by an angry husband. We'll know if we have to do anything else by looking at Grangers' share price when the story breaks."
Graham sighed in resignation and Steve sent Tom a text telling him that it would be beneficial for him, and Grangers, to meet up at the Bear at nine that evening.

Tom didn't recognise the mobile number that sent him the text and was obviously wary when he saw that the meeting place was at the Bear. The bar was public enough, and it was in Oxford City Centre, but the alleyway before it was well known to be dangerous, especially if the sender's intent was different to that in the message. Fortune usually favours the brave, so Tom's initial feeling was to look for rapid assistance in case anything kicked off. Luckily Dave answered on the third ring. Tom quickly explained what he wanted, but Dave was more concerned that Tom was.

"The Bear? You're mad. I wouldn't go anywhere near that alley in the dark on my own. It will probably be safer if you go up from Blue Boar Street instead of the High Street."

"No, they'll expect me to go down Alfred Street. Wait for me at Carfax, and I'll walk past you at 8.50. Follow me at a close enough distance not to arouse suspicion and shorten the distance between us when I turn off the High Street."

"Ok, but I still think that you're mad."

Tom answered the text, agreeing to the meeting.

At five to nine Tom entered the tight alley way. He hadn't made any sign to Dave as he passed him talking to his girlfriend at Carfax and ignored the stocky man stood at the junction of Turl Street and the High Street when he turned right into Alfred Street. He felt the presence of someone close behind him before he saw the large outline of someone else blocking his way. As soon as Tom stopped, he was grabbed tightly from behind. Tom was punched in the body and face by a man who seemed to know what he was doing. Dave quickly caught up with the man holding Tom, and one downward blow on the back of the head of the man holding Tom's arms resulted in Tom being free to fight back. Three punches from Tom knocked Steve to the ground before Dave had the chance to join in.

"Stop!" Steve had assessed the problem quickly and had to avoid it getting worse. "We were told to tell you to stay away from work for a few days, and to give you a few incentives to do so."

"Who by?"

"Someone gave us an envelope in our local pub last night containing your details and £200 for each of us to scare you off work. We weren't going to do you any damage; if we were going to do that, we would have used knuckle dusters or a knife." He didn't mention the damage he'd planned with his boots once Tom was on the ground.

"You'd better look after your friend he doesn't seem to be able to take a punch as well as you." Tom backed away, watching Steve trying to resuscitate Graham, until he and Dave were out of sight.

"How hard did you hit him?"

Dave showed Tom his cosh, before hiding it in his jacket. "I take it that you haven't been put off work."

"They will need to try harder than that, whoever 'they' are."

Steve was back at work the following morning, but he didn't see Graham again, for reasons that he didn't know at the time. He blamed Graham for the failure the previous night and resolved to go back to the controllers for another team. If he could set up another contact with Grangers, it would give him much better leverage to dictate his new terms of contract, and could result in him being a team leader, instead of being a follower. He opened the list of Grangers personnel on his laptop and looked at the names of those who Tony had thought would be able to provide them with the type of information which would be useful and could be most likely to be open to blackmail, and the best way to catch them. A broad smile appeared on his face as he drew a ring around the name of someone that fitted the bill. He was surprised that Tony hadn't set up the man before.

Steve had also used the increased budget to buy the state-of-the-art camera that he'd seen Tony with, and put in place his plan for the next contact in Grangers. He had found a room in the building on the other side of the road from Grangers' main office and had located the target straight away. Amongst many items of clothing and equipment that Steve had kept when he left the Army was a powerful pair of binoculars, and he watched the target for the next two nights. Like most married men of a certain age, the target preferred to spend more time away from the marital home, and each evening he was one of only a few people left at work, and they were soon outnumbered by the cleaning staff. Despite telling his wife that the reason that he worked late was that the lack of staff resulted in making him really busy, he always stopped work to talk to the cleaner when she was in his office. Even Steve could work out what to do. He opened up Tony's list of 'assistants' and found one who looked close enough like the cleaner to take her place.
On the third night, a different cleaner entered the office block, the woman who usually cleaned the same floor as the target had happily accepted the £20 that Steve had given her to stay at home, Steve had told her that she would still get paid for her shift, and no questions would be asked. Her supervisor had better things to do than to speak to every one of the cleaning staff that she was responsible for, if they didn't turn up for work the security staff at each company would pone her to let her

know, and she would find a replacement. She would soon find out if the cleaning hadn't been done. The replacement cleaner wore no make-up and was the same height and shape as the usual one, she made her hair look similar, and she carried the usual cleaner's pass, so security took no notice as she entered the building; they would have seen the difference if both women had turned up wearing only the clothing underneath their cleaner's uniform, and if the new cleaner had her usual hair style and make up. She spent an hour cleaning the offices and toilets in her area as quickly as she could so there would be no complaints about the work not being done before she applied some red lipstick, smartened up her hair and hitched up her tunic to show off her bare legs just above her knees before going into the target's office. The man working late in the office noticed straight away that the cleaner was not the usual one, and Steve congratulated himself on how the plan was going. He couldn't hear the discussion but could see from the body language of the target that it was going the way it should.

"I'm sorry to disturb you sir, I didn't expect you to be working this late."

"Where's the usual cleaner tonight?"

"She phoned in sick, so they asked me to do her shift."

"And you didn't mind?"

"Oh no sir, I'm glad of the work, it's a bit scarce at the moment."

"I'm sure that someone as pretty as you would have no problems finding work."

"It's not so easy when you have two young children, and their father's run off with someone younger without leaving me any money. The money from the government isn't anywhere near enough to keep the

kids fed and clothed, so I have to take any type of work that's going, usually low paid. I'd do anything for some extra money"
"You need to be careful saying things like that."
"Why, it's true."
"Someone might misunderstand what you mean by 'anything'"
She smiled, knowing that he had taken the bait. This one would be very easy to reel in. "What? Sex? Chance would be a fine thing. No-one's interested in me anymore. That's why my husband's left me and I'm doing cleaning jobs."
"I would imagine that there are lots of men still interested in you."
She smiled at him. "Does that include you?"
"Yes, definitely!"
"Thank you, but I have to get on with the cleaning or the supervisor won't let me work here again." She started up the vacuum cleaner and went around the office carpet quickly. She could feel his eyes on her and bent over forwards on a regular basis to show off the top of her legs. She stopped the vacuum cleaner, picked up the wastepaper bin and emptied its contents into the black bag that she'd brought into the office. He was still watching her. "Is there something that you want me to do for you that is better paid than cleaning?"
He was stumped for an answer. He'd often thought about offering the usual cleaner a few quid to brighten up his life, but never expected anything to happen. This one was much better looking than the usual cleaner, and he probably wouldn't see her again. He had become more aroused than he'd been for a long time. "What are you offering me?"
"I could find the time to give you a blow job for £20"

"In here?"
"Why not, you're not expecting anyone, are you?"
"Do you mind if I turn the main light off?"
"You carry on, I can pretend that you're Brad Pitt if it's dark."
The darkness had no effect on the camera, and Steve watched as the girl went through her 'job' with the expected skill. After about twenty seconds she stopped, and Steve thought that it was all over.
"I haven't had the chance of anything as big as your cock for ages, would you like a shag for no extra cost?"
Without waiting for an answer, she opened her cleaner's tunic, took out a durex from her pocket, unwrapped it and rolled it over his todger before he could think about changing his mind; but there was very little chance of that happening. She also had time to put some moisturiser on the outside of the durex, which would be more efficient than spit, and she was moving her body against the office wall as soon as he was inside her. Steve was enjoying watching this as much as the couple in the office were doing it and was more upset than he thought he would be when the target pulled his trousers back on and took out his wallet.
"Are you expecting to work here again soon? I work late most nights."
"Probably not, but I'll make sure that I clean this office area if I do."
As Steve had arranged with her, the rest of the cleaning had already been done before she went into the target's office, so she pocketed the £20, zipped up her tunic, and left.
Steve had paid the two women, so all he had to do was get back home and put the next plan in place. The train didn't take long to get into Paddington, so he had time to

drop off the camera in the office safe, and go for a few celebratory beers in the pub. He hoped that Graham would be in the pub already so that he could give him chapter and verse on how it had gone with the new target.

Steve had enjoyed watching his first attempt to bring in a new contact and was looking forward to a long session in bed with his new girlfriend. He hadn't felt this good for months, Graham hadn't turned up at their usual drinking hole, but Steve was smiling broadly as he left the pub to walk to another pub where he had been chatting up the barmaid for the last few nights. She had finally agreed to meet with him after the pub closed and go for a meal and then back to his flat. Steve hadn't had much success with the women lately, but it was better than when he was still in the Army, as most of the local women were put off by his reputation, which he always felt was unfair. Even as a corporal he knew that to get the young soldiers to do what he wanted them to do he had to give them a certain type of motivation, the lazy ones often needed two fists to get them to understand the error of their ways. When he was helping with the training, he had been taught to treat the young soldiers like old-style computers and punch the information in. It was also the case for his wife as well, and Steve thought that she'd got the message and things were finally going well until she packed her bags and left whilst he was away in Afghanistan. Her note merely stated that she wanted nothing more to do with him, and for him to stay away from her. Her note also told him that she would be filing for divorce, what it didn't say was that she was six weeks pregnant and didn't want to bring up a child with a father who had such a violent temper.

It hadn't been difficult to find Steve, and the man appeared from the shadows before Steve had travelled very far, and then moved back out of sight, giving Steve a quick glimpse to let him know who he was, and that he was there, without drawing attention to himself from anyone else. As ever, although Steve had seen the man on business a few times before, he was ready to defend himself in case something kicked off. He disregarded the fight with Tom which he blamed Graham for losing and was confident that he could still look after himself with his hands as well as anyone he knew, but he knew well enough to keep his distance when knives were involved. Despite the action movies showing the unarmed hero despatching numerous knife-wielding 'baddies' with immaculate style, he'd seen the statistics regarding those both with and without his training in unarmed combat who had tried, unsuccessfully, to beat the odds against people with knives. He held his course looking into the darkness from where the man had appeared as the distance between them reduced. The man called out quietly to Steve to join him; if he'd wanted to be seen in the open with Steve, he would have met him in the pub. Steve looked around him to assess the danger and to see if there was anyone else close-by who might cause him problems, but it was quiet. If they were going to shoot him, he was already an easy enough target for the distance between them. He'd had more than a few beers but was still sober enough to know what was happening as he disappeared into the darkness, and he kept out of arm's reach from the other man. If they wanted to play quietly, Steve could reciprocate just as easily.

"What's up?" he whispered.

The answer was as quiet as before, "We need your help to find Tony."

"And?"

"Your presence has been requested, and it would be better if you came now."

Steve was still more in favour of a legover. "I'm busy now; can't it wait until tomorrow morning?"

"Probably not, I've been asked to get you to the office tonight, and your future employment could be affected if you decide otherwise. It won't take long."

Steve shrugged acceptance, he was still in a good mood, and the car appeared next to them from nowhere before he had time to change his mind and drove them to the underground car park of the office block which, amongst many others, contained the controllers' head office. Steve followed the man up the dark stairway to the rear entrance of the office, where they were met by another man who Steve recognised.

"Sorry about this Steve, but they asked to see you asap. I've seen you around at a couple of meetings, but we haven't been introduced. I'm Jason and this is Dave."

Steve nodded. Jason did all of the talking and Dave showed very little interest in what was going on.

"I'm sorry to drag you in at this time of night but all Hells broken loose since Tony disappeared, and we need to find him. I've called the boss and he'll be here soon, do you want a drink while you're waiting?"

Steve was a beer drinker, with the occasional Grouse chaser, so the large glass of single malt was gladly accepted, and was emptied and re-filled quickly, as they made the usual 'heavy' small talk.

"Can you still remember your SAS selection, Steve?"

"I'm not suffering from dementia yet, you know."

"We have a problem with our new interrogation tool?"

"And?"

"We thought that it would be fool proof, but when we tried it on someone last week, we didn't get all of the information we needed?"

"So what can I do?"

"You must have got through the interrogation phase to pass selection. If you have a look at our apparatus, you could give us a clue where we're going wrong. After last week's fuck up, your name was mentioned by the bosses, not only to improve our methods of obtaining information, but also as the person to extract it. It could be a nice little earner for you."
Steve perked up again. The decent whisky and the opportunity to dish out some violence for cash agreed with the expectations he had when he started working with Tony.
Jason looked at his watch. "We've got a few minutes now if you could look at it for us."
"No problem, where is it?"
They went back downstairs, but this time, below the car park level, through a heavy door, and further into another, window-less room which was cold, and had an 'uninviting' feel about it. In the middle of the room, a hoist was attached to the much higher than usual ceiling, but, apart from that, the room was empty except for a table next to the door, and a closed locker. Steve was unimpressed.
"What's frightening about that? The first thing you need to do is to scare the shit out of the stooge before you start putting any pressure on him."
"We didn't have time to prepare for this; we have a selection of sharp implements in the locker that we would have laid out on the table. We don't use them, but they scare the shit out of me."
Steve nodded his approval and waited for more information from Jason.
"When the apparatus gets going the odd movement is unexpected, and causes more confusion than pain, leaving the victim more or less unmarked."
Steve looked around for the usual white noise generator, or such like, but when the locker was opened, the main item on view was a strait jacket, as

well as the tool kit and a large bucket. Steve was still underwhelmed. "It's not easy to get someone inside anything like that."
The two men looked at each other, taking in Steve's comments. "We've had to drug the two people we've used it on."
Steve could see how they could use his expertise, as these two were morons. "If you kill someone on this thing, the drugs will be found in his bloodstream by the doctor doing the autopsy."
"But we don't intend to kill anyone, we just want information."
"You won't get any information if they think that they're not in any danger."
"So how are we to get it on him then?"
"You tell the bosses that I'll give them assistance, but I'm not going to tell you that for nothing."
The two men looked at each other, and Jason took out a small pocketbook and pen. "I think that we need to make a few notes. Could you give the machine a quick try for us, and then let us know what you think in a few days? I'll make sure that you get well paid for your time."
"Just make it quick."
"Put the straight jacket on, so that you get the full effect of the hoist."
Steve took off his jacket and held out his arms until the straight jacket was in place, and secure. "You also need to have an idea of what you want to know before you start asking the questions and be able to identify whether what you're being told is true and what isn't."
"Ok Steve, how about, where is Tony, and what do you know about his disappearance?"
"That's too fucking easy. I haven't a clue where he is, I don't care where he is, and he made himself scarce when he lost his bottle on the last job. Try something else."

"Ok, we'll ask you about the latest job. Can you lie on the floor, please?"

Steve did as he was asked, and the other two connected the hoist to his ankles, and it pulled him upwards until his head was two feet above the floor. The lights went off, and the room was now pitch black, with no gaps of light around the door. The machine spun Steve round in differing directions, moving him up and down and varying speeds, until he had no idea how far he was above the floor. After about thirty seconds, the lights came back on, temporarily blinding Steve, but not the other two, who were now wearing dark glasses. Jason started the interrogation. "Did Tony have anything to do with the change of plan for your latest job?"

Steve had little problem focusing on the question and could keep up the treatment for hours. "Tony wouldn't have anything to do with the extra business that we were asked to carry out, I told you earlier, he lost his bottle and left in a huff."

"Did he have any part in the death of Thomas Harbod?"

"He knew nothing about it, I was the one asked to divert his attention. I received some information about how to get into the old man's house. it was my idea to carry out a simple robbery to distract him from his work, which went wrong, sadly for the old bloke."

"How did you get the information?"

"From the contact at Grangers. He told me that someone at the team building event said that a bedroom window in Thomas Harbod's house had been set up so that it could be unlocked from the outside, and the burglar alarm had been disabled at the window."

"Who was with you when you robbed his house?"

"No-one."

"How did you kill him?"

"I didn't; he caught me in his house and tripped over his cats and fell down the stairs."

The lights went off, Steve was lifted upwards again, and the machine started to spin him faster and faster, until Steve lost track of time. The bright lights came on at the same time that the machine stopped twisting and sent him rapidly downwards head-first to the ground, before stopping inches above the floor. Steve was starting to feel sick, but his head cleared quite quickly.
"How did you kill Thomas Harbod?"
"I didn't kill him, he tripped over his cats in the dark, fell down the stairs and broke his neck."
"Did you leave any trace of you having been in the house?"
"Not a chance, I wore gloves all the time I was there, and had plastic covers on my shoes. I left a picture on the floor that had fallen down from the wall due to an old picture hook at the bottom of the stairs, which people will think woke him up and made him get out of bed."
"Who is your point of contact giving you the information from Grangers?"
Steve didn't expect this question and giving up the name could result in a loss of the promised bonus. "I'm not at liberty to tell you that. Ask me something else."
"I think we'll stay on this line of questioning for the next spin around the room. We'll also step up the programme by introducing some water."
The lights went off again, and Steve was spun around much faster than the last time. When the machine came to an abrupt stop a minute later, Steve had lost his senses and felt really sick. The lights came on and Dave restrained Steve, whilst a bucket of water was pushed upwards by Jason so that Steve's head was completely submerged. Steve was powerless from preventing this happening, and the water went down his nose whilst he started to struggle for breath. After a minute, the bucket was removed from his head, and Steve coughed his heart up."

"Maybe you'll be more helpful now. Who is your point of contact at Grangers giving you the information?"
"Fuck off."
"We can do this for as long as we like, and it gets worse every time. You'll tell us in the end, so why not tell us now?"
"Go fuck yourself."
The lights went off again, and the bucket was pushed upwards putting all of Steve's head in the water. Steve had completely lost his good mood and tried to move his body away from the water, but he was held securely in place. He tried to pull his legs upwards and jerked his head and shoulders from side to side. His frantic struggles started to recede after two minutes, until he eventually became still, his last thought being that the two idiots were getting close to drowning him. He died without realising who the idiot was. The machine lowered Steve slowly to the floor to prevent any marks and bruises appearing, the straight jacket was removed and replaced with Steve's own one. The bucket was still almost full of murky water. When Steve's body was found in the Thames a few hours later, the autopsy would reveal that Steve had a large amount of alcohol in his bloodstream, and the large amount of water from the river Thames in his lungs made it look as if he'd drowned there.
It didn't take the two men long to clean up the room, and dump Steve's body in the Thames, and despite their late finish, they were both in the office at eight o'clock to discuss how their interrogation of Steve went with Gerald, a sharp-dressed member of the hierarchy.
Jason gave Gerald a bag containing Steve's mobile, his bank cards and a bunch of keys.
"We changed these for the ones that you gave to us yesterday."
"Well done. What did you find out?"

As before, Jason did the talking. "Steve's story backed up what we expected. Tony's in the clear, and so is Graham. The death of Thomas Harbod was an unfortunate mistake, caused by Steve, which both Mr Harbod and Steve have paid dearly for. Steve was asked to distract Mr Harbod so he put in place a pretend robbery, but Mr Harbod came out of his bedroom, tripped over his cats in the dark, and broke his neck when he fell down the stairs."
"Were there any fresh marks on Steve's body that were not consistent with him falling in the river?"
"Not at all."
"Did you put him in the same part of the river that you took the water from?"
"Yes, and before you ask, no-one saw us fill the container up, or put Steve in the river."
"Ok, thanks Jason. Could you please give me a full report of everything that Steve said. I'll tell HR to take Steve off of our list of contacts, and we'll bring Tony back into the fold, so don't kill him the next time that you see him." Gerald gave the two men a bundle of money each and walked off to join the rest of the management team.
The two men were happy with the outcome from a few hours' work, plus what was left of the whisky. Killing Steve, even though they knew that he was a member of the team, was second nature to them.

The management team were dressed in expensive suits and were drinking top of the range bottled water when a smiling Gerald joined them in the plush boardroom.
"We've had a discussion with Steve about Thomas Harbod's death, and there's no evidence at the house to make it look like the death was suspicious."
Christopher, a large, sour-faced man was not convinced. "He was a rich man. His family will want a full investigation into his death."

"They'll get that but it won't find anything. He lived on his own in a big house and tripped over his cats late at night and fell downstairs and broke his neck."
Some people in this line of work have a dark outlook on life, Nick was one of them.
"Cats! I always said they were bad news."
Gerald tried to move away from the new topic of conversion and get to the main part of their business that morning, but Trevor cut in before he had the chance.
"My mother adores her cats they can't all be bad."
Nick was having none of this rubbish. "Ok, not all of them, but eight out of ten cats will ignore you, even if you feed them, and they will do whatever they want to do." He paused for a second. "And they're no good for protection, not like my Rottweilers are."
Gerald banged the table. "Gentlemen, the main point of this meeting is that we can bring Tony back to the team, he's in the clear."
This pleased everyone apart from Christopher. "That's a mistake; if you trusted him, then you wouldn't have sent people to bring him in earlier."
Gerald was always surprised by Christopher's open hatred of Tony, so wanted to keep him out of the process of getting back in touch with Tony. "If you remember, it was me who supported Tony when the decision was made to drag him in. I also said that he would be too clever to get caught, which he was. Tony's always played it straight with us and is the best at what he does. I'll put out the word that I want to speak to him, he trusts me. We'll need to give him a new team, Steve went for a swim in the Thames last night and won't be returning."
Christopher struggled to keep his calm. "What about the work that Tony's team were doing before Tony made himself scarce?"

"We'll draw a line under that for now, but Richard is heavily involved with Grangers, so we'll see what he thinks. The company changed the details of our arrangement, and they'll have to live with the consequences. If there's nothing else, I have other things to do."

TEN

Richard made no comments regarding the bruises on Tom's face when he entered Tom's office at lunchtime on the day after Tom's meeting with Steve. Jerry was already there, discussing how they could carry on with their current workforce without any foreseeable increase in work. Grangers had already reduced the workforce by not recruiting when people had left, usually to retire, and laying off any staff at the moment would be noticed and would have a detrimental effect on their share price which they were trying as hard they could to protect. Although Richard had arranged with Thomas for Jerry to work at Grangers for only two weeks some time ago, Jerry had stayed working with Tom, and the two of them had become a very efficient management team.
Richard's mobile made the standard 'pinging' noise when he received a text.
'Need to spk with 5, suggest 5 at 4.15'.
Richard hadn't received a text from Gerald since just after Thomas died, but was pleased that it was Gerald, and not Christopher who was getting in touch, especially if they wanted to talk to Tony. Richard changed the code in the text and forwarded it. Tom stopped talking and looked up from the reports they were discussing.
"Sorry about that, important business, outside of ours. Carry on."
They were interrupted again within seconds. It was already Tuesday, so Richard was surprised for the second time that morning when Tony agreed to meet with Gerald at three the following day, but he wanted Richard to be there as well, and for them to meet in Richard's car. Richard texted the response, and continued, uninterrupted this time, with Tom's latest plan of action to save the company. The press release regarding Tom taking over as the chairman of Grangers was a great success, and coincided with the award of a

substantial contract, assisted by the incorrect costing information passed to Steve, but it was still not enough. The price of Grangers' shares stirred from their death bed and took a sip of broth. It was early days, and Grangers was still in danger, but Tom was encouraged by the good news, and had other plans that might improve matters further.

Tony arrived at Richmond station an hour early and walked down the Quadrant with his usual air of indifference. A minute after walking past McDonalds he doubled back and went inside for a coffee safe in the knowledge that he was not being followed. He sat upstairs waiting for the large hand on the clock to move around, wondering why Gerald wanted to speak with him, if it was to tell him that he was no longer in danger, then a text message would have been sufficient. The controllers had always gone about things in a strange way, especially when he was recruited. He had a rough understanding of their existence but had no idea that they knew of his. He'd been a surprise to everyone since the day he was born, his father expected a larger baby in line with the rest of the males in his family. As Tony grew up, the difference in size and appearance between him and his elder brother became more and more apparent, and his performance in school was much better than anyone in his family had ever achieved. The rest of his father's family and his brothers played truant more often than attending school, and Tony was the first to stay on at school over the age of sixteen. His father, and grandfather were more than happy with their lot of mechanics, and his father couldn't see any reason why Tony needed to go to university, but Tony's mother put her foot down, and eventually got her own way. Tony's father started to talk to him when he realised that Tony could be more interesting than the rest of his brothers, and Tony started to watch television with his father more often, as his father was more likely to talk when the plot in an action film became unbelievable, especially when the action contained cars. "That's crap. If I was driving a car that fast, and went round a bend that sharp, there's no way that I could stop it from going off the road."

"But dad, that's what makes it exciting. People would get bored if James Bond slowed down to a snail's pace when the driving conditions became difficult."

On another film, the car crashed and burst into flames. "That wouldn't happen. It takes more than a few bumps before a car would catch fire."

"Why not. At school they taught us all a fire needs is fuel, oxygen and heat."

"You can stick with your school lessons if you want boy, but they only teach you theory. This is real life."

"But Dad, the three requirements for a fire are present."

"The petrol is in the fuel tank; it takes a lot to split it open."

"But car fires are reported on a regular basis."

"It only appears that way. Car fires only happen in a very small percentage of crashes. The fire is usually caused by something other than the fuel. The internal combustion engine works by exploding the fuel vapour, which is inside the engine compartments, not the fuel itself. And you don't often get flames when you crash a car."

"So why do the cars explode then?" This was the longest conversation that Tony could remember having with his father.

"Problems with the wiring loom around the engine causing a few sparks, or better still a leak from the brake fluid or from the power steering containers onto a hot engine. If they get going, the vapour in and around the engine will increase the fire, and the vapour in the fuel tank could make it explode. Then you might have a fire."

The beatings from his father stopped as their conversations grew, but they were replaced by those from his elder brother, which were far more vicious. Tony found a few ways to reduce the damage from his brother's fists, but none of these were as successful as just keeping out of the way, spending most of his spare time out of the house taking photographs of anything that took his fancy worked well. The best way to keep out of the way was to go to university. He didn't make many friends during his three years at university but at least the beatings stopped. He had no idea what he was going to do when he left university, and nothing interested him except for a visit from an Army officer who he'd spoken to afterwards, the main selling point being that he would be able to live wherever the Army sent him, and he wouldn't have to go to live back at home. His latest first for the family was his completion of officer training at Sandhurst Military Academy. Some of his father's family had spent a few years in the Army, and one had even reached the rank of corporal, before being thrown out.

Tony's mother wore her best dress for his passing out parade at Sandhurst, which was expected. What Tony didn't expect was that his father would be there, wearing a suit. His mother finally had a chance to talk to him when his father disappeared to find a toilet to get rid of a few too many beers in his bladder.
"Your father's really proud of you, although he doesn't know how to show it."
"He's never treated me as his son, so why should he start now?"
"He could never understand why you're so different to him and your brothers, so he's always believed that you aren't his son. You've finally given him something to be proud of."

"Does he believe that he's my father now?"
"I don't think that he ever will. I've never really been unfaithful to him."
"So, is my father then?"
"No, he isn't." She took a deep breath. "Your biological father is one of the managers at a company where I used to do the cleaning."
"What? Do I know him?"
"No, you've never seen him. We were short of money, so I took on a few cleaning jobs in the evening. Your father's a good mechanic, but drinks too much and takes more time off work than he should. I noticed your biological father watching me whilst I cleaned his office each night, and he eventually started to speak to me. The conversation became more familiar until he offered me some money if I would have sex with him, and you're the result."
Tony would remember the discussion for the rest of his life, for more than one reason.

Bullying had always been seen as the best way to get people to do things in the Army, and Tony, despite being an officer, quickly discovered that he was not exempt from adverse treatment by those senior to him, and surprisingly from the senior ranks who he was supposed to be in charge of. Having a university education didn't help him, and it took him some time to harden his character and learn how to manage those beneath him. He didn't like much of what he encountered in the Army and had already started to consider another occupation when he discovered one of his sergeants being attacked by two men on his way back to the barracks late one night. Another man was motionless on the floor. The sergeant was the hardest soldier in his company and was putting up a good fight but was being gradually overpowered until a kick from behind brought him down. Most of his Army colleagues

would have rushed to his aid, but Tony took out his mobile phone, held it in the air and shouted at his best parade square voice.
"Stop! I've phoned for the police, and they're on their way, so I suggest you fuck off now."
There was time for a few kicks into the body of the sergeant before the assailants picked up their colleague and ran off. The sergeant looked around, seemed to smile when he recognised Tony, and slowly pushed himself up from the ground.
"Hello sir, nice night for a stroll."
"What was that all about?"
"Some people that I encouraged to do something they didn't want to do decided that they weren't going to do it after all and wanted to show me that they had changed their minds, and they set their dogs on me to reinforce their point."
"Do these people only react with strong-arm tactics?"
"Absolutely not sir. They usually do what we want them to do at the first time of asking. We used to have someone who would set up people in compromising situations and give them photographic evidence to encourage them to do what we wanted, but he came to a sticky end last month, unofficially of course, it was made to look like an accident. We're good at that sort of thing. We're also looking for a replacement if you're interested."
"It would take a hell of a lot of money to entice me into getting into that sort of business."
"Oh, don't worry about that sir, the pay is unbelievable."
"What's the point of being paid an unbelievable amount of money if you don't live to enjoy it?"
"The photographer we had was stupid and paid for his mistakes. If you can keep your head down, you'll probably go unnoticed for a very long time. It looks like our photographer told the heavies who attacked me who I was, and how to find me. Those three were good at

what they do, but so are we. I'll have to make sure that I'm not out on my own late at night for a while, but I'll have to change Regiments sooner rather than later."
"At least you managed to put one of them down."
The sergeant pulled up the sleeve on his right wrist. "This is a new miniature TASER, I try not to leave home without it. Unfortunately, it's only good for one go. If I'd had another one, they would all be on the floor, and I'd have been tucked up warm in bed ages ago."
Tony looked distinctly unimpressed.
"Look sir, I've known you for some time, and you're different to the usual officer we get, you know what makes people work, and you don't take any shit, despite your size, if you'll excuse me. We really are looking for someone like you, do you want me to set up a meeting?"

The sergeant was spot on with his assessment of Tony, and the following few years after changing from the uniformity of the Armed Forces to the rapidly changing environment of blackmail and extortion saw a substantial increase in his personal skill of choosing victims who could be enticed into doing things that they didn't want to do by obtaining evidence of certain activities that they wouldn't like other people to find out about. His offer to destroy the photographic evidence generally resulted in Tony getting what he wanted. He'd improved his expertise at photography more than he thought possible, and his colleagues, who were much more physical than he could ever aspire to be, taught him a few tricks to protect himself, should he ever find himself at the wrong end of an attack that he couldn't run away from, or talk his way out of. Tony had seen the Kung Foo films along with most of the population but didn't believe that a little old man could over-power the usual huge muscle-bound beast with a few 'wax on, wax off' exercises. He was much better at concealment and thought that he was invisible to people outside his usual narrow circle of work so was surprised to find the envelope that had been pushed through his letterbox when he arrived home one evening. He'd rented a flat in London when he left the Army and was quickly successful enough to buy a flat in Kensington which he thought no-one knew about. The envelope contained a return train ticket, the key for a locker in Kings Cross station and a short note informing him that it would be beneficial to him if he took three days away in two weeks' time. He only required a small bag containing his washing and shaving stuff, and a change of clothing, everything else would be provided. Further details would be placed in the locker an hour before the train left Kings Cross.

Tony was always in the 'nothing ventured, nothing gained' camp, and when he opened the locker at Kings Cross before catching the overnight train, he found a large book on photography with a post-it note on the cover telling him to read the contents fully, as questions would be asked during the following three days. He had barely an hour's sleep before getting off the train at a previously deserted Kingussie train station in the early hours of a cold and wet morning in the Scottish Highlands. Eight others followed the old man to the waiting mini bus which rattled around the countryside for an hour, until they arrived at a large old house which appeared dilapidated from the outside and was not much better, or warmer, when they stepped inside the building through the large creaking doors. The minibus driver had left them in the company of a tall, well-built man in an expensive suit.
"Good morning gentlemen, my name is Donald, we have a lot of work to get through in the next two days. He gave each of them an envelope with a number on it. "You don't need to know each other's name; your room

number is on the envelope, and the door key is inside it. When we speak to you, we will use your room number. Get rid of your luggage and do what you need to do as quickly as possible. Leave your mobile phones in the room. We'll meet back here in fifteen minutes."

Tony was surprised at the stern voice, and the lack of please or thank you. Even when he was being bollocked rigid at Sandhurst the staff retained a semblance of politeness. All nine of the recent arrivals were back downstairs within the allotted time.

"The rest of the morning will be spent on written tests in the large room on your left, we'll break for lunch at twelve thirty for half an hour followed by a psychometric test. After that we'll see how you perform on our command tasks outside."

The man next to Tony was the first to speak. "When are we going to talk about the small arms book that I read on the train?"

'Small arms?' The penny hadn't dropped yet that they had been given different books to read, but the confused look on every one of the attendee's faces helped Tony realise that they had been given something to keep them occupied during their journey instead of getting their heads down and arriving as fresh as possible from a train journey.

Donald pointed at the room on their left and waved them onwards. "Everything will become clear as time progresses."

Despite Tony's Army training he expected to be tired, but the lack of food and the coldness in the room sharpened his wits.

The man waiting for them in the next room was smaller than Donald, but also wore a sharp suit.

"The first part of today is relatively straight forward. All you need is the pencil and the booklet on your desk. I will tell you when to start, and when to stop. The target is to complete as much of each part of the section in the

booklet in the allotted time. When I say stop, put your pencils down and go to the start of the next section in the booklet and wait until I tell you to start again."
Tony had seen this type of tests before, and as promised, they were relatively straight forward. The first part was a few pages with words on the left-hand side, and a space after each of them underneath a heading 'One-word definition'.
One of them looked up from the book. "What are we supposed to do?"
The man in the front of the room looked at the man asking the question and wrote down his table number. "Do whatever you think that you need to do."
Apparently being able to work out what you needed to do was part of the test. Tony went through each part of the booklet with relative ease. The list of numbers in the part labelled 'Sequences' started of very easily, 2,4, 6, 8, 10..., 1, 4, 9, 16..., 0, 1, 1, 2, 3... were simple enough, but became difficult when the numbers in the sequence were hidden as being the second, fourth and sixth in the list, and then more complicated when letters and numbers were introduced together, such as T3, S4, P5, S6, H7. Tony thought that if the number connected with 4 was R for Rhombus instead of S for square, he might have taken more time before he wrote O8 to show that there were 8 sides to an octagon. Tony had just finished when the man told them to stop, but a few of those taking part turned over a few of their pages of their booklet until they reached the start of the next part.
They had more problems with the next part, which was a long list of sequences of numbers and letters. These also started off easily, 7 C O T R could only be '7 colours of the rainbow' but Tony had to think about 1000 W A P I W until he remembered to song in the seventies made famous by a bald-headed actor playing a TV detective who had a hit record speaking the words 'If a picture is worth a thousand words'. He followed these

words with 'If a man could be in two places at one time, I would be with you tomorrow and today.' Tony understood that this was one place at two times, but it didn't stop Kojak getting to number one in the charts.

They were given five minutes for a quick piss break before they were given two books of information relating to two sides in a conflict and a map of a fictitious country and a booklet of blank pages with the instruction; Write a report describing the strengths and weaknesses of both sides of the conflict, provide reasons why which side will receive support from the United Nations, and how you would advise the leaders of both sides on their strategy to win the conflict, or how to avoid it, and the most important factor, how to obtain support from the media and the general public. Time allotted one hour. When Tony finished his report a few minutes before being told to stop, both of his arms were aching One of the very few benefits of being left handed was that he was made to write with his right hand when he learnt to write at school so he could write with both hands. He was more than ready for lunch.

They were kept busy for a few hours after lunch before being taken into a changing room where they were given a pair of overalls and what looked to Tony like old-fashioned Army boots before being led in turn to a small room with a large door which was the entrance into a small grassy enclosure containing numerous command tasks.
"Leave your watches here, as they might become damaged, you'll get them back later. Each of the tasks are numbered, attempt each task in numerical order. You have five minutes to complete as many tasks as possible, with any luck some of you might start a second circuit before your time runs out. If you can't complete any of the tasks don't stop, move on to the next task."

Tony went into the toilet and for the first time in more than three years outside of his bed, he unstrapped his TASER from his left arm and hid it behind a pile of toilet rolls.

There was a one-minute gap after each participant had finished before the next one entered the area. Some of the tasks had a high degree of difficulty, both physical and technical, other tasks, such as the two heavy weights with hand grips on the top which were carried around a small circuit back to their pick-up point were there to take up time and tire them out. There was a large tree in the middle of the weight carrying circuit that he had a good look at on his way round. A thick rope hung from a large branch, with a small brass bell at the top of the rope. At the bottom of the tree was a sign 'ring the bell'. There were steel footholds in the tree, going around and upwards to assist those that were unable to climb a rope to the top, but progress would have been much slower. As he finished the climb up the rope to the high branch in the tree and back down again, Tony saw that the next task was a simple high jump, but with no sandpit or cushions on the other side, and the words 'jump over' next to the activity number. Using the Olympic high jump method would have winded him and slowed him down. He had become adept at the high jump at school despite his lack of height and had studied the method first used by Dick Fosbury in the 1968 Olympics that won the athlete a gold medal and had been so successful that it became the style used by every athlete he'd seen since. The Olympic champion must have been happy that his surname was adopted for the name of the Fosbury Flop, instead of his first name! The bar was far too high for Tony to hurdle, so he dived headfirst over the bar, followed by a forward roll to cushion his body on landing enough to enable him to move on quickly to the next task. He'd seen the three vertical ropes when he applied for his Army training and quickly swung in his best Tarzan style from one rope to the other and his momentum took him quickly up and over the six-foot-high wall as he sprinted to the long jump to start a second circuit. Tony was puffing hard when his five minutes were up, but he had completed another three activities on his second circuit and was happy with his achievement.

The command tasks were followed by more hanging around until later that evening. They were still in their overalls and boots, and their watches had yet to be returned when they got into the back of minibus which drove off into the darkness. It was cold and dark inside the minibus, and they could barely see anything outside. The cross-country journey quickly became bumpy and uncomfortable and it took a few minutes until someone finally broke the ice.
"What's all this rubbish about? Does anyone know why we're here and what we're doing?"
There was a minute's silence until someone answered.
"Hopefully, we're being subjected to a new type of job interview for something out of the ordinary."
"I have no idea what the written tests will prove. Luckily, I did ok on the command tasks."
A voice from another dark part of the minibus joined the conversation. "I almost completed a circuit, the ropes fucked me."
Tony kept quiet.
"The ropes were a piece of piss, I had to stop for a breather after the high jump though; I'd have completed a circuit if I hadn't been winded when I landed."
"It took me ages to climb the tree, I've always been shit at climbing ropes."
Another voice joined in from the darkness, "What's so relevant about the ability to climb ropes anyway?"

The minibus stopped, and they became aware of the man sat in darkness in the front passenger seat. "Right gents, you'll be leaving the bus with a few minutes interval between each of you. Your target is to find your way back to the hall, preferably before it gets light. There are people in the woods who will try to capture you, it would be advisable to avoid them wherever possible. Number seven will go first. Good luck."

There were only three people left in the back of the minibus when Tony was told to leave. He'd noted where the last two had got off and followed in their direction so that he could get a warning if they were caught. He'd organised this sort of thing for his soldiers, and usually searched them for hidden compasses and such like before letting them loose into the countryside, it was amazing where people could hide things. He didn't know that the last two stars at the bucket end of the plough constellation were named Dubhe and Merak, but he did know a few things about the sky at night, the most useful fact was that he could find the Northern star by drawing a line upwards from the two stars, the Northern star would be about two and a half times further awat compared with the distance between the other two. The minibus had changed direction a number of times, but Tony thought that he was about three miles to the west of the hall. He ran as quickly as the narrow winding paths allowed him, stopping every thirty seconds or so to listen. After ten minutes he could hear someone about a hundred yards in front of him, two minutes later he could hear the commotion of the person in front of him being attacked and dragged away through the undergrowth. Tony moved quietly in the opposite direction to try to catch up with the next person in front of him. The minibus had changed direction when each person was dropped off, but Tony had no problem working out their location with respect to the hall. Another two runners were taken away from the chase whilst they were about fifty yards in front of him, and he had the uneasy feeling of being watched, but he kept moving quickly enough to keep out of the way and after two hours of changing direction he was hidden in the middle of some bushes within sight of the front door of the hall. A small movement in the darkness by the entrance gave away the presence of a guard, and he saw the dull glow of a cigarette end in another guard's cupped hand at the bottom corner of the hall. Tony sat in silence waiting for their next move. He could barely hear the movement behind him of more than one person getting slowly closer and closer, and he knew he would have to make his move soon or he would be captured. All sounds stopped except for a rustling to his left as one of those taking part burst out from cover and sprinted towards the entrance to the hall. Two people behind him joined three people to the right of the front door, and the sprinter was swiftly hauled to the ground. A hood was put over his head, and it took all five of the pursuers to drag him around the side of the hall. Tony wasted no time in exploiting the unexpected opportunity and ran around the other side of the hall towards the command task area, past the obstacles and through the door into the room to reclaim his TASER and strap it out of sight beneath his left elbow. He was sitting down in the dining room when he was set upon by two of the pursuers. Although he made an effort to fight them off, there was no great point in upsetting them, or their loved ones, by re-arranging their genitalia. There seemed no need for the thick hood on his head, but they put it on anyway, and then twisted his arms behind his back and

frog-marched him out of the room, across the reception area and downstairs. Tony's wrists were put into tight handcuffs attached to a chain to what Tony expected was a thick wooden table. He heard the two men leave the room, and he was left in darkness and silence for about ten minutes, most of which he was wishing he'd taken the opportunity to have a piss whilst he was in the toilet. The lights were switched on, but he didn't realise how bright they were until the hood was pulled off. Tony could see the outline of the man sat in front of him, but the detail was limited due to the light shining directly into his eyes.
"What's your name?"
Tony was pleased that the man had started with an easy question, because he had no idea what they wanted to know.
"Why do you want to know my name?"
A sharp pain travelled up his body which was inflicted from someone out of view behind him.
"You're right, we don't need to know your name, we know everything we need to know about you. Especially that you cheat your way to get whatever you want, without considering the consequences."
Tony sat in silence, waiting to find out what this was all about.
"I'm going to take you outside again and turn you loose. This time there will be added pressure, most of the others are back in the house now so there are going to be more people looking for you this time, all of them will have an added incentive to hurt you as much as possible before bringing you in. It will be even worse for you if you do anything stupid before I drop you off. Follow me."

The man unlocked the handcuffs and Tony followed him upstairs and outside. The man walked to one of the Land Rovers parked at the back of the hall. "Get in the passenger seat."

The man drove off at speed and didn't slow down for at least ten minutes.

"Could you tell me what this is all about, please?"

"This is a special selection course for people who we would like to recruit into our business."

"Why do people who work for you have to run around a forest in the darkness trying not to get caught?"

"The chase adds pressure to the interview when you're caught, especially if we prevent you from sleeping for over a day."

"But I didn't get caught."

"You will this time. There will be plenty of people looking for you, and we will be checking your movements on the close-circuit cameras around the area."

"Why was I chosen?"

"I made sure that you were on the list this time."

"You're going about things in a strange way if you're trying to get me to join."

"That's not why you're on the list."

Tony had no idea what was going on. "So why bother?"

"Can you remember George Reeves?"

"No, should I?"

"He was my brother. You entrapped him with a young boy and blackmailed him to give up secrets in his business."

"That's not true. I don't use children to entrap people, If I've taken photos of people having sex with children, they've arranged it themselves and I've caught them at it."

"That's bollocks, things like that don't happen by chance."
"I've caught a few paedos. When I draw up a list of possible targets, I also look into ways that they can be induced into helping us. If I find out that they have sex with children, they do half of my work for me. It's easy to find out where they do what they do, which is always away from their home."
"How many of them have killed themselves because of what you did?"
"None that I know of."
"Well, he did. He was my brother."

Tony tried to move the LASER further down his arm without the man noticing.
"Stop fidgeting. I warned you not to try anything stupid."
"My wrists still hurt from the handcuffs."
"Live with it, we'll be there soon."
The Land Rover carried on through the dark forest for another ten minutes until it pulled over and the man got out. "Get out and stand over there."
By the time that Tony was out of the Land Rover the man had a gun in his hand pointing towards him. He didn't know that Tony had moved his left hand out of sight inside his sleeve and was holding the TASER towards him.
"I promised my dead brother at his funeral that you would be joining him in Hell."
"How do you know that you're not being watched on one of the cameras?"
"Do you think that I don't know where the cameras are?"
Those was the last words that the man ever spoke, as he fell, quivering, to the ground. Tony had to make up his mind quickly what he was going to do. If he left the

man and escaped in the Land Rover, the man would, no doubt, continue to come after Tony until he was dead. He'd never killed anyone, but Tony could see no other option which kept himself alive. The man was much heavier that Tony, but was eventually back in the driver's seat, with his gun back in his coat pocket. Tony never expected his father's comments to be any use, but the ones about cars bursting into flames when they crashed on TV shows came to mind. Tony opened the Land Rover bonnet and found the brake fluid and the power steering fluid containers and took the tops off. He closed the bonnet and went back to the driver's seat and leant over the body of the man behind the steering wheel. He let off the hand brake; the vehicle started to roll forward slowly. He pushed the clutch in with his right hand and put the Land Rover into second gear with his left. He released the clutch and pushed down the accelerator until the vehicle was moving too quickly for him to keep up, and he watched as the car went over the edge and flipped over a few times until it actually burst into flames. Tony quickly buried his TASER and the fluid container tops in the woods away from where they had stopped and ran for help. He was caught within a few minutes and dragged to the interview room.
"I don't know what I did wrong. He said that I had to do the exercise again. He drove for about twenty minutes then threw me out of the Land Rover and drove off at speed. He'd only gone a few yards before he went over the edge."
"Why did you get taken out again?"
"I don't know. I don't remember him saying why when I was here for the first time. What was on the recording?"
Tony wasn't too surprised to be chosen as a successful candidate, despite the sour-faced Christopher being

convinced that he had something to do with the accident, and the death of his friend. The tape of Tony's interview before going out into the woods again backed up what he had told the others, and it was treated as an accident. The body in the Land Rover was badly burnt, and his pistol was taken away before the police arrived. It was easy for the police report to show that it was just a tragic accident, and the death was kept out of the news.

The remnants of Tony's coffee had gone cold, and it was time to leave. He wanted to reach the car park for the meeting in plenty of time to check it out and find a good place to stay out of sight. The Old Deer car park was as busy as ever, but Tony had walked up from McDonalds fifteen minutes before Richard's car arrived, closely followed by Gerald's. Gerald parked up, paid for his parking and casually walked over to Richard's car and got in the passenger seat. Richard drove off, returning ten minutes later to collect Tony from further down the car park, and left through the exit again. No-one came out of hiding when Richard's car left the car park for the first time, and Tony could see that the area around where Richard's car returned to was clear.
Tony wore jeans and a baggy top, and a dark wig, but was easily recognised by the other two in the car.
"Afternoon Richard, you seem quite cosy with Gerald, especially after you told me that you stay well away from the controllers. How can I help?"
As Richard was only the conduit for the meeting, he left the talking to Gerald.
"We thought that it was time you came back. Are you ready to return?"
"I'll need a new team. One that listens to what they're being told this time."

"Steve's no longer available, his contract was permanently closed by Jason."
"Will he be traced back to me?"
"No, he shouldn't be. Apparently, he fell into the Thames after having too much to drink. The water in his lungs came from the same area of the river in which he allegedly fell in."
"The police already had his picture from the death of Thomas Harbod, they came to my office and showed it to me. Apparently two people had told them that I knew Steve."
"They haven't been able to name Steve from the photo, and there won't be any problems with his accident, it was Jason's usual handiwork, and we've got the local plod to push it through as misadventure, with only a brief mention in the news, so it's doubtful that anyone will link Steve to Thomas Harbod's death. They've probably lost interest in him already."
"Ok, that's cool. What did Christopher have to say about me coming back?"
"He didn't seem to be too pleased about it."
"I expect that to be an under-statement."
"What's his problem with you?"
"When I first joined your gang, Christopher and I had a disagreement. He never said why he didn't like me, but he said that I didn't have the physical requirements for the job and punched me to prove his point."
"Only once? He's quite a handful and has a shitty temper. I've seen him in a few fights, and he's had to be pulled off if we wanted to keep the other person alive."
"He's a bit slow, and predictable. I knew that he was going to punch me, I didn't have the time to get out of the way but managed to move my head down far enough so that his fist connected with the top of my head. I wasn't knocked completely senseless, and he stopped for a few seconds as he'd hurt his hand. He

went to punch me again, but was too confident, and left himself open. One of the beneficial factors of being left-handed is that everyone in a fight expects to be hit by their opponent's right hand. I managed to sidestep him to left and dodged his right hand and punched him as hard as I could on his throat. It's a trick that I learnt from a cage fighter, he made me practise it until I got it spot on and it's been usual a few times. The lack of motivation to move after you've been punched in the throat is quite amazing. I left before he could start again."

Richard finally had the chance to join in the conversation. "I've had dealings with Christopher. He's a nasty bastard and wouldn't leave things unfinished."

"He tried to get me at our next meeting and was told in no uncertain terms to leave me alone, so he paid someone to beat me up."

They were on their way back to the car park by now, and Tony saw Richard's eyebrows go up in the rear-view mirror. "Were you badly beaten?"

"Christopher chose someone who knew me quite well, and he told me what he'd been paid to do."

This was all news to Gerald, and he listened to the conversation in stunned silence. Richard had problems with the traffic, which was already building up towards rush hour, but wanted to know the rest of the story.

"Did you pay him more than Christopher did to stop him from hurting you?"

"God no. Christopher would have just sent someone else. I told him to tell Christopher that he'd given me a hell of a beating, and that he'd told me that the beating was a present from Christopher, in case I'd pissed off other people as well."

"Didn't Christopher find out?"

"I made myself scarce for a week. I was overdue a holiday anyway. When I returned, I asked a friend to add some colour to my face to look like faded bruises.

Christopher was very pleased with himself when he saw them."

"They must have looked convincing."

"People see what they want to see. It was a good job though."

"Do you have his details; I might need him for future work?"

"It was a she, and she's no longer around. You might remember hearing about her husband? He disappeared some time ago, and a man who worked with him was jailed for his murder."

Richard nearly hit the car in front. "Peter Stevenson from Oxford?"

"Yeah, that's right. It was his wife that did the makeup job."

Richard tried to focus on his driving. "Good grief, it's a small World. I knew Peter, I also knew the bastard who's in jail for his murder."

Gerald could finally add something to the discussion. "I had dealings with the pillock who murdered Peter Stevenson. A nasty bastard called Kevin. He wanted us to do some work for him once to help him take over a company. But his plan was half-baked, and we told him to get lost."

Richard didn't want to say too much, as he was one of a small group who knew what actually happened between Kevin and Peter, so changed the subject.

"Are we doing anything for Grangers after the attack on their business?"

Gerald turned his head to look at Tony in the back seat. "We'd like you to redress the balance of things, if you could. The company who hired us has gone further than we agreed, and they need to be taught a lesson. Would you be willing to do this?"

"No problem with that. Any ideas what you'd like me to do?"

Gerald nodded his head. "Richard and his associate Jerry are heavily involved with Tom Harbod at the moment, I'm sure that they could think of a few things." Tony raised his eyebrows and looked at Richard. "Gerald seems to know a great deal about your work." Richard remained calm; Tony was not the only person in the car who was good at poker. "I'll speak to Tom later and ask him if there's anything special that he'd like. I'm sure that he'll have a few good ideas."

Tony needed more information before he could do what they wanted. "Did you bring Steve's mobile phone with you?"

Gerald had expected this request and took the phone out of his pocket. He had no problem giving it to Tony. "I've had a quick look at this but let me know if you find anything on it that might interest us. It didn't take too long to access the contents, his password is 5892, which were the last four numbers of his Army number."

Richard was surprised again. "Surely you left Steve's mobile with his body, otherwise the police would have been suspicious. Everyone has a mobile phone these days."

"We left a mobile phone in Steve's jacket pocket, but one that would be almost impossible to trace. We'd damaged it, so there was no way to extract any information from it. We tore his back pocket to explain why he didn't have any bank cards on him but left some notes and loose change in his other pockets so that it wouldn't look like he was robbed."

Tony nodded. "What about his house keys?"

"Yes, we also took the keys to his flat and changed them for ones that won't open anything now and had no markings. We'll have a look round his flat to see if there's anything useful there before anyone notices that he's gone."

Richard didn't know Steve but had problems believing that he wouldn't be missed by anyone. "There must be someone who will come looking for him, surely?"

Gerald had a sound knowledge of everyone who worked for his company. "Most of our people won't be missed. Steve's wife left him years ago, and is not claiming maintenance, he has no real friends in the area since settling in London after leaving the Army, and he's not in touch with his family. We'll take his belongings out of his flat late at night, so when the landlord comes looking for unpaid rent, it will look like he's done a midnight flit."

Tony was happy to be back in the fold. "Ok Richard, you have my new mobile number, send me details of what Tom Harbod wants. Don't make them too explicit, in case they get compromised. A meeting with you and Tom would be good, the sooner the better, I just need to get a few things sorted tonight. Gerald, if I have to report the point of contact from the other company to the police are you ok to keep whoever will be taken to court from mentioning my name?"

Gerald smiled at this. "It would be good if one or two of them ended up in jail. They were told not to try to get more than we'd originally agreed, so it will act as a deterrent for others who think that they might want to try the same. We'll just tell them that if they mention any of us to the police, their stay in prison will not be a happy one, and they probably won't make it out alive. That usually works, if not I'm sure Tony can find other ways that they can be dissuaded from mentioning our involvement."

Tony looked up from Steve's mobile phone. "Funny you should mention it, there just might be."

Richard had driven back past the entrance to the Old Deer car park and wanted to speak to Tom before it got too late. "Where do you want to be dropped off, Tony?"

"Anywhere around here is good. Kew station is just up the road." The car pulled over to the kerb as Tony phoned Gerald from his mobile. Gerald's phone rang. "That's my new mobile number Gerald, I hope to hear from you soon, don't forget that I need a new team." He turned to Richard. "Let me know what you want me to do to help to put right the problems caused to Grangers."

ELEVEN

John the Accountant and his father had been going to Newbury's Saturday horseracing meeting in August for as long as John could remember. As they went past the East Ilsley turn off on the A34 John's father said the same thing that he always did.
"That's the old A34, it used to take us ages to get to Newbury races before they put in the dual carriageway. I used to go to see the Hennessey Gold Cup with my father, and when Arkle was racing there in the nineteen sixties, we would be in a traffic jam for about two hours trying to get to the racecourse. He was the best horse I've ever seen. I've seen hundreds of top-class horses and he would have beaten all of them. Everyone thought that Mill House was unbeatable after he won the Cheltenham Gold Cup in March 1963, but after I saw Mill House beat Arkle at Newbury when they raced against each other for the first time in the Hennessey Gold Cup later that year, he never beat Arkle again."
John smiled at his father's comments, which he'd probably heard twenty times before. John knew a thing or two about horse racing and usually won enough to pay for his entrance to the course and his lunch, but his knowledge was nothing compared to his father. They walked back to the entrance after parking up in the large field, trying to escape the lady selling lucky heather for an exorbitant price, and went into the course. John's father made his usual comment again about the course and they entered. "That old derelict building on the left used to be the Tote. You could bet win or place for four shillings or a pound, which was a lot of money in the sixties."
"You don't bet much more these days Dad."
"I don't come here for the gambling, I come to admire the horses and jockeys. I can't afford much more than £2 each way these days anyway."

"But if you have a horse which you think is a dead cert, surely you'd put more money on it."

"No, not anymore, I've had so many horses which I thought couldn't be beaten, and put a day's pay on it, after which I had to explain to your mother where my wages had gone."

They walked round to the grandstand. They were early enough to go around the back of the grandstand to look at the horses in the parade ring before going back to the lines of on-course bookmakers between the grandstand and the racecourse. John's father looked at the odds for the favourite for the first race and shook his head.

"The starting price is far too short."

"If I put on £50, I can win £25, and I can't really see it being beaten."

John's father was looking round for a bookmaker who was offering the 'betting without the favourite' option which was quite common when they also thought that they stood too much to lose on a horse that would most probably win. He looked at all of the large bookmakers' boards but couldn't find one that advertised what he was looking for.

"It's not really worth risking my £2."

"Choose a horse with a better price then."

"I'd rather bet on a short-priced winner than a longer-priced loser."

"If you've already chosen the horse that you expect to win, but the starting price is too short, you can't wait around until the price is right, it won't happen. Put your money on the best price you can find, or better still, why not choose a horse that you expect to come second to the favourite and put them in a forecast on the Tote?"

John and his father held this discussion whenever there was a short-priced favourite, but John was the only one who remembered it. They both went their own separate way to place their bets before returning to the grandstand to watch their choices win. After the third race they went into the bar underneath the grandstand for a beer.

"How are you doing today Dad?"

"Fine, I'm nearly £10 up."

"You'd have a won a lot more if you'd increased your stake."

"Maybe so, but I could also have lost more."

"What's the most that you ever won on a bet?"

"I won nearly £30 once, but that was inside the bookies in Oxford when I actually had three winners in a £1 Treble. I watched them win on the television in the bookies, it was quite scary watching the race whilst the third horse in the treble won."

They re-started their usual moves from the parade ring to the bookmakers to the grandstand for the final four races. When they were looking at the horses going around the parade ring for the final race John's father looked at the racing page of the newspaper that he'd brought with him, and back to a horse as it passed him for the third time.

"The horse named Deck Chair is twenty to one, but it looks really fit and healthy and very interested. It has no form but has dropped in class for this race."

"Let's have a bet on it then."

"I'm not sure of that. When I looked at the horses in this race in the paper this morning, I chose three others. I usually go with my first choices unless they're non-runners or they don't look right in the parade ring, it's bad luck to change your mind."

They went back and made their bets before moving to the grandstand to watch Deck Chair win the race quite easily. John's father stood open-mouthed as he watched the horse go past them well ahead of the others on its way to the winning post. He looked at John and shook his head, "I told you that it would win."

He hadn't said that at all, but John didn't mind. "It's worse than that." John's father couldn't understand how it could get any worse. "You owe me five pounds."
"How can I owe you five pounds?"
John handed his father one of two winning tickets that he held in his hand. "Because I put £5 to win for both of us on two separate bookmakers offering odds at twenty to one. When you take your ticket to the bookmaker and he pays you a hundred and five pounds, a fiver of that is mine."
John's father checked the winning ticket three times before starting to cry. "I can't believe it, I've never won this much in one day ever."
"I also won the same, so I'm glad that you pointed it out to me in the paddock."
They collected their winnings and started to leave. John turned back to the grandstand.
"Wait here for a second please Dad, I need a quick wee before driving home. No doubt we'll be caught in traffic on the way out."
John's father was smiling broadly as he watched his son disappear into the toilets as the rest of the crowd were walking towards the exit.
"You look happy old man, have you had a good day?"
John's father looked at the young man stood close to him. "My son just put five pounds on the winner of the last race for me and didn't tell me until it had won."
"You didn't expect to win then?"
"No."
"Then you won't mind handing over your winnings to me."
"I couldn't do that."
The young man pulled out a knife. "I think that you can. I wouldn't want to hurt you, but I will if you don't give me your money."
"It's the most I've ever won, and my son would be upset if I gave it away."

The young man's voice changed from his friendly tone to one much more menacing. "Your son will be much more upset if he has to take you to the hospital." John's father tried to move towards the toilets, but the man stood in his way. He pushed the young man away as hard as he could, but it only made things worse. He felt the sharp pain and looked down at the blood as it started to flow down his shirt. The man took the money from John's father's pockets and walked briskly away, just before John emerged from the toilets. What had been one of the best days of his life swiftly changed to the worst day ever. He fumbled with his mobile as he selected 999 and asked for an ambulance, whilst shouting for help. Two of the course medical staff arrived and managed to staunch the bleeding before the ambulance arrived and took John's father to the hospital. He was dead before the ambulance could get him there.

The following morning John's wife woke up to find herself alone in the bed. He had been inconsolable after he returned from the hospital the night before, so she thought that he'd got out of the bed to be alone. He wasn't in the kitchen or the garden so she suspected that he must have gone for a walk. It wasn't until he hadn't turned up half an hour later that she went to check the car and found him hanging by his neck on a rope from the garage roof. The upturned chair underneath his feet covered a piece of paper containing the words I CAN'T LIVE WITH WHAT I'VE DONE.

TWELVE

Tom was still in the Chairman's office late in the evening when Richard walked in. The box and remnants of a large takeaway pizza were on the small meeting table, and a large sheet of paper was on the other table, next to Tom's grandfather's notebook which Tom had found in his grandfather's study whilst they were clearing out his house. The notebook was scrap book size, over fifty years old, and contained Thomas Harbod's ideas from a very young age until recently, including a very old design for a hybrid car with an electric motor providing the power to the engine and the electrics and a small internal combustion engine with a generator charging the battery whilst the car was in motion. There were also three designs for a method of preventing the car from being driven by a person whose alcohol level was higher than the permitted level. Tom already knew that his grandfather was well ahead of his time in the world of engineering, but this was a revelation to Jerry. Tom had his grandfather's notebook open in the 'Electric Car' section. The top heading on the large piece of paper on the table next to Thomas Harbod's notebook was 'ELECTRIC CAR - BATTERY'. Underneath the heading the page was divided into four parts with a large cross in the centre dividing each of the sections into a SWOT analysis. There were more Strengths than Weaknesses, and many more Opportunities than there were Threats. Most of the headline points for each section had been taken from Thomas's notebook, with a few added ones, mainly from Tom. Details relating to the headline points were written underneath the analysis. Tom had smiled when he first read the notes in the SWOT analysis, as the first Strength listed was 'Tom'. Tom had also added a few more notes in the 'details' area, and Jerry had made his own contribution, plus a few updates and amendments to those of Tom and his grandfather.

Richard looked down at the busy sheet of paper and realised that Tom and Jerry had become a very efficient management team.

"Electric car batteries? I think that ship has already sailed."

Tom looked up and smiled at the welcome visitor. "Not necessarily, electric cars will be huge business in the near future and will remain so for a long time. I've spoken to a few people who think that they've invented the optimum battery, but nothing has been agreed yet. We've missed out in the production of whichever battery is chosen, but if we can match the design of our models of electric cars, lorries and military vehicles so that they can be fitted with the chosen battery, we will be ahead of the game."

Richard agreed with Tom. "It won't be that easy to make that choice. Sony thought that they'd done that in the 1970s with their Betamax video cassette, which was reported as the best system, but it was outsold by the VHS system because VHS had a much better marketing campaign. The companies using the Betamax system lost out on a hugely lucrative business."

Tom smiled at his older colleague. "Young people can learn from history, even if they didn't make the mistakes themselves."

"If you are going to market a new product, you have to remember that there are many different types of people that might buy it."

Jerry picked up the empty pizza box. "In this case there are only two types of people, those who eat salad cream with their pizza, and those who haven't tried it yet."

Richard shook his head, but the other two laughed out loud. Tom was the first to stop.

"What brings you here this time of night?"

Richard put the CCTV picture of Steve on the table. Tom looked up in surprise. "How did you find out about him?"
"Find out what?"
"He's the man who attacked me outside the Bear."
It was now Richard's turn to be surprised. "You were attacked outside the Bear?"
"Yes, the night before the morning that I turned up to work with a few bruises on my face." Tom tapped the face of the man in the CCTV picture. "He told me that he'd been asked to dissuade me from working for a few days. Unfortunately for him, I could punch harder than he could. So why do you have his picture?"
"He's the man who was in your grandfather's house on the night that he died."
The happy mood was lost. "What!"
"He's the man who was in your grandfather's house on the night that he died. The photograph was taken late at night in the street where your grandfather lived on the night that your grandfather died."
"How do you know this?"
Richard was always prepared to tell the occasional 'white' lie if the truth was more harmful. "I was given his picture today by someone involved in stealing company information to allow another company to win bids for work which should have gone to Grangers and Robertsons."
"Has he been arrested yet? I have a few questions that I'd like to ask him."
Richard shook his head. "Unfortunately, he won't be answering any questions. His body was dragged out of the Thames in London a few days ago. He has yet to be identified."
"Yet to be identified? He must have had a mobile phone and bank cards in his pockets."
"Apparently not. His mobile phone was broken and full of water and he didn't have a wallet. His house keys

had been swapped for an old set that couldn't be traced."

"How do you know this?"

"Someone told me."

Tom was only just getting to know an idea of what Richard actually did to earn his money and had more than an idle suspicion that some of the work was more than slightly outside of the law. "Do you know who he was?"

"No, but I know a man who does."

"Do you know who he was working for?"

"That's easy to work out, the company who outbid you for the contracts for work over the last year. Unfortunately, it will be difficult to prove that they did anything illegal to win the bids."

"So why are you telling me this?"

"I know a man who might be able to put things right for Grangers. If he could make things happen, what would you want him to do?"

"Bringing my grandfather back would be a good start."

Jerry had been quietly making notes for the last few minutes. He wasn't as emotionally involved as Tom, so was able to make more business-like decisions. "Could your friend get the contract awards changed so that they are given to Grangers and Robertsons?"

Tom still hadn't been able to come to terms with the fact that his grandfather might not have died of natural causes. "That's all very well, but can your friend prove that the other company is to blame for my grandfather's death so that those who organised it are jailed?"

Richard needed to bring a semblance of reality back to the discussion. "Tom, your grandfather was an old man who had a heart attack and fell down the stairs at home. I doubt if any court would be able to find a person carrying out a burglary in his house at the same time as being guilty of murder."

"So why did you show me the picture?"

"Because the person who gave me the picture may be able to get the company responsible for stealing your contracts to compensate Grangers."
"How do you intend to do that?"
"I don't. But the man who gave me the picture can be very persuasive."
"When can I meet him?"
"Are you free tomorrow or the day after?"
"Any time after six o'clock."
Richard looked at his watch and shook his head. Despite it being a Rolex, it didn't give him the option to choose a time that he would prefer it to be. "It's eleven o'clock already, I'll send him a text to see when it will be worth our while to meet up. I probably won't get a response until tomorrow morning." It only took Richard a few seconds to send the text.
'I have spkn to my friend they are v keen to discuss ways to put things right. When can we meet with you, pref evening?'
Although it was late at night, it took less than a minute for Richard to receive a response. 'Same place as today but on the side of the road going west, 400m from the entrance to avoid any cameras. Five hours later for tomorrow. Your car.'
"Ok, we're on for tomorrow night, we need to be in London at eight o'clock. Are you joining us Jerry?"
Jerry nodded, pleasantly surprised that he was back on task with Richard. Working on company business with Tom made an interesting change, but he much preferred the scary side of Richard's business. He suspected that it was Tony who they were going to meet with the following evening. Jerry had heard so much about Tony, and it would be good to finally find out why everyone had such a high opinion of him.
"Ok, I'll pick you up from here at six thirty". He left the office with one of Jerry's favourite comments, "you two need to get some sleep, you can't burn the candle at

both ends, especially if you're not dipping your wick! See you tomorrow."

After Richard dropped him off at Kew, Tony caught the tube to just outside his office and walked past the main entrance three times in twenty minutes wearing a different coat and hairstyle to see if anyone was waiting outside for him. His first port of call was his clandestine office to retrieve his laptop. He then went upstairs to his normal office to check out the safe. As expected, there was no sign of Graham or any cash in the safe, the bonus find next to Steve's laptop was Steve's new camera. He was more than happy to be back at work but wanted to make himself scarce as quickly as possible in case there was anyone still looking for him. He put the two laptops and the camera in his bag and went to the underground to catch a train back to his flat where he could look at the information he'd collected on his laptop that he could use against the point of contact who had asked them to obtain information from Grangers and Robertsons.

Tony knew from experience that sometimes you need to dig up some dirt on certain people in case they caused problems. Tony had a bad feeling about the contact when he went with Steve to their first meeting with the person looking for information on Grangers and Robertsons. The man introduced himself as Colin when they met in the pub car park, which was his actual name, backed up by the business card which he gave to Steve and Tony. They moved to a room in the back of the pub to discuss business in the company of a bottle of single malt whisky. Steve was eager to please in those days and listened to Tony when he told Steve that it would be good practice for later work if he took the lead in the early discussions. Tony had gone through the initial meeting procedures a few times with Steve until he was confident that his performance matched his appearance. Neither Steve nor the contact knew that Tony was recording the conversation and taking photos throughout the meeting. This was the first job that Steve had worked with Tony, and he talked too much. Fortunately, it was the first time that Colin had dealt with this type of work, and he was impressed by Steve's physical size, his forthright manner, and the way that he did business, and disregarded the smaller insignificant man who had hardly anything to say. The only thing that he said to Tony was "If you're not going to anything constructive, you might as well make yourself useful and pour the drinks."

Tony made up his mind at the meeting that he did have something constructive to do, and that was to make sure that the contact didn't cause them any future problems. It was easy for Tony to find out where Colin lived. Colin didn't notice him at the supermarket when he carried out his weekly shop with his mouse of a wife, and a few weeks after the meeting Tony followed Colin's car out of London up the M1 until the car disappeared after St Albans. Tony didn't want to drive around the smaller roads and meet up with Colin's car, and he already had enough information to speak to another of his business acquaintances so went home to make the phone call. The phone was answered immediately.
"Hello Jock, are you busy at the moment?"
"I'm never too busy if it involves money."
Although he was Scottish, Jock had lost his accent when he joined the Paratroop Regiment as a Crow, a name which Tony had learnt from the infantry soldier's dislike of the 'special' forces not long after joining the infantry from Sandhurst. He thought that the term 'crow' came from the derogatory statement that the only things that fell from the sky were paratroopers and bird shit, but it was an acronym for Combat Recruit of War, one of

only a few non-offensive terms given to anyone and anything by the Paras. Tony remembered when he met Jock when they worked together for the first time. He was shorter than Steve, but probably more powerful. Tony's sergeant in the Army was instrumental in Tony changing occupations, and Jock was one of the first members of the team he was introduced to. "This is Tony, who has taken over as our photographer. This is Jock, who can get you information that you wouldn't believe existed."
"I prefer doing my work, it's a lot safer than getting close-up photographic evidence."
The first thing that Tony noticed was that Jock's name didn't match his accent. This could have been due to the Army nickname system of calling people the opposite to what they actually were, such as 'lofty' for short people.
"Jock?"
"Yes, I am Scottish, I lost my broad Glasgow accent almost as soon as I arrived in Aldershot, no-one there could understand me so I thought it would be easier if I started to talk like them instead of trying to get them to talk like me. The only problem that I had was when I went home on leave, I'd often be beaten up by the people who didn't know me, or didn't recognise me, because they thought that I was a Sassenach."

Tony had come to ask Jock for assistance on a number of occasions, and he had never failed to provide the information that Tony was looking for.
"What do you want to know?"
"There's a person I'm interested in. I followed him up the M1 this evening but lost him after St Albans."
"What is he like as a person?"
"What has that got to do with St Albans?"
"If you want me to answer your questions, you need to answer mine first."

"He's a bully and seems like an arsehole. Is that enough?"
"Is he married?"
"Yes, does that make a difference?"
"It might. What's his wife like?"
"Small, quite plain, doesn't speak much, she looks smart but doesn't dress in expensive clothes or wear lots of makeup."
"That fits."
"Fits with what?"
"You're right about the bully part, he likes to dominate people, which is why he has a timid wife, and why he was out by St Albans."
"What's so special about St Albans?"
"There's nothing special about St Albans. After the St Albans turn off from the M1, miles from anywhere, is a bunch of sheds owned by people that cater for men who like to have sex with young girls. He's probably gone there."
"Young girls?"
"Yes, most likely illegals who are too afraid not to do what they're told to. He would be able to dominate them and would probably knock them around a bit as well."
"How do you know all this?"
Jock shrugged his shoulders. "Not from personal experience. A few people that we have obtained information from have been persuaded to help us when they've been shown photos of them with the young girls there."
"How do you get the photos?"
"Each of the rooms have closed-circuit television in case the client starts to get too rough. The owners don't seem too bothered if any of their girls gets smacked around a bit, but they need to protect their assets to keep them working so they keep an eye on them. For a monkey I could probably get a few photos for you. Do you have a picture of the man that you're interested in?"

Tony handed over a clear photo of the man from his inside jacket pocket."
"Nice photo, much better that the ones that I usually have to work with. Did you take it yourself?"
"Yes, at our first meeting. He didn't know that I took it."
Jock nodded. "That's why they have such a good impression of you. I'll probably be able to get the photos to you in a few days and bring them to your office Thursday lunchtime. Are you ok with the price?"
Tony had heard somewhere that the old five hundred rupee note in the time of the British rule in India had the picture of a monkey on it, and a monkey now meant £500.
"No problem, I'll have the cash with me. See you Thursday."

Jock had no problem obtaining the pictures, he expected people who made money selling young girls to perverts would have no problem earning extra cash by selling a few photos. The quality of the pictures wasn't up to the normal standard of Tony's, but the CCTV pictures never would be. The pictures were still clear enough after Tony had scanned them into his computer, and there was no denying that the person with the girls was Colin. It was money well spent, as Tony would find out later. It was no coincidence that the police raided the site three months later after an anonymous tip off, freeing the girls held captive and arresting the men in charge.

The first thing that Tony did when reached his flat was to look at the messages in Steve's phone, he didn't want to be caught on the underground cameras looking at Steve's mobile so it stayed firmly in his bag with the laptops. The extra work started some weeks before Tony had stopped getting information for this contract, and the messages were incriminating, but only for Steve and Colin, Tony wasn't mentioned. Tony printed off the pictures of Colin with the young girls and a few pictures of Steve and Colin from the initial meeting to set up the contract to get business information from Grangers and Robertsons. He printed off the text messages between Steve and Colin and added them to the photos before getting some sleep. It had been a long, busy day which had ended much better than it had started. The following morning was spent looking at the photos in Steve's new camera, which were interesting to say the least. He recognised the young lady in the cleaner's uniform in compromising positions with Frank Harbod but didn't expect to use the photos at this or any future time. He then had a long look at the contents of Steve's phone, he would probably have to hand it over to the police, so wanted to make sure that there was nothing incriminating in any of the messages or photos.

Rush hour in London had been and gone, and the traffic was light enough to allow Richard's car to pull into the side of the road just after the Old Deer car park at Richmond at precisely eight o'clock. Tony stepped out from behind the large sign as Richard's car approached him. Tony didn't expect any problems now that he was on good terms with the controllers but was over-cautious by nature. He quickly got into the back of the car next to Jerry, and Richard drove off towards the M3. Richard knew where the Automatic Number Plate Recognition cameras were situated and had chosen a route to keep this meeting as covert as possible. Tony became acquainted with the other passengers whilst Richard navigated his way to somewhere where they could carry out their discussion without being seen or disturbed.
"Hello Tom, I've heard a lot about you from many different people. Have you considered coming to work with us?"

"I've had a few offers from most people that I meet, I'm quite happy to stay where I am for now thanks."
"What about you Jerry? I'm sure that I would pay you a lot more than Richard does?"
Richard looked at Tony in the rear-view mirror. "This is a meeting to discuss how you're going to get us out of the mess that your team put us in, not to steal my staff."
"Don't listen to Richard guys, I'm not the cause of the problem, I'm the solution. We'll talk about that when we've parked up somewhere a bit quieter."
Jerry remained silent in the hope that he might learn something from Tony that would explain what had happened, who was responsible, and what could be done to get back some of the work that had been stolen. Tom was still more interested in finding out what happened to his grandfather.
"Are you saying that the person whose body was pulled out of the Thames wasn't working for you then, Tony?"
"He started off as a member of my team, and then decided to take some more work off-script without telling me. There's not much we can do about him, as he's dead, but there are some other people that we need to focus on."
"Were you involved in his death?"
"Certainly not! I don't go around killing people, that's well outside my job spec. My speciality is finding ways to get people to provide information that gives our customers a business edge."
"Will you be able to get information so that anyone involved in my grandfather's death will be put in prison?"
"That's highly doubtful, Tom. Your grandfather's death was a terrible accident, there's no physical evidence to prove that Steve was actually inside the house at the time of your grandfather's death, or that Steve was the cause of your grandfather's death. There is the CCTV picture of Steve close to the house, and I can provide some details to clarify who told Steve to be there, but it's

doubtful that the police will be able to charge anyone apart from Steve with your grandfather's death, or conspiracy relating to his death. We'll cover all of this when we've parked up."

Five minutes later, Richard pulled off the main road, and went down a side street towards an old building. He drove around the back and parked up out of sight. It was getting dark by now, but they could all see Tony's pictures and messages on the back seat.

"This is the initial meeting to request business information from Grangers and Robertsons. You can see Steve quite plainly in the picture along with a person named Colin from the company trying to get illegal business information. The messages show the instructions from Colin to Steve asking for other information."

Tom was sceptical. "Is that all you have? How can that be useful to us?"

Tony picked up print offs of the mobile phone messages and put them in the centre of the back seat. The first print off showed the request that Steve pay a visit to Thomas Harbod and leave a subtle message inside the house to divert Thomas's attention from what was happening inside Grangers."

"How did he get inside my grandfather's house? It was locked up every night as tight as a drum."

"All of this work was done without my knowledge. I spoke to an associate of Steve's named Graham last night who told me that Steve was given details of how to get inside the house by someone who went to the team building."

Tom went quiet. He knew that the information would have come from him, and there were only a handful of people left in the bar that evening who could have passed the information to Steve. Tony pointed to the second print off.

"This is the request for Steve to attack Tom in Oxford and put him out of commission for a few days. Please note Colin's comment asking Steve to be careful, and not to have the same ending that happened to Thomas."
Tom was still unimpressed. "That won't help us either. You have information showing only one person was involved, we need to show that the senior management of the company would be found guilty in court, and to get the contracts that were stolen awarded to the correct companies."
Tony agreed. "The only way we can get that is to pressurise this Colin to give evidence against them."
"So there's nothing that we can do then."
Tony opened his final envelope and took out the top two CCTV photos of Colin, the first one showing him having sex with a young girl, another showing him giving her a beating.
"I have more of these, and we should be able to get Colin to give us evidence of the involvement of the senior management, and get him to make statements to the police in return for them giving him amnesty from any charges relating to this matter."
Jerry had disregarded Tom's pessimistic comments, as he could feel that Tony was building his case stage by stage. He spoke for the first time since they had parked up.
"How did you get all of these pictures and information?"
"That's what I do Jerry."
Jerry was impressed. He had no idea how he himself would have even started to produce all of the information on the back seat.
"But surely the police will have to arrest this Colin when they see the pictures of him having sex with an underage girl."
"They won't see those pictures unless Colin declines my offer to help us. That's what I'll tell Colin if you want me to continue with this work."

"How did you arrange for these pictures to be taken?"
Tony went quiet for a few seconds as he remembered telling the man in the Land Rover in Scotland that it was easier to obtain evidence of people who paid for sex with children because they set up the liaisons themselves instead of the ones set up by Tony himself employing the local working girls. This was just before the man's Land Rover hurtled over the cliff.
"I didn't arrange for those pictures to be taken, I don't agree with that sort of exploitation of young children, but there are always those that do, and if we suspect someone of having any kind of perversion, we can usually find evidence of it quite quickly and easily."
It was finally Richard's turn to add his comments
"I've seen this happen once before, and when the court case was over, the company were told to give the contracts to the companies that they had stolen them from. Would you be happy with that outcome Tom?"
"Will that also apply for the contracts for Robertsons?"
"I can't see why not."
"Will anyone go to prison?"
"I can't guarantee that Tom, but their lifestyle will definitely deteriorate."
"How much will it cost me?"
Richard looked at Tony for the answer. "This is free Tom. I've been asked to help you out, and I'm happy to do so for nothing. I'll get more than enough brownie points from the people that I work for."
Tony took everyone's silence as their statement of agreement for him to set things in motion. "Ok Richard, that seems to be our business concluded. If you could drop me off on the side of the road close to Kew tube station, I'll send the good news to Colin. I'll be in touch in about three days to let you know how things went.

The following morning Tony was waiting, out of sight, across the road from Colin's house. Colin left his house at 7:45 and walked to the tube station with Tony about twenty yards behind him. Tony was across the road when Colin returned home at six fifty-five that evening, he stopped the next young lad walking past and waved a five-pound note at him.

"There's a man who lives at number eighty-seven over the road that I need to get this letter to him without his wife seeing me. It's worth five pounds if you'd put it through his letter box, preferably without being seen."

"I think that's worth ten pounds mister."

Tony smiled and changed the note to a tenner, "Ok, if anyone asks you who gave you the letter, tell them it was a big black man. Ring the doorbell just before you walk away from the house."

He watched the boy walk over the road and put the envelope through Colin's letterbox and then press the doorbell. The boy walked off into a small crowd of pedestrians and a few seconds later Colin came out of the house holding the letter. Tony had already set up the text message 'look in the envelope' from his own mobile and pressed 'send'. He watched Colin read the text and then look up and down the street. He ripped open the top of the envelope and had to support himself on the railings when he saw the first of the handful of photos inside. Tony called Colin's mobile phone and heard it ring three times whilst a shell-shocked Colin stared open-mouthed at the photo of him with the young girl.

"Hello?"

"Hello Colin."

"Who is this?"

"You don't need to know who I am. What you need to know is that you are in deep shit."

"You don't know who I am either, but note this, I'm not frightened by anyone too cowardly to speak to me face-to-face."

Tony had dealt with plenty of bullies before, he had Colin where he wanted him.

"Unless you listen to me, you are going to jail for a long, long time, and trust me, they don't treat paedos too well in prison."

"Fuck off!" Colin closed the call and disappeared quickly inside his house, but Tony stayed where he was for ten minutes in case Colin was looking out for him. He used the time to compile and re-read his text message before he pressed 'send'.

'Colin, I hope that you liked the pictures, and the messages between yourself and your business spy. The police are very interested in your company, especially after the death of Thomas Harbod. It's not you that we're after but your bosses. Phone this number back in the next five minutes or I'm sending the photos to the police and it'll be you in court instead of your bosses.'

A small crowd of people approached Tony and he used them as cover as he walked away from his hiding place. He'd almost reached the steps down to the tube station when his phone rang.

"Hello Colin, are you ready to listen?"

"What the fuck do you want?"

"Your bosses have reneged on their contract."

"I don't know what you're talking about."

"Yes you do, the photos of you with the man who killed Thomas Harbod show that."

Colin didn't dispute that he knew that the other person in the photo with him was present when Thomas died.

"What contract?"

"You asked the man in the photo to get confidential information from Grangers and Robertsons, but you went behind the organisers' backs and tried to get more than they agreed."

"That wasn't me."

"The texts to your contact and the photos of you with him show otherwise. You also arranged for the visit to Thomas Harbod's house, and the attack on Tom Harbod."
"I was just the go-between."
"The police will get those messages and the pictures of you with him in five days' time, and they will come looking for you. If you can give them evidence showing that your bosses were the initiators and sign a declaration that they forced you to set up the fraud, you will probably be let off."
"I won't be able to do that."
"That's up to you. If you don't, I'll send the police the photos of you with the young girls, and they will add the charge of underage sex with that of fraud and conspiracy. You probably know what will happen to you in prison."
The phone went quiet. Tony was used to this and knew that Colin would be the next to speak.
"I'll need more than five days."
"No you won't. The office will be deserted this weekend, you can get it them. Don't bother trying to phone me back because this phone will be destroyed when I hang up after this call. We'll be watching you to make sure that you and the board members don't do anything stupid."
"Such as what?"
"Such as you doing a runner, or you warning the board and them trying to get rid of anything incriminating. Remember, we have more than enough evidence to get you convicted, just make sure that you have enough proof to implicate the board when the police come for you in five days' time, otherwise we'll send them the other pictures."
Tony hung up and went down to catch his train home.

THIRTEEN

It had been a long day, and although Tony's day was nowhere near as traumatic as Colin's, it was far from over. As usual, Tony left the underground station some way from his house and walked one of the various routes that doubled-back on itself to check whether anyone was following him. He turned off the burglar alarm and checked the tell-tales around the house and poured himself a single malt quickly followed by a deep hot bath to soothe away the grubbiness of the city and his job. He had no problem going to sleep despite the ear plugs he fitted in his ears to warn him of anyone entering the house. He checked the ear plugs on a regular basis, but this was the first time they had actually woken him up for real. The person downstairs was almost silent in the darkness but different noises in his ears warned Tony of the location of the intruder. Tony switched on the dim bedside lamp which was enough for him to see the life-size dummy next to the bed and place it underneath the duvet with what looked like the top of Tony's head on the pillow. He turned off the lamp and moved to the chair hidden from the bedroom door by the wardrobe and sat there waiting with his left hand holding his TASER pointing towards the door just out of sight. He had long ago followed the belief that having a second TASER available was a huge improvement on his chances of survival, and his spare was hanging on his side of the wardrobe next to a sharp knife within easy reach should he need them. Tony had a good view of the bedroom in the small mirror on the bedroom floor next to the bed and could see the bedroom door slowly opening, the darkness in which Tony was sitting kept his position secret. The silhouette of a tall man wearing night vision goggles entered the room, the pistol in his right hand held firmly on the body in the bed whilst the man checked out the

room. Despite being fitted with a silencer, the noise of the three rounds leaving the handgun was heard clearly as they hit the dummy. The man could see the blood appear from the wounds in the target's head and chest, and he stepped forward to check out the victim as Tony fired his TASER. The next thing that the man knew was that he was bound hand and foot by strong plastic ties which held him firmly on the chair that Tony had moved away from the wardrobe. When Tony had taken off the night vision goggles to muzzle the man's mouth, he saw the face of someone he recognised from his photographic gallery of people to beware of. Tony was on the phone to a colleague, the gag in the man's mouth prevented him from interrupting the conversation.
"Gerald, it might be a good idea if you could come to my house as quickly as possible, there's someone I think that you should meet."
"Does this mean that you're finally going to let me know where you live?"
"I suppose I'll have to. I'd prefer not to leave our guest alone whilst I come and pick you up." He gave Gerald his address and the best place to park. "It should take you less than twenty minutes for you to drive here at this time of night. Phone me when you arrive, and I'll let you in."
The man's senses had cleared by the time his expected victim was joined by his associate, he wasn't sure if this was good news or not when the man entered the bedroom. Gerald looked at the man strapped to the chair in disbelief.
"What the fuck is Jason doing here?"
"I have a good idea, but shall we ask him?" Tony looked at the man on the chair. "If I take off your gag, you're not going to make too much noise, are you?"
Jason shook his head. Although they had never worked closely together, they knew all about each other. Jason was the person who was hired if they wanted a death to

look as if it was due to natural causes or an unfortunate accident and had recently proved his expertise disposing of Steve. He had an encyclopaedic knowledge of drugs and poisons but could also set up a car crash and make people think that it was driver or mechanical error.

"I'm sorry Tony, I didn't know that it was you that I was shooting."

"So what did Christopher tell you?"

"What makes you think that Christopher hired me?" Gerald knew the answer to this one. "He's always hated Tony and he thought that we were finally getting rid of him, but Tony persuaded us otherwise."

"He told me that someone had gone off-script and was being disrespectful. If we allowed it to happen then it would open up a huge can of worms."

Tony was still interested in why it needed such drastic action to get rid of him, when a P45 would have been just as affective. "I'm surprised that he didn't want you to let me know that your visit was a present from him."

"Why would he do that?"

"Because he has a nasty, vicious streak. He once paid someone to beat me up so badly that I would be out of circulation for a few weeks and told the person that he paid to assault me to tell me that the beating was from Christopher. Luckily the person who he chose was someone I knew, and he warned me off. I went away for a week and arranged for someone to make my face look as if it had been severely bruised and re-arranged."

Jason knew that Christopher was an unpleasant, cruel bastard, but the only time that he'd been asked to do anything like that was from a rape victim after the rapist was found not guilty in court.

"Christopher told me that you were tricky and said that it would be better if I concentrated on the hit."

"Didn't you ask him who the target was?"

"Of course I did. He just said that it was better if I didn't know until afterwards."
"What did he tell you to do with my dead body."
"He told me to leave it where it was. The standard two bullets in the heart and one in the head would send out the required warning."
"Didn't you expect any questions coming your way after they found the dead body with three bullet-holes? Your speciality is knowing how to get away with murder without anyone being suspicious."
"Not really. Christopher told me that there would be a long list of suspects, which didn't include any of us. He gave me a large pack of H to put your fingerprints on and hide in the house." He looked at the cable ties keeping him strapped to the chair then at Gerald and Tony.
Gerald had never experienced anything like this before. "Don't look at me, I haven't got a scooby about what happens next."
Tony pulled the long knife from the side of the wardrobe next to the spare TASER and walked back to Jason. Tony always looked after his weapons, as his life could depend upon them being in the best working order, the knife cut quickly and easily through the plastic ties, and Jason shook his hands to restore his circulation.
"I take it you're not going to kill me then?"
Tony kept the knife in his hand. "Gerald can kill you if he wants to, as long as he cleans my house and gets rid of your body, but I think that you'll be more use to us alive. Could you do me a favour?"
"Anything."
"Could you promise not to take out another contract on me please."
"I didn't know that you were the mark, I wouldn't have taken it if I knew."
Gerald was still uncomfortable with what had happened. "When I said that I don't know what should happen next,

I meant it. Tony, you seem to be happy that Jason walks away from this, but what about Christopher. Sooner or later he'll find out that you're not dead, so he'll try again until he's successful."

"So I have to go into hiding for the rest of my life?"

"One of you needs to disappear."

Tony and Gerald looked at Jason.

"What?"

Tony was thinking the same as Gerald, it was Gerald who said it first. "How would you get rid of Christopher if someone asked you to?"

"Christopher would be easy. Everyone knows about his short temper, his blood pressure must be sky-high."

"You can't give him a heart attack by walking up behind him and shouting 'Booh'!"

"I could give his heart attack a kick-start though."

Gerald was still asking the questions ahead of Tony. "And get away with it?"

"Easily."

"How much would it cost?"

"Are you being serious, because I could end up in trouble with the bosses."

Gerald tapped himself on the chest. "You're talking to him. Christopher has overstepped the mark too many times, and this is the last straw."

Jason looked at Tony. "Are you ok with this?"

"I wouldn't lose any sleep if I didn't have to worry about Christopher anymore."

Jason knew that this would be Gerald's decision. "If you want Christopher to have a fatal heart attack, I can do it tomorrow morning. I've already been paid for tonight, so it would be free."

Tony had wanted to ask earlier, and now the chance returned. "How much was I worth?"

"Ten grand."

"Is that all!"

"That's standard for me. Any more than that and I would definitely needed to know who the target was."
"How are you going to do it?"
"Simple enough, I'll give him something in his coffee when we meet up. I'll need to increase his blood pressure to help it to work, but that should be easy with Christopher,"
Gerald knew how distrustful Christopher was, and couldn't see how Jason could pull it off. "How are you going to get him to drink a coffee that you give him?"
"He's suspicious of everyone. We usually meet up early in the morning at somewhere secluded, so he always likes me to turn up with my hands already occupied with something. I've brought him a coffee to our last two meetings, I'll give him a little bonus this time."
"You won't be able to get anything that would work in a cup of hot coffee."
"Luckily for me, that's what most people think, including Christopher. I have an early start tomorrow morning, do you mind if I leave?"
Tony was stunned at what had just been agreed, Gerald seemed to take it in his stride. "Do you want a lift somewhere?"
"No thanks Gerald, it would be better if we weren't caught together tonight. I'll see you two sometime soon, hopefully in more pleasant circumstances."
All three of them knew that they wouldn't get any sleep for some time, and Gerald left a few minutes after Jason. No further words were exchanged, but they all knew that their future depended upon Jason's success in the next few hours. Tony also knew that if Jason was successful, and he usually was, he would need to find another new house. If Jason failed, and killing Christopher might not be as easy as Jason said, he would need to speak to Richard about another identity.

As usual, Christopher was early for his meeting with Jason, as he was with everyone. Jason turned up exactly on time with two coffees and sat next to Christopher on the park bench. Both of the men were wearing large hats which covered most of their faces when viewed from above. They also knew that there were no cameras covering this part of the park. Jason looked a bit old to be wearing a baseball cap, but it did what it was supposed to do. He could see beneath the hat that Christopher had his standard frown.
Christopher took a sip of his coffee, decided that it was cool enough to drink, and took a mouthful. He swallowed some more and started to appear less miserable.
"How did it go?"
"It was a good job that you warned me that I needed to focus on the job, it was just a pity that you didn't warn me that it was Tony."
"He's had it coming for years now, I can't believe he lasted this long."
"What exactly has he done to upset you so much?"
"He killed a friend of mine."
"Tony? He's not the killing type. I should know, I've killed a few."
"He sent my friend over a cliff in a Land Rover and he got away with it. Everyone knows he did it, and they covered it up."
"Did you bring the money?"
Christopher took the envelope from his inside jacket pocket and handed it to Jason. His hand started to shake.
Jason looked at Christopher's hand. "You need to take a break from your way of life, or you'll end up with a heart attack. You shouldn't pay to have someone killed just because they upset you. It was bad enough that you paid someone to beat Tony up."
"Who told you that?"

"Tony did."
"When?"
"This morning. Tony also told me that the person that you paid to beat him up let him off."
"That's bollocks, I saw the bruises."
"It must have been a good make-up job if it fooled you."
"I told you not to talk to him and just kill him."
"I couldn't avoid it. He had me tied to a chair."
"What the fuck are you talking about?"
"Tony caught me in his house before I could shoot him."
"So how did you kill him?"
"I didn't. You did warn me that he was tricky."
"Why did he let you leave?"
"I think that was Gerald's idea."
It was so easy for Jason to wind Christopher up. He started to cough, and his chest started to burn.
"What the fuck was Gerald doing there?"
"He was talking to Tony about you. Gerald thought that it would be a good idea if you retired."
"You don't just retire from this business."
"You do if Gerald thinks you should."
Christopher tried to take out his mobile but dropped it onto the ground in front of him. "Get me an ambulance, I'm having a heart attack."
"That's the stuff that Gerald asked me to put in your coffee. Your temper won't help, but it's far too late for you to cheer up. I'd like to say that it's been a pleasure working with you, but it never has been. Thanks for the cash."
Christopher gave out a shriek of pain and collapsed on the bench. Jason checked his pulse but was sure that the dose in the coffee was more than enough to do the job. He cleaned off the packet of heroin, put Christopher's fingerprints on it, and hid it in the inside pocket of Christopher's jacket. Using Christopher's fingers, he dialled 999 on Christopher's mobile and could hear the operator asking him what service he

required as he dropped it back onto the ground. Any trace of the chemicals in Christopher's body would have cleared by the time the autopsy was carried out. He put the cash into his jacket pocket and picked up Christopher's coffee cup and walked briskly to the exit of the park. Although it was still early in the morning, he found himself in the middle of people moving in all directions and became one of a crowd on his way to the bus stop.

FOURTEEN

Tony phoned Colin four days later to check that he was still focused on the task that he'd been given. He been waiting opposite Colin's house for almost an hour before Colin finally returned home from work and he was just about to open his front door when his mobile rang.
"Good evening, Colin. How much evidence were you able to get?"
"It's only four days, you said five."
"I'm just checking your progress. Well, how's it going?"
"I managed to get a copy of some invoices for services that we haven't received which were put through the accounts to cover the costs that we paid your company."
"What about authorisation for the payments?"
"They were authorised by Charles, the Managing Director."
"Anything else?"
"Not yet. I have been looking, but I wouldn't have kept anything that could be found either."
"Were you given any written instructions of what you asked us for?"
"Not much."
"What do you mean, not much?"
"Charles wrote me a short note of what I was to ask for, including how much we were willing to pay."
"Do you still have it?"
"Yes, it's in my office here."
"Where is here?"
"In my house."
"What about the instruction to break into Thomas Harbod's house, or to beat up Tom Harbod?"
"Charles didn't give me anything on paper, he asked me to do that when we were alone in his office discussing the increase in the attack on both companies."
"Thank you, Colin. Do you have fax machine or a scanner at home?"

"No-one has a fax machine these days."
"Scanner?"
"Yes."
"Can you send me a copy of everything that you've just mentioned to this mobile?"
"When do you want it?"
"Now would be good. A man from the police will be in touch with you tomorrow. Make sure that you have the information handy, but keep it safe until then in case someone else comes looking for it. It will save you a large amount of embarrassing questions from everyone and will probably keep you out of jail. I'll destroy all of the photos of you with the young girls after the court case."
"How can I trust that you'll do that?"
"I won't need you once this matter is closed, just remember that the only person from our company that you mention to the police is Steve and you won't have to worry about the pictures. I told you before, you are not the person that we are interested in. Make sure that you send the evidence to this mobile straight away as it will be destroyed in a few minutes. I'll be in touch with another mobile if I need to."

Tony waited where he was, out of sight from Colin, until the messages arrived ten minutes later. He forwarded the attachments to Gerald and to his laptop. The message to Gerald was simple. 'This is all we have from Colin, there is nothing in writing telling him to arrange the break in at Thomas Harbod's or the attempt to beat up Tom. Please make good use of it. Let me know on my main mobile when I can contact the police re Colin.' A 'thumbs up' emoji came back from Gerald immediately. Tony took out the mobile's SIM card and broke it into small pieces before going to the underground.

The following evening Jason phoned Charles, the Managing Director. "Good evening Charles, I need to talk to you about the work that we have carried out with Grangers. We usually deal with your associate Colin, but the original contract was made with you and we have encountered a large problem that my company and you need to resolve before the police and the Serious Fraud Office get involved."
"Can it wait until tomorrow afternoon my wife is away at the moment and I have some important work that I need to prepare for tomorrow morning." What he really meant was that his wife was away looking after her father, who was not long for the world, and he'd arranged for a female to spend the night with him.
"I only need about twenty minutes of your time and can be at your house in fifteen minutes if you could spare the time. The sooner we deal with this problem, the quicker it will go away."
"How do you know where I live?"
"We've known all about you since you requested the information on Grangers and Robertsons." Jason had also known that Charles' wife had driven away with a large suitcase two days ago, and that Charles had been home from work for the last thirty minutes.
"Oh. Well if you're not going to take long, I'm sure that I can fit you in."
"Thank you, Charles, I'll see you in fifteen minutes." Jason was parked up a street away from Charles' house. He waited for eight minutes and then put on his baseball cap, picked up his briefcase and walked to see Charles. The door was answered straight away by Charles who had yet to make an impression on the large measure of single malt in the crystal glass. Jason showed Charles his business card, and a photo of Christopher.

"Good evening Charles, we haven't met before, the original contact would have been with Christopher who can't be with us this evening."
"Would you like a drink?"
"I would, but unfortunately I'm driving. I have a lot to say, so a glass of water would be good thank you."
"Right, no problem with that. Please come into the drawing room and take a seat. I'll be back in a second."
Jason was still standing, looking at the expensive original paintings on the walls when Charles returned.
"You have a good taste in art. You must have an equally substantial bank account to be able to afford these."
"Thank you, but I'm sure that you have more important things to discuss that my paintings." Charles was keen to get rid of Jason so that he would be free when his evening's entertainment turned up.
"Could we do this in your office please, there are some forms we need to complete?" Charles shrugged.
"Follow me, this is all part of your twenty minutes."
Jason showed Charles the CCTV picture of Steve outside Thomas Harbod's house. "The police are looking for this person. He was the main contact of your associate Colin. There will be big trouble when they find out that he works for us, and he was employed by your company to get information from Grangers illegally."
"You have no problems there; I won't tell them anything."
"I didn't think that you would. Your associate Colin is expected to spill the beans in the next few days. He doesn't know of our involvement, but you do. When the police start to talk to you, we don't want any mention of our company's name."
"Christopher made it quite plain that we were not to mention anything about you to anyone."
"So if the police offer you a deal you'll keep it quiet about us?"

"Good point. How badly do they want to get at your company?"

"They've been trying to link us to a number of investigations for some time, but they are having problems distinguishing the difference between their arse and their elbows."

"So what's in it for me to keep you out of my discussions?"

"It would not be worth your while if you did!"

"You're not trying to threaten me, are you?"

"There are no threats involved, it would be hugely beneficial to you to forget that we exist."

"I might have to re-consider if their offer was worth it. And threatening me will get you absolutely nowhere."

Jason had looked at Charles' file and was expecting problems. "Could you do me a favour please, and indulge me in one of my interests?"

"Look I'm busy, and I want you to leave."

"Just two seconds, let me look at you palm, and I'll tell you your fortune. If it appears healthy, then I'm sure that our problems will vanish."

If it would make this idiot go away, it would be worth it. Charles held out his hand and Jason had a quick look at it. "You have a problem with your lifeline."

"No I don't."

Jason had the small hypodermic hidden in his left hand ready to inject Charles and Charles winced at the sharp pain as the needle pierced the fleshy part at the base of his thumb. "The problem with your lifeline is that I've just injected your hand with a poison that will kill you in ten minutes. I have the antidote hidden in my briefcase, and unless you write a statement for me about the Grangers contract, I won't give it to you."

"You're bluffing."

"I don't make threats and I don't bluff. You have nine and a half minutes."

"You are talking rubbish, I feel fine."

"That's forty-five seconds gone, you will start to feel the effects in fifteen seconds, the first is blurred vision and shortness of breath. Even if you tried to overpower me and phone for an ambulance you would become too weak to do anything in the next two minutes, and you would be dead long before the ambulance arrived."
Charles stood up, lost his balance and fell to the floor. Jason helped Charles back into his chair. "Hurry up and get your pen. Time's running out."
Charles unscrewed the top of his Montblanc fountain pen. "I'm ready."
Jason had rehearsed the letter until he was word perfect. Luckily for Charles, he was a quick writer and had finished the letter taking the blame and saying how sorry he was for stealing the contracts from Grangers and Robertsons, and for organising the break in at Thomas Harbod's house and the attack on Tom with two minutes to spare.
"Is that all you want?"
"Yes thank you."
"Well give me the antidote."
"There's not a lot of time left, so the only way I can give it to you quickly enough is straight down your throat." Jason opened his briefcase and took out a small bottle and a plastic pipe. He emptied the contents of the bottle into his glass of water and swirled it around.
"Lean back, this might hurt a little, but I need to get it into your body now. It would help if you could hold the pipe steady."
Charles leant back, and Jason pushed the pipe down his throat. The contents of the glass went down the pipe in a few seconds, and Jason sat back down opposite Charles.
"I don't feel any better."
"You won't."
"What do you mean?"

"When I told you that I don't make threats I was telling the truth. What I should also have told you is that I tell lies."

"What lies?"

"I lied about the antidote. The bottle contained a packet of super-strength sleeping pills, all nicely crushed and ready for you to swallow. When they find your dead body tomorrow with the suicide note apologising for your misdeeds, they will find the empty packet that the pills were in. The coroner will conclude that you committed suicide. The chemical in the injection had a few short-term side effects and made you feel rough, but it was not lethal. I wasn't lying about the ten-minute deadline, but that was for me, not you. The chemicals from my injection will have started to disappear from your body by now and you would have begun to recover."

Charles' voice was slurred, and his eyelids had already started to droop. "Why do you have to kill me?"

"You threatened our company and that's always a fatal mistake. You were warned when you took out the contract that our involvement was never to be mentioned. We don't take threats well and couldn't take the chance that you wouldn't keep quiet about our involvement. The most effective way of keeping people quiet is for them to be six feet under."

The doorbell rang.

Charles thought that he had one last chance. "That's my friend. Phone for an ambulance or she'll tell the police about you."

"No she won't, we already know about her, she doesn't have a key and she'll go away when you don't answer. You've already paid her, so it's no great loss to her if you can't be bothered to answer the door."

That was the last thing that Charles heard. Jason took a photo of the suicide note with his mobile, cleaned the outside of the glass and put Charles's fingerprints on the sleeping pills packet and the glass. He sent the picture of the suicide note to Gerald, and Gerald sent another 'thumbs up' emoji to Tony accompanied by the words 'call the police'.

Tony had already prepared the information that he was going to give to the policeman who had visited his office. He caught the tube closer to Colin's house and sent the first message from Steve's mobile.
'Hello DCI, hopefully you will remember your visit to my office last month, and your request for information relating to the death of Thomas Harbod. The man whose CCTV picture you showed to me is no longer with us, his body was found in the Thames a few days after we met. He has yet to be identified, but his name is Stephen James and he was in the British Army until he left one year ago at the age of forty. I am using his mobile. Please let me know now that you have received this text, I have more information if you want it.'
An immediate response was received containing the words 'please send.' Tony's opinion of the police had not changed since their meeting, so he also gave some much-needed guidance in his text message.
'Please note the attached pictures showing the deceased person meeting with a representative of a company requesting illegal information on Grangers and Robertsons and the contracts unfairly awarded to them. He is a small fish in the hierarchy. If you want information relating to the leaders of these operations, and they are not warned of your interest I would suggest that you make a quiet visit to the man in the picture tomorrow morning just before he leaves for work at 7:45. Don't turn up with your sirens blazing otherwise the people that you are trying to catch will be alerted and will destroy any evidence.'
Tony included the details of Colin in the text.
A 'thank you' response was received.

'You will no longer be able to contact me on this phone. Good luck, I will text you tomorrow morning after you have met with this man. This mobile also contains other messages relating to the visit of the deceased man to Thomas Harbod's house, and the attack on Tom Harbod. I'll send this mobile phone to your office tomorrow by messenger for your evidence.'

Tony had been waiting in his usual hiding place opposite Colin's house early the following morning for half an hour when the two policemen arrived and politely knocked on the door. The door was opened immediately by Colin who looked as if he was about to leave for work. The DCI held up his ID.
"Good morning, sir I'm DCI Fellows, this is Sergeant Rogers. Could we ask you a few questions please?"
Tony was slightly out of range to hear the conversation, but everything looked good so far. The policemen disappeared into the house for almost an hour and reappeared without Colin, but with a large envelope that Tony hoped contained enough evidence to negate the requirement for him to spend any further time and money on this particular problem, and to be able to concentrate on some of the jobs that would be of greater financial benefit. Five minutes after the police had gone, Colin left the house looking flustered and moving quickly to reach the office before being castigated for arriving late. No-one had informed Colin that his boss was also going to be late, in more ways than one. Tony replaced the SIM card into Steve's mobile and phoned the policeman.
"Good morning DCI, how did your meeting with Colin go?"
"It was interesting. We have another person who we need to speak to before we make any arrests, but it looks like the case is almost ready to take to the SFO

and the DPP. Is there any other information that you could give to us to assist us?"

"I don't think so. I'll get this mobile delivered to your office, and I expect the person that you're going to speak to next will be able to fill in any gaps when you speak to him."

"We're going to his office now before he starts filling up the shredder."

"Good luck, and remember what you promised when we last met, you won't be bothering me again for a while yet, will you?"

"We'll see about that."

Charles hadn't turned up for work when the two policemen arrived at his office. His p.a. phoned his mobile, but the call went to voicemail after a few rings.

"I'm sorry sir, he was fine yesterday. He did say that his wife had gone to look after her father, so he may have gone to see her. He would usually phone me to let me know if he's not coming into the office."

"Could you phone his wife please and ask her if she knows where he is?"

The p.a. phoned the wife's phone, this time the call was answered.

"Good morning, Jessica it's Jill. Is Charles with you, he hasn't come into work today and he's not answering his mobile."

"No, I've not seen him for three days. I spoke to him early last night, but I couldn't reach him this morning, I just thought that he was in a meeting."

"There are two policemen in the office that would like to speak to him. Is it ok if I give them the spare house key to check that he's all right?"

"That would be fine. Could you ask them to let me know how he is?"

"Certainly, I'll give them your mobile number."

The house was quiet when they opened the front door. The two policemen had knocked on the door for two minutes before making the decision to go inside and shouted from the bottom of the staircase. They separated to check out the house.

The sergeant shouted from upstairs, "Guv, I think you need to see this."

The DCI joined his sergeant in the office.

"Bollocks. Don't touch anything, we need forensics here ASAP."

The DCI took some photos, mainly of the corpse, the suicide note, the empty pill packet and the empty glass, whilst his assistant phoned the office and then both of them went to the front door and waited for the forensics team to arrive.

FIFTEEN

The next leaving do should have been Gordon's, and it was a surprise to most of the Grangers board and staff when Frank announced his retirement. Business was picking up, and Grangers had been awarded two of the contracts that they had been cheated out of. Frank had lobbied long and hard for his son to replace him on the board, but the decision to promote Anna was otherwise unanimous. Rick wasn't that bothered about promotion and had considered whether he should leave and look elsewhere, but decided that he wouldn't be able to receive anywhere near the same amount of pay for doing as little work in any other company. Despite not being the most popular person in Grangers, Frank was a member of the board, so most people spoke to him. It was never the same for Rick, so he spent the night with his father.
"I still can't understand why you're leaving, you have a good number at Grangers, with good pay and people doing all of the work for you."
"That's because I trained them so well. There aren't many other departments who could say that. If you'd shown a bit more interest in my job, I could have talked the board into you replacing me."
"There was never any possibility of that happening. Now that Tom is in charge, I wouldn't have a chance. He's never liked our side of the family."
"He always got on well with my father."
"That was probably in defiance to his grandfather. The two old men were as different as chalk and cheese, and Tom wanted to show his grandfather that he was his own man."
Rick had never had anything good to say about Tom or Thomas. "Both of them have led a charmed life all, the old man was wrapped in cotton wool from when he joined Grangers at a young age because he was

married to the old chairman's daughter, and so was Tom because he was his grandfather's blue-eyed boy. They wouldn't know what to do if they weren't so protected."

"That's not true, son is it. Thomas was company chairman through our most successful times and Tom has proved to be effective during the last year when we could have quite easily gone bust."

"Tom was lucky that the police found that we'd been tricked out of some contracts, we'd have gone under if we hadn't been given the extra work for nothing."

"That's not fair on either of them either. Both of them were always more interested in the company that I was, they knew what they were doing, and worked much harder than I ever did. They are the reason that my shares in Grangers are worth so much and I can afford to retire."

"You don't have that many shares in Grangers."

"I bought some of Tom's shares when he needed money for the deposit for his flat, and I bought most of your older brothers shares. I also bought yours when you sold them to pay off your gambling debts, more than once."

Rick stared open-mouthed at his father. "How did you know that I sold my shares?"

"There were always people who would let me know when Grangers shares were being sold. Tom got a much better deal from his shares than you did, but he always knew what was good for Grangers."

Rick was having none of it. "If John the accountant hadn't killed himself, they'd probably never found out who was giving away our information, and the police wouldn't have started looking into the fraud cases."

"It was lucky they didn't find out about the R&D information that I gave to you last year wasn't it?"

Rick went red, he thought that his father hadn't realised that he'd passed the info to the skinny man and he

didn't want to talk about the meeting that he had with the larger one who scared the shit out of him. He tried to change the subject.
"The people in Grangers never treated us with the same respect that Thomas and Tom have been given."
"Don't you believe it. I've always been held in high esteem. It wasn't long ago that I was propositioned by one of the cleaners. I'm sure that never happened to the old man."
Tom and Helen walked over to Frank and Rick's table, closely followed by Gordon and Rachid and their wives.
"Do you mind if we join you? We won't get the chance to talk to you so much in the near future."
Others joined them at the table, another table was moved over to make more room, and the topic of conversation changed to comments about Frank's style of leadership, good-hearted jokes about Frank, and how much he'd be missed.

The police were delighted at their success from solving a difficult, high-profile case so quickly, and took all of the praise from all involved with no suspicion that any of the evidence had been staged. The SFO came down hard on the fraudulent company, gave two of the stolen contracts to Grangers and another one to Robertsons, and barred the chairman from business for five years. There was not much that they could do to Charles, who'd had the decency to do the right thing, but none of this helped the fraudulent company's share price, which plummeted.

Tom had inherited his grandfather's large house and he was keen not to leave the house empty for too long. The first thing that Tom sorted out after his and Helen's important boxes had been unpacked was to make his old bedroom window secure, and to re-connect the burglar alarm. When the business ceased to be such a huge drain of his time, he re-started his grandfather's customary meals for his friends and contacts in business. One change was to move the meal to a regular Friday night dinner, every other week so that those attending didn't have to get up as early the following morning. It was also much easier to review what had happened in the world of business and the world as a whole during the previous two weeks instead of discussing what they expected to happen, and then put forward their ideas on what was most likely to happen, and how they could exploit any significant changes. The change of the day for the business-related dinners had made no difference to Helen for the last few months as she had stopped drinking alcohol when she discovered that she was pregnant, but she still enjoyed the food and good company, plus other people's views on commerce and the economy outside of those of Tom, who was now her husband, and Malcolm, her boss. The table was unusually cramped for space for this meal, and Helen had arranged for two waiters and an assistant for the chef when Tom showed her the list of attendees and asked her to construct a seating plan. Tom was pleased to see Richard for the first time since he'd left to fill an unexpected vacancy in a person named Gerald's company, and it was good to meet up with Jerry who had taken over the duties of closing down of the company that had tried to steal their business. Most of the people at the table were unaware of Tom and Richard's involvement relating to the stolen contracts that they'd been given back but were relieved that both Grangers and Robertsons were running at almost full capacity. During the increase in conversation between the main course being cleared away and the dessert being served Malcolm made a comment that he was much busier than he had been for years, and how surprised he was that the police had resolved the problem of the fraudulent bids for the contracts so quickly. Jerry looked at Tom and winked, "It's highly unusual for the police to solve anything difficult. When we had problems with money laundering in another company a member of the fraud squad told me that he could never understand why people stole money that needed to be washed."

Tom and Richard both laughed quite hard at this, but the relevance was missed by most of the people seated at the table. Helen tapped on the back of Tom's hand and looked at him with her eyebrows raised. She was always quick to understand when things weren't as they seemed. Tom had told her most of the story just after it happened but had missed out the gory details. Tom whispered, "I'll tell you later," and changed the subject.

When the meal was finished and the table had been cleared away, the arrival of the cheese and port was closely followed by the move to business-related dialogue, the main topic was still the problems caused by the loss and award of the contracts, and how both companies had re-arranged production to include the extra work, and had taken on staff where a few months previously they expected to reduce their workforce.

Tom was keen to carry on his catch up with Richard and Jerry and get the others around the table more involved in their discussion.

"What's your new job like Richard?"

"It's not much different to most of the things that I've been doing for the last few years."

"How are you getting on without Jerry? He's been working for you for some time, hasn't he?"

"He's still working for me now."

Tom looked over to Jerry. "I thought that you were involved in sorting out the company that tried to steal our contracts?"

"I am, the receiver would have taken ages to sort out the mess that was left after they lost their main contracts. The fraudulent company wasn't that old, and only had a few contracts apart from the ones that they stole from Grangers and Robertsons, and only two of those were profitable and could keep going for some time. They also had shed loads of debt."

"What has that got to do with Richard?"

"The company that Richard is working for now has a few small companies registered with Companies House, we used one of them to buy a large controlling level of shares of the fraudulent company which includes what was left of the assets, and Richard asked me to try to sell off anything worthwhile. Do you know anyone who might be interested in taking on the two profitable contracts?"

Tom looked at Gordon. "Do you think that we could manage another increase in production?"

Gordon's wife was not impressed. "He promised me that he only agreed to stay on because Grangers was going through a quiet time, and now he keeps telling me that he's been snowed under for the last six months."

Rachid was more enthusiastic with the prospect of extra work. "Gordon and I will be able to take on another contract. I've been saying for some time that we could find extra space by re-organising the stock rooms. It will be a big stretch to take on two new contracts without finding another production area somewhere else."

Gordon looked over at Rachid and shrugged his shoulders. "It's as if you never left the Production team, Tom. But I have to agree with Rachid, we could have the capacity for another contract."

Tom looked over to his godfather. "Perhaps Robertson's could take on extra work?"

Helen kicked him under the table. Malcolm was already smiling. "I'm sure that Helen doesn't have anything else planned for the next few months."

"Well Jerry, you might just have found a way to dump your rubbish contracts. Malcolm and I will need to

speak to you over the weekend before we put our ideas to our respective boards."
"I've kept my social calendar free just in case you asked. I can be here tomorrow lunchtime if you want."
"You may as well stay here for the night. What time can you get here tomorrow Malcolm?"
"I have a few things to do tomorrow morning. If I lay off the port, I'm sure that I could be back here for lunch."
Tom looked back at Jerry. "What other plans do you have with the rest of the company that you're closing down?"
"Richard and I drew up a plan when he first asked me to look at Grangers." Jerry looked over to Richard.
"My current boss Gerald spoke to me when he heard that Grangers and Robertsons were being shafted, and we expected this to happen. After the contracts that are any good have been taken over by another business, the company will be closed down and the land will be worth a small fortune for building a housing estate."
Tom never ceased to be amazed at Richard's ability to spot an opportunity.
"That's quite a long game you've been playing. Did anyone suspect your intentions?"
"Certainly not, it's good to keep a few steps ahead. I've always liked a hostile takeover!"

Printed in Poland
by Amazon Fulfillment
Poland Sp. z o.o., Wrocław